SECRETS OF THE
KING'S DAUGHTER

SECRETS OF THE
KING'S DAUGHTER

RENAE WEIGHT MACKLEY

A BOOK OF MORMON ROMANCE

Covenant Communications, Inc.

Cover image *The Fine Young Girl with a Light Dress* © Anpet

Cover design copyright © 2016 by Covenant Communications, Inc.

Published by Covenant Communications, Inc.
American Fork, Utah

Printed in the United States of America
First Printing: January 2016

22 21 20 19 18 17 16   10 9 8 7 6 5 4 3 2 1

ISBN 978-1-62108-795-3

"This book captured my heart on the first page and held it captive long after I finished the last. It's definitely one I'll recommend to friends."
—Rebecca Jamison

"Author Renae Mackley explores the world of a beautiful Lamanite princess who determines to face life's challenges and heartaches with courage and forgiveness. Interwoven with intrigue and romance, the story of Princess Karlinah is one of hope and inspiration for those who press forward in faith toward a better tomorrow and an enduring legacy of honor."
—Lori Nawyn

"Having researched and written about the events in the Book of Mormon for many years, it was a pleasure to read *Secrets of the King's Daughter* by Renae Weight Mackley. Debut author Mackley deftly brings the Book of Mormon to life as heroine Princess Karlinah returns to her homeland and tries to start a new life, after her short but tumultuous marriage to a Lamanite prince. Secrets of the King's Daughter is an inspiring story filled with danger, intrigue, romance, forgiveness, and faith—a must read for lovers of historical fiction!"
—H.B. Moore, Best of State and Whitney Award Winning author

Acknowledgments

Many have supported and guided my path in the writing of this book. I would like to thank my husband, Reo, for his support. I could not have devoted so much time to this project without him. Thanks go to critique group members that shaped my story and gave encouragement: Melissa J. Cunningham, Lori Nawyn, Shannon Cheney, Brock Cheney, Angela Milsap, and Richard Johnson. Members of Author's Incognito taught me much—thank you all. Two readers who went the extra mile were Becki Clayson and Heather Baird. I couldn't have asked for a better editor—thank you, Stacey Owen. Being part of the Covenant family fulfills a dream, and I thank them for their warm welcome. Finally, I am grateful to the writers and record keepers of long ago who left their precious stories to the future.

Chapter One

PRINCESS KARLINAH HID A SECRET that could kill her. It smoldered deep in her queasy stomach. She lowered her head as she approached her powerful father-in-law where he glowered upon his throne. His scowl mirrored her husband's when she'd fought with him last night. Shaking off the image, she bent her knees to the tiled floor and bowed. She rose when invited, tucked a strand of long black hair behind her ear, and kept her gaze below the king's eyes. "You sent for me, Great One?"

The Lamanite king of the land of Jerusalem dipped his feathered head-dress in reply and dismissed the servants waving palm fronds. He stood and motioned Karlinah forward.

Karlinah's slight frame trembled. Dread filled her as her awareness of the private nature and seriousness of the conversation increased. She felt convinced he meant to accuse her. Would she receive a trial? The king would never understand her circumstances, with the way he treasured his precious firstborn. He would condemn her to die. Struggling to push her feet forward, she took two slow breaths and looked at him.

"There is no easy way to say this." His matter-of-fact voice belied the gravity of his words. "My son is dead. Murdered."

"Murdered?" Karlinah echoed. What a strong word to describe what had happened to her new husband. Regretting that the word slipped, she covered her mouth with her hand. It might have sounded like a confession for how nervous she must look. A quivering gasp escaped her lungs as Karlinah locked eyes with his.

The king's features softened, showing that he mistook the catch in her breath for a sob. "I know," he said. He took another step forward to pat her arm, jostling his stomach, which spilled over his girdled loin skirt. "It is a shock to us all." He gave a tired sigh.

Karlinah fluttered her thick lashes and placed a hand on her smallish bosom but couldn't make any tears. Did the king expect to see them? Her knees knocked against each other under her sheath dress until she saw the sad smile crossing his face. A tidal wave of relief washed over her, which she struggled to hide. The king awarded his daughter-in-law with sympathy rather than anger and punishment.

"You have nothing to fear, my dear."

His watchful glance made Karlinah suspicious of his words. She kept silent.

"We will catch this assassin and put him to death. My spies are searching as we speak."

She nodded, her stomach clenching at his words. She managed to glide over the tile as he led her to a cushioned bench.

"Why don't you rest here?" He waited for her to sit.

Karlinah smoothed her hand over the jaguar-pelt cushion, her mind still racing.

"It appears there was a struggle in his bedchamber. Did you see anyone last night?" His lips pressed tightly together, his eyes narrowed.

She lifted her head and whispered truthfully, "No." It seemed surreal to have the king questioning her without suspicion. Could this be a test? She swallowed.

"Did my son take you to his bed last night?"

Tears spilled over as she nodded, but she kept a straight face and her eyes on his.

"And you returned to your own bedchamber, seeing no one, hearing nothing?"

"Yes." The truth came easily, giving her a measure of confidence.

The king stared off into the distance. "Masoni's skull was crushed, and his own knife pierced his side. A man of strength did this. There have been threats against *me*, but I never imagined this." He paused to gaze at her. "I shall tell you what I expect of you."

Tightness filled her chest. Going home seemed too much to hope for. She'd remain trapped in a world even more elaborate than the luxury she'd grown up with, surrounded by royalty who cared only for themselves. Conversations were superficial or instructional, if she was spoken to at all. Her purpose here was to be on display and to produce an heir to the throne. No one wanted her suggestions or to hear anything that might come out of her mouth unless it flattered them. Karlinah exhaled the heat building within and nodded. The king sat down to face her, his hefty body dwarfing hers. The feathers of his headdress intruded into her space. She bit her lower lip, knowing she must obey.

"You will be expected to walk to the royal burial grounds in the procession with the family and mingle with mourners for seven days. You are to attend the nightly feasts provided for our visiting guests. They will want to meet my son's lovely wife. You will make yourself available to receive them and listen to their consoling words with a brave face. My household will show honor. Leave the noise to the wailers."

"I understand," she whispered. The brave face would be easy enough. These citizens and visiting dignitaries meant little to her. *And then what?* she wondered as a shiver crept down her back. Staying in these palace walls without friends or becoming the property of another selfish relative of the king would be unbearable. She waited for him to continue.

"After the seven days of mourning, there will be a transitional time to decide your future."

A silent breath caught in Karlinah's throat, and she held it. Her eyes fastened to his, flicking back and forth as she took another breath and listened.

"You will remain in my household until it can be determined if you are with child. If this is the case, you will raise my grandchild in the palace. If not, you may either remain here in luxury and splendor or return to your father in the land of Ishmael. If you return to your family, the promises made between our cities will become void with no ill consequences. Our cities will remain friendly. The choice is yours."

A choice! Karlinah could hardly believe her ears. *Please don't let me be with child.* She blinked, her stare vanishing, and hoped her excitement didn't show. A placid mask composed her features—something she had recently learned to do well—and she gave the expected response. "That is generous, O King. I shall do as you say."

"Good." He rose and waited for her to do the same.

Dismissed, Karlinah backed away, retreating to her bedchamber. She plopped down on the silky bed cushion and stared at the stone wall, pondering how life could change so quickly. Four moons ago, her father had made the announcement that altered her life. She leaned against a rabbit-skin pillow and let her mind slip back to that fateful day. Her father had animatedly described their good fortune. She closed her eyes and saw the feathers of his headdress swishing back and forth around his vibrant face as he spoke.

"I have wonderful news," King Lamoni had said. "You have been chosen to become the bride of Prince Masoni, the king's eldest son in the land of Jerusalem."

She'd tried to stop her quivering chin and the tears that silently spilled over without permission.

"Stop this foolishness," he growled before softening. "Karlinah, you knew this day would arrive. I waited as long as I dared."

It was true. He had waited until she turned sixteen to increase trade with this great city. He sent gifts and held a feast in honor of the king of Jerusalem to cement their relationship. Lamoni achieved the best he could for his eldest daughter while making an even greater alliance between the lands.

"Masoni is the firstborn. You shall one day become queen in a great city! It is a beautiful, rich land, with irrigation from Lake Sirlon. You will lack for nothing, and we will be but a day's journey away." He laid his heavy hands on her slender shoulders. "If I could keep you under my roof forever, I would, but I need grandsons in superior lands. This is for the best, Karlinah. You will see."

She opened her eyes and attempted to shake the memory from her head. It might have been for the best if the king's son behaved more like her older brother, Lamonihah. But no, Masoni was haughty and cared more about appearances than her feelings.

She remembered trying to please him when she first arrived at the palace—wearing her hair how he liked it, joining in conversation or remaining silent as his mood dictated. Instead of growing closer to him, the more she learned about her husband, the more afraid of him she grew. His temper flared when he drank, and he could smile at her one minute and yell at her the next. Karlinah learned to stay out of sight as much as possible and made small efforts to please him when she could, but she set her mind against abiding those wishes that humiliated or caused her pain.

Karlinah wiped fresh tears from her cheeks, the memories still vivid. There were so many directions her life could take. Would her future lie in Jerusalem or Ishmael? Touching her abdomen, she wondered if there was life inside. Could she love and nurture a child of Masoni's? She hoped she wouldn't have to.

Chapter Two

KARLINAH FOUND SOLACE WALKING THE palace grounds where she could think better—breathe better, away from the burning incense. She wasn't required to be anywhere before tonight's reception, when the citizens would file past Masoni's body and give the family words of consolation. The prince's death would be announced at noon through the long, mournful sound of a ram's horn and lamentations of hired musicians outside the palace doors. Runners had been sent to surrounding cities so that dignitaries, arriving anytime within the week, may come to pay their respects. She brightened at the prospect of seeing someone from her family.

As Karlinah wandered between irrigated rows of plum, guava, and pabapira trees, a tapping sound broke through the din of city life. The staccato beat continued, so she followed it, passing four gardeners, who lowered their heads as she passed. At the far end of the grove, a young man artfully embellished a stone bench with his hammer and chisel. Curiosity led Karlinah closer.

She watched for a moment and then huffed, disgusted by yet another example of the finery the king insisted upon to show off his city. Remembering her initial pleasure at seeing the magnificent city, it saddened Karlinah to see her perception had changed in such a short time.

The craftsman must have heard her, for he stopped hammering and turned. At the sight of her richly colored robe and jewelry that glinted with the sun, he bowed and waited for her to pass, but she didn't. After straightening, the young man fixed his eyes on his sandaled feet. No greeting or thought escaped his lips. Perhaps he would have had something to say to her if he knew of the events within the palace. In either case, Karlinah would rather hear his true thoughts than obligatory consolation. Here in Jerusalem, Karlinah felt like a jeweled box that no one could open to see the value inside. She must lift the lid herself or remain secluded in darkness.

Karlinah ventured to break the awkward silence. "Sorry to disturb you." It occurred to her that the artisan, not much older than she, couldn't share blame for the haughty attitude of most royals in Jerusalem. He simply performed his trade as hired. She took three steps closer and examined the detail and precision with which he executed the work in progress. "It's lovely." The words sounded too casual, too hollow to express such skilled labor.

With head down, the man replied, "Thank you."

His voice held a note of pride, and Karlinah knew he took the compliment sincerely. In that moment, Karlinah realized he had his own ornately carved box that remained hidden from her perusal by the same laws that blocked him from befriending her.

She studied his profile for a moment. A strip of leather secured shiny, black hair out of his eyes, revealing small ears that stood out from his head like butterfly wings. Smooth, rounded muscles gave sturdiness to an upper body that glistened in the sun. A wave of heat touched her cheeks, and she averted her eyes. Something important about him lingered under the surface, taunting her. A shake of her head still didn't bring clarity, so she gazed at him again, unable to identify her interest. Perhaps she had felt mistreated for too long to ignore him.

While his eyes remained hidden, she judged the outline of his nose and chin as handsome, though it made no difference. Masoni had been handsome. If only she could have seen deeper into his box before she'd had to marry him.

It struck her how different this skilled, humble man appeared from her late husband. A desire welled up to know more about such a commoner as he. It reminded her of the servant Isabel, her only friend in the land. Could *that* be the underlying feeling she sensed in this man—he might be her friend if circumstances were different? Did he and Isabel represent all the nameless, wonderful people with whom she could not get close? If she stayed here, none of the relationships which society deemed proper could satisfy her need for a deep, human connection.

Loneliness poured over her like honey, dripping into every crevice of Karlinah's soul. This man probably had many close companions while none of hers resided in Jerusalem. He had only lowered his head out of respect and custom. Perhaps he fared better than she.

But a friendship with him would never transpire. If she stayed in Jerusalem, the king would never allow her to consort with commoners or servants. She missed her sister, Hepka, and maidservant, Abish—her closest friends. She could only hope to return to her own land. The thought gave her feet mobility. She thanked the worker for his service and strolled away.

***

Cumroth chiseled at the granite bench almost absentmindedly. His hands knew what to do, and his mind focused on the shocking death of the prince. He couldn't get over the fact that Prince Masoni's grieving wife had stopped to take notice of his work at such a time. At Cumroth's last assignment, the king had only clapped his hands, declared the artisan's efforts as 'splendid,' and walked away, telling the servant at his side to pay Cumroth. It seemed as if the king had merely added it to his tally and already forgotten what the carving looked like. The princess had taken several minutes to study his work, and it filled him with pleasure.

The immerging rose petal needed smoothing, so he took out a small tool and scrubbed at the surface. A gentle voice repeated in his head, *It's lovely.* She had meant it. He hadn't dared speak with her about it, wouldn't know what to say. She was a princess, after all. He promised himself he would return her kindness at tonight's reception with just the right words. He considered for a moment what he could say. It would be easier if he knew more about her.

What did the princess do all day besides taking walks in gardens? She didn't lounge around eating rich foods—not with *that* figure. Whatever she did, he wouldn't trade his life for it. Simplicity and avoiding pretenses described what Cumroth valued. He and his father had the freedom to go anywhere they wanted, creating lasting beauty everywhere they went. Cumroth felt glad they would soon finish this job and leave for Shilom. He was ready for a change.

Chapter Three

"Father!" Karlinah shouted it before remembering she was in mourning.

The servant who showed him the way now left them alone. Lamoni opened his arms for a hug, and it sent all the emotions she had tucked away streaming down her face through tears. She wiped them away and put on a smile so her father would know how glad she was to see him. "You came alone?"

"Yes, well, besides my escorts. Your baby brother has a cough, and the queen didn't want to leave him. I left them home with Lamonihah in charge of the city." He returned her grin.

It amused Karlinah that her father still referred to her two-year-old brother as a baby. How she wished she could see all of them. If the king's decision to give her a choice held and she wasn't with child, her wish would soon come true. She refused to think of either of those options blocking her desires—at least not when she could spend time with her father.

"Tell me," he said, removing his plumed headdress. "How are you dealing with all that has happened? I have heard that the prince was murdered."

Karlinah pulled him over to sit at a bench. "It's . . . it's hard to think about that. But I am managing well enough. Thank you for asking."

It hit Karlinah that she sounded as stilted as she had last night at the first reception. She'd used some of the same phrases over and over, with two exceptions. Her maidservant, Isabel, had actually given her a hug. It was bold, and it snapped Karlinah out of her stupor so that she could feel the compassion the girl had for her. The other was the stone artisan, whose name she still didn't know. Even though he seemed to be looking at her chin instead of her eyes—a commoner's habit she disliked—his tender words touched her. She couldn't recall her reply to him, but it was much more natural than the answer she had just given her father.

"Sorry, Father. I'm a little tired."

He gave her a sad smile. "And certainly a little tired of questions too."

Especially the ones from the king's guards, she thought. They had pushed her for anything she might know. How long had she been in his bedchamber? Where did he keep his knife when he changed to bedclothes? Where was the statue placed? How soundly had she slept? And on and on. Her father's sigh drew her attention.

"But I will ask one more, and then we can discuss pleasant things. I will stay until after the burial tomorrow."

Karlinah bit the inside of her lip. She'd remained calm before the guards, but could she do so now with her father, who knew her so well? Not if he asked the first question that came to mind.

"Will you continue residing in Jerusalem?"

She blinked. "Uh, yes. For now. The king will speak with me about it later on."

"Of course." Lamoni patted her hand, apparently satisfied with her answer.

It stung a bit that her father fretted so much over the relationship between their two cities. At least he had asked about her first. She shrugged it off, knowing he didn't understand her life here. She turned the topic to their family, and the two enjoyed an hour of conversation before parting to dress for the feast.

Isabel came in with the tailors' recent creation from fabric that had been fitted to her last week. The sheath dress, dyed blue, was pulled over her head. Isabel tugged at the cord concealed in a casing until it cinched her waistline comfortably tight. No girdle was needed. The cap sleeves that protruded from her shoulders were balanced by a band of embroidery and a fringe at the hemline. Jewelry adorned her arms, neck, and ears. Isabel also freshened Karlinah's eyeliner. The girl stepped back and pronounced the finished look as "beautiful."

Too bad Masoni can't see me in his favorite color. The wicked thought made Karlinah's mouth curl into a smile. "Thank you, Isabel." The maidservant dipped her head and retreated.

Karlinah found her father waiting at the entrance to the great hall. He escorted her in and deposited her at the head table meant for the king's family. Karlinah took her spot on the left of the king, and Lamoni found a place at another table. The king's married daughter and her husband sat to Karlinah's left. Younger sons and a daughter flanked the queen on the other side. Karlinah had never sat next to the king before; Masoni had sat between them. The king was handsome, like his son, with straight black hair framing angular features. He acknowledged her with a nod and then watched the room fill.

While servants came around with fruit and wine, Karlinah gawked at the finery she saw. Gold and silver, jade and turquoise, feathers and abalone shell adorned the guests. The king stood, and the room suddenly hushed.

"My dear guests, I thank you for coming to honor the memory of my son Prince Masoni of Jerusalem. The queen and I will always treasure him, as we do your friendship. Though we lament his loss, please make yourselves merry and partake of this glorious feast in his honor, for Masoni loved festivities. The wailers will return in the morning, and then the processional will begin."

A dozen servants arrived as if on cue. They set down platters of roasted peccary and venison. The flesh was followed by a variety of vegetables and then breads. Enticed by the smell, Karlinah tasted everything—even something new to her, something called pickled cacti. She chewed, smiling at her father and thinking of her family.

"Enjoying yourself, my dear?" The king's low voice hinted at disapproval.

She stopped midchew to consider her answer. Was merriment meant only for the guests? Surely he didn't want her to appear grief-stricken. Wasn't that what he had meant by putting on a brave face? She finished chewing and swallowed while composing a neutral answer. "The food is very good."

"I am pleased that you have an appetite."

Karlinah couldn't tell by his tone if he was pleased or not. She simply nodded and slowed her eating. Thankfully, the king went back to ignoring her. Twice he talked through her, as if she were invisible, to his daughter and son-in-law. His sparse remarks never made her feel included.

The feast ended with more agave wine and little cakes made from oats and honey. The king's mood had lightened, and his conversation grew louder with each cup of wine. Karlinah let the king see her cup get refilled once, but she didn't drain it. Her slender body couldn't handle more.

When half the guests had departed, Lamoni came forward to thank the king and let his daughter know he wanted to retire for the evening. Karlinah sent him a half smile, trapped until the last guest left or until the king dismissed her.

"You have a good-looking daughter," the king said to Lamoni in too-loud a voice. "I know Masoni thought so." He grinned and wiggled his eyebrows.

Heat rose to Karlinah's face. *Don't say more. Say good night.*

"She gets it from her mother." Lamoni chuckled. "I hope she will continue to be useful in your kingdom, in accordance with our bargain. Again, I wish to express my sorrow over Masoni's death." He bowed and backed away. Karlinah breathed a sigh of relief that her father wouldn't hear more of the king's loose tongue.

"Too bad I have no sons old enough for you, my dear."

The pressure in Karlinah's chest increased. "Yes, Great One."

"But you would probably be barren for them too."

Karlinah took in a deep breath and clamped her mouth shut. Barren? Four moons of marriage, and she was already barren? *How dare he!* If she was not with child, of course it would be considered her fault. He would never blame his precious son. She said nothing and waited to be dismissed.

***

Karlinah arrived in the entry vestibule in time to hear first, then see the king yelling at the minstrels and wailers to take their noise outside. At least he hadn't been yelling because of anything she had done or neglected to do this morning. He put his hands over his ears. *Too much wine the night before*, she figured. She turned before he could see her and went to the cookery to ask someone about her duties for the procession. There she found Isabel gathering spices.

"Stay here. I'll be right back," Isabel said once she learned Karlinah wanted to speak with her. She almost galloped down the hall as she spoke. "I must get these to the servants so they can rewrap the body with fresh linens, as required by the king."

Karlinah huffed. It was just like that man to make the servants redo the disconcerting task so his son's body would be its most presentable.

Isabel returned shortly, bringing with her the scent of incense on her clothes. The royal body needed to be buried by the third day or the incense would no longer mask the odor. Commoners' bodies were typically buried on the first day.

Getting the directions she needed, Karlinah thanked Isabel and sought out her father. She had one hour before the procession, where they would follow the bier carrying Masoni's body for burial in the cement building at the far end of the fruit groves.

She felt too nervous about leading the processional with the king and queen to enjoy this last bit of time she had with her father. He must leave directly afterward to get home by dusk. "Take me with you," she wished she could say to him. Never mind that the king wouldn't allow it, her own father would refuse, desiring her to stay and produce grandsons in superior lands. Was she doomed to such a life in Jerusalem forever?

***

Waiting for the signs of being with child proved a trial of Karlinah's too-little patience. Now that the week-long feasts were over and visitors gone, she'd had to find other things to occupy her time. Walking in the gardens held less pleasure now that Masoni's body rested nearby. She avoided the king, but the queen permitted her to read some of the writings in her possession. They told of legends Karlinah found interesting, allowing the pleasant passage of a small chunk of time.

She worried that the guards would drag some poor citizen in to the king and present him as his son's murderer, but so far they hadn't. Now her three weeks of vigilance were finally over. She sat in a chair beside her bed, anticipating her maidservant's arrival.

When Isabel entered to tidy the room, surprise registered on her face. "Forgive me," she said and backed away.

"It's all right, Isabel," Karlinah said. "I wanted to catch you before you take my bedcovers for washing." She pulled the blanket down to reveal the soiled, red spot. "The queen's handmaiden will want to witness this that she may inform the royal great ones."

She bobbed her head once. "I'll let her know right away."

"If you can be present to observe a reaction from the king or queen, I would be interested to know of their countenance."

The girl nodded. She obviously knew about the difficult temperament of the king and more so of his son. Isabel had seen the bruises on Karlinah's body when she assisted at the baths.

"I expect that the king will be calling for me. I will be walking in the gardens."

"Of course." Isabel withdrew from the chamber, and Karlinah followed her out.

As she strolled past cultivated gardens of trees and flowers, Karlinah hardly noticed the beauty. She worried if the king would be angry with her or retract his previous generosity. Her childless condition was certainly not anything she could change. He had to accept the situation for what it was. The thing he still could do was change his mind about allowing her a choice. Isabel found her nearly an hour later.

"The king wishes you to come to the throne room right away," Isabel said, her eyes wide with apprehension.

"What is his mood?"

"His eyes glinted with annoyance at first, but he recovered quickly. You shouldn't keep him waiting."

"Thank you, Isabel. You are a true friend."

The maidservant's face radiated with pleasure at the praise. Karlinah would miss her the most.

Karlinah scurried to the throne room, wondering which of her practiced responses she might need. If the king stayed true to his initial arrangement, fear would not claim her. But rulers frequently changed their minds, as she knew from her father.

The possibility of facing disagreeable circumstances remained, but Karlinah gathered courage and marched up to the guards. As they announced her, she took a deep breath and slowed her steps to enter with restraint. It was important to appear submissive, though her mind fixed on leaving. She sank to her knees and bowed all the way to the cold, mosaic-tiled floor.

"Ah, Karlinah." The king raised his jeweled staff and motioned her forward. "Have you decided to stay here in Jerusalem or return to Ishmael?"

She blinked at his directness then hid her eagerness with a slow reply. "I thank you for your generosity, my king. I wish to return to my family."

His face remained as rigid as stone. "Very well. I will send a runner ahead to let King Lamoni know of your arrival. In three days' time you will be accompanied back to your father. You will give him my best regards and apologies concerning our original agreement."

"Yes, my king. I am certain he will be sympathetic to your—our—loss. My father would want you to be reassured that a visit from you would be a welcomed honor anytime." Karlinah waited for any last words before bowing, but he simply dipped his chin. She turned and managed a slow retreat, keeping the smile inside from bursting out and spreading across her face. Three days would not come soon enough.

Chapter Four

THE JOURNEY HOME PROVED TIRESOME, even though Karlinah lounged on a shaded litter carried by six men. Their movements were anything but smooth, with the quick pace they maintained. She would have preferred to walk, but the guards had their orders. Her former father-in-law likely insisted on her proper treatment and a showy entrance to the city. Mosquitoes buzzed around her head until relief finally came in the form of a light rain.

Familiar landscape beckoned, and Karlinah sat up straight, her eyes darting everywhere as the company reached the edge of Ishmael. The smell of smoke filled her nostrils, but Karlinah could see workers controlling the plume. Slaves and servants had piled logs from the largest felled trees into fencing to keep out deer or other animals. Branches and waste burned in a pile in the center. The cleared land would become new maize fields, with ash from the fire to be turned into the dirt by fire-hardened sticks. The enriched soil would be raked into rows waiting to accept dried kernels before the season of heavy rains. If Chaac, the rain god, favored them, the sacred crop would succeed.

Karlinah couldn't help grinning as she passed the onlookers who gaped at the approaching company. Being among her people filled her with warmth. She chuckled, certain she presented an odd spectacle to behold. In front of the litter marched four spear-carrying soldiers. Behind her tramped others who carried sacks with gifts and trading goods. At the tail tread four more soldiers, their spears aimed at the cloudy sky.

Thatched huts periodically lined the dirt highway. Adults and children stopped what they were doing and came out from dwellings or fields to view the procession. Soon, houses made of limestone, clay brick, or cement appeared, clustered like leaves on a branch. The gathering of citizens grew.

"It's the princess!" someone called.

Karlinah's eyes darted to both sides of the road as she heard her name shouted. She recognized many faces but realized she must refrain from waving during her time of supposed mourning. Word could reach her former father-in-law that she exuded happiness above regard for the memory of her husband. The king's guards searched to accuse someone, and she didn't want to give any cause that might lead them to her. The secret inside her must never reveal itself or the king would surely kill her. His words, calling Masoni's death a murder, rang in her ears. Her stomach roiled at the thought that she could be known as a murderer, regardless of the reasons. She shuddered. This secret must be protected at all costs.

When the litter was set down in the dirt courtyard in front of Karlinah's stone house, she looked at it longingly. Though the grandest in Ishmael, it paled in comparison to the palace she'd left behind. Several of her family members ran down the steps to greet her. Her mother, Queen Mierah, whom Karlinah most resembled, grinned broadly and carried her youngest child, Tobias, on her slender hip. Karlinah gladly received her mother's embrace.

"Thank the gods for your safe arrival." The queen patted her daughter's cheek. "We've missed you, dear. How are you?"

"I am well," Karlinah said, fighting tears. "It's good to be home." She then kissed Tobias on the cheek and ruffled his hair.

He squealed in delight. "Linah home."

Hepka's hug came next.

"I have something to tell you!" Hepka whispered in her ear. "After we hear all about Jerusalem, of course." Hepka's round face shone with the enthusiasm that Karlinah lacked. She had no desire to discuss Jerusalem or the events that brought her home, but she knew it was inevitable. The family knew she was returning as the widow of a murdered husband but knew little else.

Karlinah's younger brothers, Ishmael and Jarom, circled her, jumping up and down and asking if she brought presents for them.

"Of course," she told them. Tobias squealed again.

Karlinah knew there were questions to answer, but she would wait for the privacy of their living quarters. After their greetings, she and her mother ordered servants to attend to the needs of Karlinah's escorts. When her father and elder brother arrived, she would explain that this was not merely a visit to console her in her time of supposed sorrow.

She was home—a widow at sixteen . . . with a secret.

Chapter Five

SUNLIGHT STREAMED THROUGH NETTED OPENINGS high on the gray stone wall of Karlinah's bedchamber, nudging the princess to pry herself from under the soft rabbit skins. She opened her eyes and smiled at the safety of her childhood bed—no Masoni to fear. She snuggled deeper into the furry indentation of her pile of skins, suppressing a twinge of guilt as his image floated behind her closed eyes. Further sleep instantly vanished.

Relishing her surroundings, Karlinah mused about what she would do today. Certainly Hepka wanted to spend time with her. It would be fun to shape clay beads to decorate new hair ties. Karlinah took pleasure in etching designs into the clay before fire hardening and sliding the beads onto the ends of woven strips of cloth that kept her plaited hair in place. Masoni had thrown away the ones she had taken to Jerusalem, saying a woman in the king's household should not be seen wearing something so childish. She twisted her mouth in anger at how much control he'd had over her. Anger at being forced to face harsh realities.

A knock at the door captured her attention. It seemed too early for Hepka. Karlinah stiffened. Father? She knew he wanted to speak with her, but all he'd had time for last night was a family meal. Surely he would want a report on Jerusalem. And what else?

"Come in," Karlinah called hesitantly.

Abish, the twenty-seven-year-old maidservant who had mothered her and Hepka as children, poked her head around the heavy plank door. "Sorry to disturb you, but the king wants to see you before his court agenda fills."

"Abish!" Karlinah stood up and reached for a hug.

"That's my girl," Abish said tenderly and released her. "We need to hurry. What do you want to wear today?" Abish's long fingers grasped Karlinah's hand, pulling her to the garments hanging from pegs mortared into one wall. Sometimes her favorite servant had the persistence of a bee that buzzed in her ear, but Karlinah couldn't blame Abish for father's command, and they certainly didn't want to make him angry.

Karlinah wished the two of them could sit and talk awhile. The time for that would come, but she wouldn't share too much. She couldn't stand to have their relationship ruined if Abish didn't understand her relief over Masoni's death. No one who hadn't gone through the same suffering could know the depths of anguish Karlinah endured. She could picture the look of horror on her maidservant's face at learning the cold thoughts of the princess's heart.

Karlinah studied her maidservant's kindly dark eyes then gazed down the wide, flat nose to thick lips spreading into a broad smile. She matched it, wishing time permitted past recollections, but Abish needed an answer.

"A simple tunic of drab color. I'm tired of dressing like a peacock."

Abish laughed. "I've missed you."

"Oh, you have no idea how I've missed you!"

Abish took a brown cotton sheath from a peg on the wall and slipped it over Karlinah's head. She combed out her mistress's shiny black hair with a seashell comb. Stepping back to view the results, Abish shook her head and made a clucking noise with her tongue. "The king will not be pleased." She quickly went to the baskets on the floor along the wall's edge and plucked three bracelets from one and a red girdle from another. "Wear these. Your father will think you look naked without them."

Karlinah slipped a thick, gold bracelet over one elbow and two of abalone shell on the opposite wrist. It reminded her of when Masoni had servants drape colorful fabrics and gemstones over her; the servants made marks for fitting and then sent the clothing away to complete the creations. She could still hear his words in her mind. "My wife is the most beautiful in the land," he'd boasted, making her twirl around in her finery. It was fun at first, until she learned the truth. Though Karlinah knew she possessed a measure of beauty, Masoni's words were not meant for her benefit. He only said such things in front of others, never complimenting her when they were alone. His eyes only held lust at such times, and he concentrated on his own pleasure.

Abish tied the sash around Karlinah's trim waist. "We must put some flesh on your bones. Didn't they feed you in Jerusalem?"

Karlinah looked down at herself, considering this. Maybe eating had lost its pleasure in her former household, but she didn't think she looked much different than a few months ago. "Everything from roasted wild boar to sweet bread with honey and enough agave wine to make me dizzy." The wine had served to dull her senses. She smoothed her tunic below the sash, swallowed hard, and padded barefoot down the hallway to the throne room.

At the entrance, a heavy, woven tapestry draped across the archway. A guard pulled it aside and allowed Karlinah access. As King Lamoni looked up from a piece of bark parchment, a warm smile crossed his round face. The tightness in her chest gave way to a long exhale. He had not yet put on his feathered headdress, and Karlinah could see the balding spot on the top of his shortly cropped hair. She bowed. "Great One, I came as soon as I could."

The king stepped from his throne and took Karlinah's hands in his. "Are you well, my daughter?"

"Yes. It's good to be home again."

He squeezed her hands, let go, and took his seat, leaving her to stand before him. "It is good to have you with us."

The words only partly rang true; her presence worried him. She could see it in his pinched forehead, his firm grasp on the throne armrest. It was a good thing he valued her worth as the eldest daughter. He would naturally be disappointed over unfulfilled promises with Jerusalem, but was there more? Did he already concern himself with finding Masoni's replacement? Karlinah watched his rare set of straight teeth as he talked, taking her mind off her churning stomach.

"I stayed up most of the night, worried over our relationship with Jerusalem. We have no one to make certain trade will continue, no protection against war if aggressions increase. Tell me more than the brief story I heard last night. Has the prince's murderer been found?"

"No."

King Lamoni let out an exasperated breath. "Did the king have no other sons for you to marry, no reason to let you stay?"

"Only young sons. He would have let me stay if I had wanted, but it didn't make any difference to him once he learned I was not with child." Karlinah let her voice take on a measure of annoyance. "An heir mattered most. *I* was insignificant."

"Of course." Lamoni nodded, unaware of her pain. "Losing a firstborn and his seed would be devastating. The lack of an heir nullifies our agreement, but I hope your presence was regarded as a step toward unity and not against." He tapped at his lip. "This offer for you to stay, did it feel forced? What was the king's mindset in letting you return here?"

"No. It meant nothing to have me there, so he graciously gave me a choice. He has no fondness for me or complaint against me, only the wish for an heir. I'm sorry you will not have grandsons in Jerusalem, but the splendor there is diminished by the people's haughtiness. Believe me, Father, you don't want Ishmael to become as Jerusalem. It is much preferable living here."

His sharp tone bit through the air. "Do not presume to tell your king what is best. You have not the wisdom of years nor experience in political matters."

She smothered the spirit rising in her and bent low. "Oh, Father, do not be angry with me."

It was pointless for the king to see her view. It went against tradition and would only infuriate him further. Even a princess was required to submit to her husband. Her father expected her to embrace the life of luxury and title as future queen with gratitude, as a gift from the gods. He had made the bargain of his lifetime. Too bad Masoni loved himself and his vices more than her.

Karlinah inhaled sharply. "The gifts! Did you not see the gifts the king sent?"

Lamoni's face brightened. "No. I would have slept better had I known of this cordial response. I better see what was offered so I can reciprocate with double."

"The servants left them in the vestibule last night."

"I came in through the side entrance." He creased his brow and tamped his staff on the tile. "Which servant neglected his duties in not allowing your escorts to present gifts to me? Death to the servant who caused this." He pounded his fist on the chair.

Karlinah held her breath for an instant. "It was mother and me," she suggested. "We ordered rest and refreshment for the caravan before any-thing else. You and Lamonihah were busy in court at the time, remember?" She watched her father's irritated face as she raced on to explain. "The men were shown to rooms for the night. They are probably still here since they brought items to trade in the market. You can still prepare parting gifts."

King Lamoni growled for a servant, who parted the tapestry and entered. Lamoni's jowls relaxed when he learned that those from Jerusalem were indeed still in the city. The servant listened to Lamoni bark commands and scampered off to fulfill his duty.

"Forgive me, daughter," he said, his voice returning to normal levels. "I must make arrangements before these men depart. I will speak with you later about new events that concern you. Go."

The king dismissed Karlinah from the cavernous room. *What events?* She bit her lip.

Believing Hepka still slept, Karlinah headed to the front porch for some fresh air. She stepped out into the cool shadows and drew in a deep breath. Instantly a heavy scent caught thick in her throat, and she started coughing.

"Princess?"

A tall, slender figure appeared at her side, and she took a step back, frowning. It was Japethihah, the high priest who performed blood offerings at the sacrificial altars of the house. He hurriedly set his perfumed oils and pottery down on the porch, his eyes only leaving hers to place his torch in the holder on the wall. It seemed he feared she might disappear if he looked away.

"I heard you were coming home. Is everything all right?"

His melodic voice dripped with concern as it lilted along. Karlinah liked to hear him speak, especially when he chanted a prayer. It was the only thing about him that she found comforting. "I'm fine. I have returned because my husband died." The words sounded strange in her ears, and she searched the priest's eyes for a reaction. Had she sounded too cold?

"I'm so sorry," he gushed.

Karlinah saw a flicker in his small, shining eyes, a twitch at the corner of his thin lips. People were always interested in death. "He was . . . accidently killed." She silently scolded herself for these words as soon as they were out of her mouth.

Japethihah didn't blink. "Such a tragedy. You must be devastated." His beady eyes gazed down then up, taking in the full length of her body and pausing at her abdomen. "I take it you are not with child."

"No."

He stared at her face with intensity. "It is a blessing from the gods that you have returned, though new challenges await you. I can help you through this period of adjustment. You will undoubtedly need spiritual advisement and comfort. My services are readily available—day or night."

Masoni had given her that same hungry look. Apparently Japethihah did not have priestly services in mind. Karlinah felt heat creep into her face as he undressed her with his eyes. A sudden wish to don a cloak enveloped her, and she vowed not to reveal so much information to him or others in the future. "I'm managing, thank you." Turning her head toward the entrance, she said, "Well, I'm going see what the servants are cooking."

He bowed his head. "Good day, Princess. I am truly pleased to see you again."

She gave a slight nod and strode into the house. The sound of his silky voice echoed in her head like a ripple of water lapping again and again at muddy banks. At what point would these welcoming phrases dip into monotony? How many people today would say they were glad she returned home? How many would mean it truthfully, without concealed motives? She felt like a caged quetzal on display. Once again she was single, a prize to win, like a beautiful bird to be captured and locked inside a cage. She ran down the hallway to her bedchamber, her hands covering her ears.

Karlinah stayed in her room until Hepka sought her. After an embrace, they sat cross-legged on the floor, facing one another.

Hepka took Karlinah by both hands, her face beaming with anticipation. "So, tell me what it's like to be married."

Karlinah shrugged, letting her hands fall into her lap as soon as Hepka let go. She stared at the floor. "It's nothing special to become a man's property. You do what he says and try to please him." Her gaze shifted uncomfortably back to Hepka.

"I know *that.* I've seen how Mother stays out of sight until Father demands her presence. But Masoni was rich and handsome. Won't you miss him? Aren't you sad?"

Karlinah pondered her response while her sister waited. She must not give away too much but didn't want to foster disillusionment either. It wouldn't help Hepka to fancy marriage as romantic and then be let down when her turn came. "Handsome or not, it was a political marriage. Love was never part of the bargain."

"So you're not downhearted?"

The simplest response was best. "No."

"Good." Two dimples deepened in Hepka's cheeks as her eyes brightened. "I have something to tell you, and I made everyone promise that I could be the one to do it. But I didn't want you to feel sad when

I told you because it's wonderful news. Ready?" Her eyebrows flicked up once. She waited for Karlinah's nod then said, "Remember how my interest in Jaros deepened before you left for Jerusalem?"

Karlinah bobbed her head again.

"Father has granted permission for us to marry. I'm betrothed!"

Karlinah gasped, sucked into the excitement. "That *is* good news! Jaros is a good man." Her voice squeaked higher. "I'm so happy for you."

Karlinah rocked forward onto her knees to give her sister a hug. Karlinah stood and took Hepka's hand, dragging her over to sit on the bed. "Are you ready for marriage?" she asked, her head tilted.

The younger sister's words took on an offended tone. "Of course I am. I'm in my fifteenth year, and half my friends are married." She paused and gave a shy smile. "We are in love. Jaros's father is a successful merchant with enough economic influence to please Father. Since Jaros is training in the business, Father found him acceptable."

"Then the gods have blessed you." The praise gave way to sadness, which flooded Karlinah's chest. "I came home just in time for you to be taken away from me." Her lower lip pushed into a frown before she continued speaking. "It's not fair. When is the ceremony?"

"In two months' time. But don't be sad. Jaros and I will make our home in the family compound like Lamonihah and Evah. We will see you all the time."

We. The word struck in the pit of her stomach with strange finality. *We* no longer meant the two of them. It meant Hepka and Jaros. Karlinah put on the false smile she had mastered, and loneliness seeped back into her heart.

Chapter Six

AT SUNSET KARLINAH SAT IN the eating area of the cooking room, scooping out the last of the black beans in her ceramic bowl with her fingers. She savored not only the flavor but her freedom to find her meal without restriction. It wasn't where she wanted to be often, but it suited her this once. On her way out, a servant boy found her. He stared at her with round eyes, a dreamy look on his face.

"What is it, child? Are you hungry?"

The boy shook his head. "I'm not a child. I bring you a message. Uh, King says to find high priest."

Did she understand him correctly? "I'm to find the high priest—now?"

He grinned and bounced his head vigorously.

Karlinah chewed her lower lip. "Is there any more to the message?"

He shook his head slowly this time, as if sorry for the conversation to end. When she simply stared back, he turned and ran out.

Quickly forgetting the boy, Karlinah went to find the high priest. She would see what Japethihah had to say and be gone quickly. She asked a guard in the vestibule if he knew the location of the high priest. He directed her to the altar at the side of the house. There she found Japethihah kneeling on a rug, worshipping at the altar with soft chanting. Eerie shadows from a beeswax candle danced onto his face when he rose to full height at the sound of her footsteps. The flicker of light created deep crevices, aging the priest beyond his three decades. She wondered how a man so young had been chosen to be high priest.

"Karlinah, thank you for coming." He smiled down at her. "You are ready, then?"

"Ready for what? I was only told to find you at my father's request."

"The king has ordered me to purify you for a new beginning of the next phase of your life. I have agreed to perform the bloodletting. This will cleanse you from all traces of your former marriage. You will be a pure virgin before the gods."

At the word *bloodletting*, Karlinah felt her throat close, her body stiffen. She silently cursed herself for her sensitivity to blood. At least Japethihah functioned in a controlled, priestly manner now, his eyes not probing. She wanted to get this ritual out of the way without his sensing her distaste.

"All that is required," she heard him saying, "is a few drops of your blood for burning upon the altar. We can do this from your earlobe."

Good, Karlinah thought, *I won't see any blood from there*. She tucked long strands of hair behind both ears and lifted her chin.

Japethihah touched both lobes, drooping with heavy, jade rings. He caressed the skin for a moment. "Soft," he whispered then closed his eyes and inhaled deeply, sending a shiver down Karlinah's spine. His breath let out slowly as he opened his eyes and straightened. "I shall do the right ear. There is no need to remove your earring."

He took an earthen dish and set it in Karlinah's trembling hands. His hands pressed around hers, and he gazed into her eyes. "There is nothing to worry about, my dear. It will be over quickly."

Karlinah could only swallow.

He pulled a blade from the leather scabbard at his side and tugged lightly at the right lobe with his other hand. Leaning in, his breath warmed her neck.

It was impossible not to squeeze her eyes closed. Karlinah clamped her teeth tightly together as the blade slid under her ear. The sting caused her to flinch, but true to his word, the pain ended quickly. Worse than that was a lurch in her stomach as she thought of both the warm trickle creeping down her neck and Japethihah's nearness. She squeezed her eyes tighter until Japethihah released the lobe and touched her clenched fingers to obtain the dish from her hands. The dish pressed cold against her jawline, and she imagined red droplets pooling inside.

Japethihah slowly set the container on top of the altar of carved stone.

The warm drip of blood dried on her neck as she watched Japethihah. He poured a few drops of melted beeswax into the dish and stirred it with a whittled stick. The priest then touched the tip of the stick to the candle flame, using it to ignite the contents of the cup. They watched the small burst of flame consume the mixture and die out to charred nothingness.

Japethihah shut his eyes and put his palms together in prayerful fashion. "May the former marriage of princess Karlinah become void before the gods. I proclaim her purified against those influences tainting her body and soul. May she go forward with blessings from the gods in a new life of her father's choosing." He paused and then turned to her. "You are purified—clean as a chaste virgin, ready to marry another." His mouth slid into a smile. "Would you like me to wash the blood from your neck?" He looked at her with shameless eyes that felt more troublesome than the thin, red crust against her skin.

"No. I'll take care of it." As she turned away, Karlinah wondered if the purification included forgiveness for causing Masoni's death.

***

A knock sounded at Karlinah's door as she readied herself for bed. Upon opening it, she found a messenger girl who explained that the king desired Karlinah's presence in the throne room. What late business did father have with her? It wasn't his custom to simply wish her a good night. Obeying quickly, she found a tired smile on his rounded face.

Her father took a few of the long dark strands of hair she had released from her plait and held them out to the side before letting go, watching as they fell into place. "Sweet daughter," he said, cupping her chin, "the high priest has informed me of your purification."

"Yes, Father, according to your command." She stood with confidence. Better to show herself as a sturdy branch than a bendable green twig. He might allow her a voice in the matters on his mind.

"And I suppose Hepka has told you of her betrothal?"

A smile quickly found its place on her lips. "Yes. I am so happy for her."

"As am I, but it brings to light a difficulty that concerns you."

Karlinah lifted her brows and waited to hear the forthcoming explanation.

King Lamoni took a deep breath then slowly let it out. "As you know, the eldest daughter of a king must marry first." His eyes searched hers for a reaction, but she hid her emotions.

"Of course, Father. I *was* married first."

"That marriage no longer exists. And you have been purified"—he crossed his arms—"that the gods may bless you in a *new* marriage. The eldest daughter must still marry before the younger." His tone had turned firm.

Karlinah fluttered her lashes in disbelief. Did he expect her to remarry before two months' time? To whom? A strangled gurgle escaped her throat as her mouth fell open. *He can't mean it!*

Her mind started spinning. Helami had shown her some attention, bringing flowers to welcome her home. If she were allowed a choice, Helami would make a gentler husband than many others she could think of. Though Helami was from a noble family, she couldn't believe Father would see him as anything but weak. Maybe she could convince him of the advantages—a man like Helami could be shaped.

The king continued. "I will delay Hepka's marriage, of course, to prepare for yours. Though it will upset her, she must wait until a suitable match for you has been made." His small eyes widened, and he leaned forward as if to tell a secret. "Possibilities have come to my attention, but one worthy contender is of particular interest. Such an honorable position he holds." He chuckled, seemingly pleased with himself.

Karlinah stared back. "Who?"

"The high priest is a most excellent choice."

"Japethihah?" Her composure crumbled, and Karlinah wrung her hands. "Oh, Father, no! Please, no." When he didn't explode with anger, she pled her case further, grateful the guards waited outside the doors. He never would have tolerated her behavior in front of others. "He's much too old for me, and you'd have grandchildren as tall and skinny as tree trunks."

Her fretful outburst transported Karlinah to another time and place for a moment. She cringed and covered her face with her hands, expecting a slap across her face as if it were Masoni in front of her. Her father's laughter brought her back to here and now.

"Tree trunks." He shook his head and flashed those strong, straight teeth Karlinah wished she'd inherited.

Daring to test his jovial mood, Karlinah asked, "Have you considered the nobleman Helami?" Karlinah's voice took on a singsong quality. "I could sway him to agree with whatever you wanted."

"Helami?" He frowned. "When you could have one as respected as the high priest?" He tsked. "There are several army captains who might do as well. Hmm. I shall look over the choices within our borders. There is no time to search beyond." He sighed, seeming to think aloud. "I am still disheartened by our diminished favoritism in Jerusalem. Hopefully, Jaros can strengthen trade there."

"Of course, Father." Though glad he would consider other choices than Japethihah, Karlinah doubted Helami had much of a chance. How could she avoid a marriage to a man who reminded her of Masoni? The whole mess upset her stomach. If only Hepka wasn't already betrothed.

After returning to her chamber, Karlinah lay awake on her bed for a long time. When she did fall asleep, she fell into fitful dreams of Japethihah lunging at her, grabbing her by the hair, and tearing at her clothes.

***

When Karlinah arrived at the family bathhouse, Hepka already soaked in the large square pool. A mist rose from channels leading to the pool from the adjoining brick furnace. Karlinah ignored her sister, who hadn't spoken to her for three days. Staying angry over something they had no control over was ridiculous. If there was more to it than that, right now Karlinah didn't care.

Karlinah unfastened her skirt and stepped into the water. She sat down, leaning against the backrest, sinking into cozy warmth. A contented sigh escaped her lips. The floral scent filled her nostrils, and she noticed shiny droplets of perfumed oil resting on the surface. A glance at Hepka told Karlinah the recent hostility continued. Her sister flicked her eyes away and lifted her chin. *Fine,* Karlinah thought with annoyance.

It was stupid. *She* should be the one who was angry, forced to remarry so soon—against her wishes. Hepka ignored that Karlinah had feelings too, blamed her, and had stormed off when Karlinah explained their predicament. If someone needed to own the blame, it should be their father. Or perhaps tradition. The sisters had been caught in the middle.

Did Hepka worry that something would happen to revoke her betrothal with Jaros or that Karlinah would refuse one candidate after another? Yes, she had a stubborn streak, but Father would never let her wriggle her way out of such an important tradition. Surely Hepka must know that. The eldest daughters of royal families—of most families—had been married before the younger daughters for hundreds of years. It was probably written in stone somewhere.

A maidservant entered with an armful of wood for the furnace. Carefully stepping over the lowest end of the sloped channels, she crossed to the furnace and tossed one piece of wood at a time into the hungry fire. Then she rolled the disc back from the channel, releasing a stream of hot water to flow into the pool. Just then Abish appeared, setting out robes and drying cloths. She turned and saw both girls watching her. She studied them for a moment, placed her hands on her hips, and said, "No laughing? No splashing? Okay, out with it. What is it between you two?"

Karlinah waited for Hepka to speak first. It would be interesting to see what, exactly, they were fighting about. As the sisters locked glares, Karlinah gave a challenge with the raise of one eyebrow, instantly loosening her sister's tongue.

"She's spreading lies about me so Jaros won't marry me. She wants more time before she has to marry."

"What?" Karlinah shouted. She stood, her hands balling into fists. When the cool air hit her wet skin, she sank back into the water, but her eyes narrowed to slits.

Hepka didn't take her eyes off her sister. "Either that or she wants Jaros for herself."

Karlinah scoffed. "I do not. You know that."

"Then why did Jaros's father ask me if it's true that I need a lamp burning through the night and a guard at my door? He thinks I'm a baby! Someone told him I'm afraid of the dark, and he's worried about the cost of oil. Can you believe it? I've never been so embarrassed in my life!"

Abish sniggered but quickly turned it into a cough. Karlinah might have laughed too if the accusation had been targeted elsewhere. "I never said any such thing," she said.

"You won't admit it!"

"Hepka, I'm sorry at how awful this is for you, but I'm telling the truth."

"Then who did?" Hepka sniffed back a tear.

Karlinah could only shake her head.

Hepka's sharp voice returned. "I can't think of anyone with a motivation but you. You're the one who's telling me not to be in a hurry to marry. It's a cruel way of stalling."

"I'm not stalling. I merely want you to enjoy your freedom as long as you can. We've been lucky not to marry sooner. Enjoy this gift, Hepka. You don't fully understand what you're getting into. But I would never stoop to childish plotting."

Abish stared at one girl and then the other with her mouth hanging open.

"You're just jealous that I have a better arrangement, that I have someone who loves me, and you're stuck with the old priest." With this pronouncement, Hepka stood and hurried toward Abish, who snapped out of her astonishment in time to help Hepka slip into a cotton robe.

Karlinah's mouth pinched as she sank deeper into the water. *Let her think what she will—it's her problem, not mine.* But as Abish guided Hepka toward the massage bed, Karlinah caught a frown from the servant as she glanced over her shoulder.

Chapter Seven

THE NIGHTMARES, WHETHER OF PRINCE or priest, had diminished, but Karlinah still didn't like getting ready for bed. In the darkness, she sat on the bed cushion in her rabbit-skin robe and combed through her hair. Suddenly the hallway outside brightened. Someone approached. Did her father send for her with news of a betrothal—at this hour? Maybe Hepka came to apologize. She gulped. What if guards from Jerusalem had come to drag her away for sentencing?

Her brother, three years older, knocked lightly then slipped his head through her open bedchamber door. "Karlinah?" he whispered.

Karlinah exhaled the breath she was holding. "I'm awake. Come in." They had only spent a couple hours together since she'd arrived, and she welcomed his presence.

Lamonihah lit the torch on her wall with the one he carried. The scent of oil and dried male flowers of the breadfruit tree burning to repel mosquitoes lingered in the air. Flames illuminated the stone wall with dancing shadows. Golden light revealed a sympathetic look on his glowing face. An uneasy sensation filled Karlinah's gut. Lamonihah was not here to share something funny or ask a female's opinion concerning his wife. Too bad; she liked being his confidant.

"Dear sister," he said shaking his head. "Evah thought I should wait until morning to tell you, but I think I shall burst if I wait. You've hardly been home and now Father is at it again."

"At what?" Her eyes narrowed.

"Marrying you off. We had an unusual visitor today, and I asked Father to let me tell you about him. A Nephite prince arrived from far away to befriend the king and live among us. Obviously you were considered as a gift to him. Father offered you to a Nephite."

At this news, Karlinah flew from her bed, knocking a basket of jewelry on the floor. She glared at Lamonihah. Her hands clenched tightly until she felt her fingernails press into her skin. "Father did what?" she cried.

"You heard me," Lamonihah said with a hint of laughter behind his cocoa eyes. "He offered you as a wife to a Nephite." A deep chuckle erupted from his throat. "A Nephite!"

The chilling words sent a shiver down her spine. Karlinah didn't know which to be angrier with—the message or the messenger. Not another loveless marriage for political benefits; the thought repulsed her. And to a Nephite! How did that happen? She shuddered.

How could her father consider such a thing? A Nephite—a descendant of those who told lies to benefit white men, who'd stolen the best lands from her people long ago, and who had broken away to selfishly prosper. Father couldn't be *that* anxious to marry her off. She hoped Hepka hadn't pushed him into this. Heat prickled on her neck. The entire household tired of Hepka's petulance.

"Ugh!" Karlinah moaned, clawing at her hair. Regrettably, King Lamoni *would* do such a thing—had done it to her once already—especially when he thought it a good alliance. Did he think such a marriage might keep the land of Ishmael safe from future wars with the Nephites? Would he stoop to this solution to stop Hepka's pestering?

What would Father do to her if she refused? Karlinah wiped the moisture from her forehead. No one refused the king. Even death was a possibility. She swallowed.

Although she had avoided seeing the many executions conducted at her father's hands, she knew they existed. It remained a king's prerogative. Many servants took pleasure in carrying out these commands, but a Nephite remained intrinsically worse than any of her father's bloodthirsty servants. Karlinah's chest heaved as her anger rekindled. It would be worse than being tied to Masoni. At least *he* had been Lamanite. No! She would not become this Nephite's wife even if it meant her own death. She crossed her arms and lifted her chin.

"You can tell Father I refuse to marry the Nephite." Karlinah stamped her bare foot on the dirt-packed floor. Life with Japethihah sounded better than death, but the king had already spoken the offer to the Nephite. Nothing could be done. She bit her lip to keep tears from forming. "Who is this Nephite?" she whispered, defeated.

The mischievous grin faded from Lamonihah's face, and his muscular shoulders sagged under his scarlet cape. "His name is Ammon, son of King

Mosiah in Zarahemla. But he did not arrive as a prince. He came alone. Our guards bound and carried him to the king at midday. I witnessed it."

"Ammon." Karlinah spat out the name.

Lamonihah shifted his weight from one sandaled foot to the other. "Father somehow took an instant liking to the man. Ammon was both bold and friendly. Strangely, he put me at ease as well. Father questioned the Nephite for more than an hour. Ammon stated his wish to live among us and be the king's servant, perhaps until he dies. How could Father reject that offer?"

Karlinah gazed at the earthen floor and shook her head, stunned.

"That's when Father asked him to take one of his daughters to wife."

Karlinah's head snapped up, and she glowered at her brother.

"But don't worry," Lamonihah quickly added. "Ammon answered that he would only be a servant."

"What? You mean the Nephite rejected Father's offer?"

Lamonihah's head bobbed up and down as he smiled. "I think Ammon recognized it as a gesture of goodwill more than anything." He playfully wagged a finger in front of her face. "But he could have said yes."

Tension released as she exhaled through pursed lips. "So"—she took a confident step toward her brother and poked him in the chest—"you came to my chamber with the intent of making me believe," her voice rose in pitch and volume, "that I would have to marry a Nephite?"

Retreating under the press of his sister's finger, Lamonihah tried to speak. "I—"

"Not enough excitement for you?" As she continued forward, Karlinah caught the musky odor of perspiration mixed with the smell of burning torch oil. She gave another poke. "After consorting with warriors, bossing servants, or whatever you did today, you feel a need to torment me?"

A silly grin came over Lamonihah's face as he shrugged. "How often does Father offer his daughter to a stranger—a Nephite, no less? I couldn't miss the opportunity to tease my favorite sibling."

Karlinah's hands were on her hips now, but she let a forgiving smile slip. She wagged a finger at him. "Some king you will make—letting a woman push you around." She gave one last push to his chest with her fingertips.

"My wife knows to show proper respect. You could take a lesson from her, you know."

"I like Evah. Father chose well for you."

Lamonihah lowered his voice. "Want to know a secret?"

"Need you ask?"

"Father didn't exactly *choose* Evah for me." A mask of concern replaced his smile. "But you can't mention it to him."

"What are you talking about? Did you make a request of him?" She remembered her hint to Father about Helami.

"No." The smile returned. "I suggested her to mother."

Karlinah gasped and tucked away this useful information. "Why, you cunning little thing." She erupted in a hearty laugh, which soon came to a halt. "But why would father choose the Nephite for me?" True, he was a prince, but any Nephite commanded far less honorability and respect than a priest. Father must be consumed with forming strong connections to other lands.

Lamonihah lifted a shoulder. "I wouldn't worry about it. You know Father has whims that come and go. Since Ammon declined, Father will concentrate on the local men."

He didn't sound convinced to Karlinah. "I hope you're right," she sighed.

"Father knows there are many good contenders around. I could put in a good word about Japethihah to him for you." He wiggled his eyebrows.

An involuntary flinch took over. "No need," Karlinah said flatly. Why did men think that one's position made for good marriage prospects? Didn't conduct account for anything? She pushed that irritation away for another. "Still, it bothers me that we'll have a Nephite in the servant's quarters. How am I supposed to sleep tonight?"

No matter what her brother's and father's impression of Ammon, she wouldn't put it past the Nephite to find her bedchamber. He was probably even more selfish and controlling than Masoni. She decided to place a chair against her door to warn her if he should try to come in.

A terrifying thought occurred. *What if Ammon changes his mind?* Father would likely honor his original offer. A wave of nausea hit, and Karlinah cast herself on her bed.

Lamonihah must have thought her tired. "Well, I'll leave you alone now, but it's good to have you back home. Good night."

"Good night."

Lamonihah covered the torch to smother the flame and left Karlinah lying in the dark to speculate over what evil might come from having a Nephite serve in her father's household. Or worse—what if Ammon decided to marry her after all?

Chapter Eight

Weak from days of fasting and travel, Ammon dug into his gourd bowl of thick vegetable soup spiced with chilies and morsels of flavorful meat. He soaked up the last of the broth with a piece of flat maize bread and wiped at the drip on his protruding chin. Now he wanted more.

Ammon rose from his perch on the floor and snaked his way around the Lamanite servants who stood or sat shoulder to shoulder on the earthen floor, purposefully excluding the pale newcomer. They laughed and talked between mouthfuls. Moments ago they were laughing at *him* as the maidservant sloshed hot soup onto his fingers. It wasn't her fault he had shifted his bowl. When he had cried out from the burning pain, he drew attention to himself. This time he would keep his eyes on the gourd. He got in line again, determined not to make a fool of himself.

Ammon scolded himself a second time for being startled by a custom he knew as commonplace in the Lamanite culture. The maidservants in the hot cooking room wore only skirts. Though he felt certain he could divert his eyes this time, it troubled him to know he would run into this problem over and over again. He came to preach to these people—including the partially clothed maidservants.

No breach of modesty existed, Ammon knew. Still, he couldn't help the occasional haunting of his former life before his conversion to the Lord, where women, wine, and idolatry occupied his leisure time. Later, he was grateful the modest clothing of the Nephite women kept his mind free from former enticement, but now he faced it again—at least with the lower class of citizens. Those with wealth prided themselves with showing off their fancy clothing.

See them as God sees them, Ammon reminded himself while he walked to the end of the serving line. This way of thinking gave him courage to overcome his weakness. Ammon kept his eyes on her face as his turn arrived, but he seemed as invisible to her as he was to the men. She filled the bowl without meeting his eyes.

"Thank you," he told her quietly.

Her head remained down; not a word passed her lips. It was hard to know which Lamanite customs he tread on or if she ignored him merely because of hatred toward Nephites. Surely his manservant status lifted him above her. Would she resent that? There was nothing he could do about it. Ammon shook his head as he walked back to his solitary spot.

No one spoke to him or caught his eye. At least no one had tried to kill him.

What Ammon needed was to speak with King Lamoni. The king had been in a jovial mood the previous day and seemed fascinated with him, asking many things about the Nephite people. If he could keep building that relationship, ways to preach the word of God would appear. If the king listened, many more would follow, like ducklings behind their mother. But Ammon must wait to be summoned by a king who possessed little reason to speak with him.

He hated waiting.

***

Head bent to watch her slow footsteps, Karlinah made her way to the throne room as commanded. This was it. Father wanted to announce her betrothal. As long as he didn't name the Nephite, she would obey. Letting numbness take over, she scarcely blinked, barely saw one set of toes moving in front of the other or the dirt change to colorful tiles. Only when its coolness touched her feet did she lift her head. The guards watched, pretending they were not. Neither they nor her father would see the raw fear in her heart. They would see the compliance of a dutiful daughter. They would see the mask she had learned to wear in Jerusalem, and they would think well of her.

A guard at the entry drew back the tapestry. Karlinah bade her feet to move faster, her body to bow before the king.

"Here I am, my father. What do you wish of me?"

He stared at her for a moment with a tilted head, and she realized she had slipped into her former obedient-wife role instead of the spirited daughter he expected. This awareness and his eyes upon her warmed the cold numbing into something more human than she wanted. This would hurt. Deeply. She silently prayed that the gods would give her strength.

"Karlinah," he said with compassion in his voice. "It is time to move forward in the matter of your marriage. Your sister has been pestering me, and she is right not to delay further. The outcome for you would be the same, so we may as well make one of you happy." A sad look briefly passed through his eyes before he continued.

"I have searched among the noble citizens with little to encourage me. It is hard for me to find anyone worthy of my lovely daughter, so I am forced to consider what would most benefit my kingdom. When the chance came for an alliance with the land of Zarahemla, it seemed a gift from the gods. But regrettably, this was not to be. I believe he would have been a good match for you."

Karlinah's eyes bulged, but she held her tongue.

"While I have tried to consider your feelings, the fact is that an honorable man of high position who desires my daughter is a better fit than one who does not. The gods have approved your union to one whose service has demonstrated loyalty and respect and whose judgment is sound. Therefore, I have agreed with Japethihah that the two of you shall become betrothed."

Had someone taken Karlinah's heart and ripped it from her chest?

"The priest tells me this is your destiny, a marriage sanctioned by the gods. Your betrothal ceremony will take place at dark in twelve days' time when the stars will be in proper alignment. That will give us time to return from my father's feast."

Nothing she could say would change his mind. In spite of her suspicions, she could not argue with her father. This decree that affected the rest of her life stood firm. All at once Karlinah felt like a child. Every maturing experience vanished, and little girl tears filled her eyes. She told herself to be grateful it wasn't the Nephite, but nothing could diminish the heavy feeling of imprisonment weighing down her heart. Dared she hope that Japethihah wouldn't beat her? His lustful, beady eyes flashed in her mind. She quickly bowed to her father and turned for the door, running on the tips of her toes.

At least Hepka could be happy.

**

Karlinah woke from a troubled sleep. She wished she could go back to sleep but knew her disquieting thoughts wouldn't allow it. Her bare feet slid to the cold floor, and she rose to put on her robe. Peering out the doorway, Karlinah saw an inviting torch burning at the end of the empty hall. If some warm goat's milk would settle her churning stomach, she might return to sleep. The thought of comfort propelled her down the hallway toward the cooking rooms. It wouldn't take much effort to revive the fireplace embers.

Halfway from her bedchamber, Karlinah reached the vestibule between the family and servant wings, where she stepped from packed dirt onto a smooth, tiled floor. Carved stonework and cushioned benches surrounded the perimeter. The public areas were decorated, though modestly, for appearance.

On her right lay the main entrance to the house, the doorway leading to an oversized, columned porch. Two arches beckoned at her left. A tapestry covered the first, blocking the view into the king's throne room. Guards flanked the archway whenever her father conducted business, but none were currently needed. The second opened to an inner courtyard containing an ornamental garden. Karlinah glanced through the arch, noting the pale gray sky to the east. Dawn approached.

A figure knelt against the stone bench at the end of a path. Karlinah stopped and squinted. *Who is this, and what is he doing?* Curiosity drove Karlinah along the path. The scent of plumeria trees filled her nostrils. She stopped, startled by mumbling coming from the man.

". . . hast preserved my life."

Karlinah didn't recognize the voice fading in and out. It didn't sound like Lamonihah or her father. The vernacular seemed odd. One of the new servants?

". . . this great work . . . truth to my brethren."

Ever so quietly, Karlinah tiptoed forward. If this were any place but her home, she might feel intrusive. For now, she simply wanted to understand what this meant. She couldn't see an idol on the bench. To whom did he pray?

"Wilt thou soften the hearts of the Lamanites with whom I serve that I may find favor in their eyes? May I—" Suddenly the man turned, his eyes locking with hers.

The Nephite!

Karlinah didn't know which emotion bubbled inside her the strongest. Fear? Anger? Hatred? "You," she seethed, pointing at him.

"Forgive me," he said gently. "I thought . . . Did I wake you?" The man rose from his knees.

Fear instinctively prevailed as Karlinah watched his brawny body come to a stand. She took a step back, spying the sling at his waist next to a scabbard holding a dagger.

His eyes must have followed hers. "I won't hurt you."

She believed him like a peccary trusted a crouched jaguar. "You try anything and it will mean certain death. All I have to do is scream. There are dozens of guards and servants who will come . . ."

The Nephite's lips quivered as if fighting a smile. The rest of his face looked harmless, but she wasn't going to let him deceive her; she narrowed her eyes.

"Yes, and I am one of those servants living here." He dipped his head. "I am Ammon, servant to King Lamoni."

Karlinah kept her arms folded. "And I am his daughter, whom you will *never* have as a wife." Her imminent marriage had at least saved her from that.

Ammon blinked rapidly then gazed up and down at her with wide eyes. One side of his mouth creased into a smile before he spoke. "I am pleased to meet you. If there is anything I can do for you, please ask." He bowed lower this time.

Karlinah snorted then lifted her chin while thick silence filled the space between them.

Ammon sliced through it, saying, "I suppose I should have prayed to find favor with the king's *family* as well as his servants." His face did not reveal emotion, but his bold words stung.

Realizing her mouth hung open, Karlinah quickly closed it and pressed her lips into a line. This Nephite not only kept his eyes lifted to hers, he spoke his mind. Her brother was half right: Ammon possessed boldness indeed, but *friendly* did not properly describe him. He turned rude as soon as he knew who she was, and all she did was make it clear he should not seek her as his wife. Truth entered her conscience. *But I'm still the princess, and he's . . . Father's guest.* Her pressed lips parted, a bit of her anger melting away.

The Nephite came forward along the path, his smile stronger. Karlinah's anger might have retreated, but her hatred burned fiercely, showing in her pinched face. This arrogant Nephite dared to smile at her as if he had won this encounter. She didn't see how it could mean anything else.

"Well then, I shall be on my way. Good day." He passed by her.

Karlinah turned to watch him, stunned.

Chapter Nine

A BOISTEROUS CACOPHONY OF BLEATING sheep, shouting men, and clicking sticks accompanied Ammon to the waters of Sebus. In spite of this hindrance, many of the servants of the king's flock attempted conversation with him. Too bad it wasn't the kind he wanted. Only a couple of men icily avoided him. Once they'd all learned he was a Christian—a believer in the prophecies of a Savior who would come to earth—nine or ten men peppered Ammon with calls to make predictions for the future, followed by hearty laughter.

"Tell me that the king will give me his riches, and I will believe you."

"Do you see the Nephite army getting slaughtered by the Lamanites? Because I do!"

Ammon's ears burned and not just from the hot sun. Some of the men spoke of their lust for women. It verified how much they needed the gospel. Would they someday let him speak of what they considered his foolish traditions without mocking him? Would they listen? He focused on the task at hand to keep positive and single-minded.

A trickle of sweat ran down his back, and he lifted the brown curls at the base of his neck to wipe at the dampness. A cotton headband absorbed moisture around his face, and his new-shaven face felt cooler. Ammon thought it better to blend in with the majority of beardless Lamanites who simply did not grow facial hair. He drew a long swallow from his goatskin pouch, glad he could soon refill it at the place of watering.

"Ammon, over there!"

Ammon snapped to attention as Ahabi, a young servant, pointed to three or four sheep barely off course. Ammon raised his eyebrows at Ahabi but played along subserviently. Ammon clicked his sticks at the sheep and moved to block their way. One had to be swatted on its haunches to get moving from its grazing stance. Another servant shouted orders to him in succession. As the new man, Ammon expected a certain amount of taunting, but this was ridiculous.

"Thanks." He flashed teeth at the short but squat young man in the group. It seemed the youth tried to look older with his bald head, but his round cheeks counteracted the effect. Ammon felt a sudden urge to grin but held it in.

Ahabi grunted then turned away.

Ammon wondered how long it might take to become accepted—if ever. After all, the longstanding hatred between the Lamanites and the Nephites had persisted since the division of Lehi's sons, Laman and Nephi, when they first arrived on this continent from Jerusalem more than five hundred years ago. The sound of his name brought Ammon's head up.

"Ammon—a jaguar!"

Pivoting on his heels, Ammon strained to find something out of place in the brush. He already had his sling out and a stone placed in the leather strap as he spoke. "Where?"

"Over there." A servant with an ample stomach pointed into the bushes. The look on the man's face told Ammon how easily he'd been fooled. The man couldn't hide his amusement any longer and burst out laughing. "I predict in the future it will tear you to pieces." He raised his hands and clawed at the air.

Ammon glared back, squeezing the stone in his hand. He imagined throwing it the laughing man's way but knew he never would, so he put it back in his pouch. *Be a good example*, he reminded himself. *Have patience.* At least no one could say he was slow with his weapon. He disregarded those who had joined in laughing at his expense and told himself not to get riled up. He needed the Spirit of the Lord to stay with him.

The scrub oak and brush soon opened up to a clearing of ferns and grass and tall, moss-covered trees surrounding a body of water. A sweet fragrance hung in the air. Ammon noted Ahabi slowing his steps while the sheep pressed toward the water. *Is that fear in his eyes?*

Ammon came around a bush and saw what Ahabi and other servants noticed. A larger group of Lamanites stood at the lake where their flock grazed. What could be so troublesome with plenty of water and pasture?

The king's servants proceeded down the slope with low murmuring. Ammon kept his senses alert. He moved closer to Ahabi. "What is it?" he whispered.

"Rimlaki's Robbers are here. They like to scatter the king's flock and plunder what they can. They find pleasure knowing that King Lamoni has put men to death for losing his flock."

A tingle ran down Ammon's spine. "Then we must keep them together."

Ahabi snorted. "You don't know these men. We would be better off turning around right now."

"But we need to replenish our drinking water and water the sheep. Working together, we can do this." Ammon realized his simple statement sounded foolish but tried not to let it dissuade his determination.

Ahabi turned to Gilgah, their leader. The two were a contrast. Gilgah's long hair reached the middle of his back while Ahabi shaved his down to the skin. Gilgah was twice the age of Ahabi and three times as serious. Only their physiques were similar. Laughter filled Ahabi's voice as he pointed a thumb over his shoulder at Ammon. "Send Ammon to fill the water pouches. He thinks he has a plan."

Gilgah pretended not to hear and set his own orders in place. "The sheep know how close they are to water and lush grass. We can't turn them away now. Samuel and I will fill the water skins. The rest of you gather for a border to keep the sheep grazing on this side of the meadow."

Contentedness swept over Ammon that the leader seemed levelheaded and not swayed by Ahabi's foolish comments. It would take wisdom to accomplish their errand.

The men quickly slid the water pouch straps off their shoulders and gave them to Gilgah and Samuel, a plain-looking man whom Gilgah trusted, before proceeding to the front of the sheep. The men held their hands out in front of the animals, talking softly. Gilgah and Samuel ran ahead to the clear water before it could be muddied by the sheep. They would avoid the stream feeding the lake since it lay on the far side of Rimlaki's camp.

Getting nearer, Ammon could see what must be Rimlaki and a few of his men lounging under a shade canopy tied to four poles stuck in the ground. One woman stood behind the leader, massaging his shoulders, while another to the side fanned a breeze toward the group with a large palm leaf. Flattened grass meant they had spent at least one night here already. He hoped they might be ready to leave today.

"They look as if they think they are kings themselves," Ammon scoffed.

All at once several of the men stopped in their tracks. "Enos," Ahabi rasped.

Ammon caught his breath at the sight which the canopy had hidden—the still form of a man dangled from a rope by his feet, his head hanging at an awkward angle a cubit above a dried, brown pool of blood on the ground. His stomach pitched. This, Ammon assumed, must be Enos.

"Enos served with us the last time we were here," Ahabi said. "He wandered into the trees to relieve his waters as we readied to leave but didn't come back. We figured he would catch up, but he never joined us, never appeared at his hut."

The dismal subject overruled any pleasure Ammon might have found from their longest conversation yet. Though not close enough to see them, he could feel enemy eyes on him, staring him down from the field as they approached. Some of the Lamanites moved out from under the canopy and gaped at the Nephite.

Ammon didn't feel so different from them but knew he must look it. His tanned skin wasn't as dark as theirs, his brown hair noticeably lighter. More than that, Ammon wore a sleeveless tunic while most of the Lamanites kept their chests bare. A simple loincloth remained adequate for most outdoorsmen while Ammon's long tunic covered his legs to his knees.

Gilgah signaled, and the men let the sheep nose their way toward the water. Once the sheep settled into drinking or grazing, the men gathered to retrieve their water skins from Gilgah or Samuel. At that moment of distraction, Rimlaki stood and commanded his robbers to run at the king's sheep.

"Aaaah!" the leader yelled, arms raised and fingers curled into claws as he stood in place. His robbers surged forward—close enough for the king's servants to see their facial features—yipping and hooting and flailing their arms. Ammon's group quickly moved to spread throughout the sheep and try to stop the scuffle. Only a portion of the flock could be contained.

The wicked men laughed as sheep darted in confusion or bumped into servants. One man roared as he saw a servant lose his footing at the water's edge and come splashing down into the mud. It added fuel to their fun.

"Charge again!" Rimlaki shouted from his cushy spot under the canopy.

Wild movement rushed at the flock.

"They think it a game," Ammon said under his breath.

It took every effort to head off and confine a small portion of the flock. Bleating could be heard far into the brush, and many animals were visible throughout the field.

Ammon's face flushed as he heard the laughing men retreating to their shade canopy to watch the plight of their brethren. He saw someone push Enos's body to send it swinging, the head flopping loosely. Laughter again penetrated the air when cries of disgust from the king's servants proved the effort was noticed. Ammon wanted to throw up but instead turned away, and the wave passed. The king's servants grouped themselves around a fraction of the king's property, murmuring over the impossible task of gathering the flock.

Ammon listened to talk of the king's wrath and heard men weeping. Voices of despair echoed one another. "The flock is scattered too far. Surely the king will slay us!"

Their lack of constructive action baffled him, and he voiced it. "Why do you not attempt to gather them instead of weeping over lost sheep? Have you never succeeded at this before?"

The servant named Samuel spoke, distaste thick in his voice. "This is only the beginning of what these men will do. Eventually they will not only scatter the sheep but drive some of them into Rimlaki's flocks. A confrontation will result with these men, who have weapons. Yet if we do nothing, we risk the king's wrath. He has put several servants to death for this."

Anger evaporated into compassion that swelled in Ammon's chest. These servants were his brothers. Maybe he could win their trust. God would aid the righteous cause of saving not only the king's sheep but their lives. Surely he had not come this far to fail so quickly. His confidence blossomed.

"My brothers," Ammon called out, "be of good cheer. We can go in search of the sheep and bring them back before it is too late. We shall do this thing for the king and our own lives."

No one moved; they stood there, blinking at Ammon.

"Ammon is right. We must try." Gilgah clapped his hands. "Now!"

The men's faces brightened with courage. Ammon led out with swiftness, and his brethren followed. As they herded groups of sheep back to the water, Ahabi bobbed his head at Ammon, a look of respect shining in his eyes.

Seeing success, Gilgah divided the men into seekers and protectors, staying to steady the gathered flock. The men worked as a team until the contented flock resumed grazing and drinking.

The offenders watched without interference, apparently enjoying their leisure while the king's men scurried about.

Rimlaki rose from under the canvas and conferred with his men. The rumble of voices grew amid the cluster on the far side of the meadow.

Ammon smelled another attack brewing. He turned to his fellowmen. "It is wrong for these men to cause our deaths. We cannot allow this." He stared over at the rebels, reading their movements. "They are not about to give up." When he looked back at the servants, their eyes met his, and their heads nodded in agreement. Ammon felt their growing acceptance of him.

Gilgah set his fists on his hips. "Neither shall *we*. Let us do this for Enos. Be ready, men, and keep yourselves between the sheep and the robbers."

Rimlaki and his robbers turned in the distance to face Gilgah's men, their stances set with malice.

"Encircle the flock so they do not flee," Gilgah ordered. "Use the shoreline to hem them in."

Even while the alarmed servants obeyed, each knew they were outnumbered and could not hold the sheep forever. If the approaching band rushed at the flock long enough, there were not enough servants to keep the sheep in check. Someone had to stop this madness.

Ammon alone held the power of God to protect them. His chest swelled at the opportunity he perceived. Was this why he had been placed with keepers of the sheep?

"I will go contend with these men," Ammon called over his shoulder.

Ahabi yelled, "Ammon, come back! They will kill you!"

Instead, Ammon continued forward, reaching for the sling at his waist and the pouch holding stones. A flash of gratitude filled him for all the target practice his father had compelled him to execute. He remembered how awkward the sling had first felt and how he'd labored to get the movements down. The pleasant memory of his first hunt sent a smile to his lips. The other men hadn't regretted his tagging along after he struck down a deer on the first day. Confidence surged through his body now as it had then.

With only a sword and the sling at his side, Ammon figured the enemy supposed him a fool to venture toward them. He could hear Gilgah angrily calling him back, certain Ammon would only stir up more trouble, yet he felt driven to continue. With one man against more than a score, the odds leaned toward impossibility. *But with God nothing is impossible,* he reminded himself. God willing, the enemy could be swayed not to fight. He must at least try.

"Brothers, I beg you to be at peace with these"—Ammon tipped his head toward the servants a distance behind him—"who have done you no harm. Enough amusement! Their deaths are no laughing matter. We do not take lightly your warning of their brother hanging from a rope. Leave now or suffer the wrath of a God who protects His people as a hen gathers her chicks under her wings."

A burst of laughter indicated what the men thought of the warning. The single rock that flew past Ammon's shoulder emphasized their response. Another stone thudded on the ground at his feet.

Help me, Lord. Ammon's weapon whirred overhead before he snapped his wrist and let go of the leather strap at precisely the right moment. His first stone took a man to the ground with mighty power. Ammon reached into his pouch for another rounded rock. The second deadly shot hit its mark, and a man tipped over, landing with a thud. As he placed a third stone into the sling, all of Rimlaki's robbers grabbed their slings. Ammon's arm swung overhead with fluid motion. A third man fell dead with a grunt, then a fourth. Astonishment stained the robber's faces. None of their shots hit Ammon. He barely had a moment to register this fact. *The Lord is helping me.*

Stones and insults continued to fly. An encouraging holler from Ahabi rose behind the Nephite. Stones pelted all around Ammon, but he didn't flinch; he focused on the robbers and not on their flying stones. *Fear not. God protects you.* The Lord had promised Ammon's father, King Mosiah, to deliver his sons, and that promise flashed in Ammon's mind as he set his next stone in place. A fifth man fell, a sixth, and still he remained untouched.

With rage at the deaths of their brethren, several of the men reached into the deep grass where their wooden war clubs were stowed. Rimlaki rushed toward Ammon, shouting and wielding his club in a menacing dance to encourage his men. Colorful feathers tied to the handle swished through the air as a focal distraction.

Ammon pulled his long sword from the sheath at his side, held its handle in both hands, and stood ready. The leader neared, raising the weapon high over his head with two hands. He brought it straight down with a fierce scream as Ammon made a calculated dodge, leaning to the side. Squatting, Ammon lowered the sword's hilt to the ground, the blade pointed upward. He shoved the tip upward, sending it deep under the leader's rib cage and into his chest until his piercing scream dwindled to a choked gasp.

Ammon braced a foot against Rimlaki's abdomen to slide his sword out of the body, which crumpled to the ground. The shining blade now dripped with bright-red blood.

Looking up, Ammon saw a man wielding a war club with a large, sharpened animal jawbone attached near the tip. He charged, and Ammon brought his sword down hard on the limb holding the threatening weapon. The blade sliced through the elbow, and the arm landed with a thump on the grass. He blinked his eyes at the ease of his success. Surely this strength was not his own. Ammon heard the man shriek, but he only had time to raise his sword again before another man charged. Grunting, he sliced through this man's arm and searched for the next who would challenge him.

He quickly wiped stinging sweat from his eyes before two approached at once. The indistinguishable cries of enemy onlookers rallied the attackers, and their screeching increased. Ammon raised his sword over his right shoulder while his left knee lifted, all weight balanced on one leg. He quickly extended the raised leg, thrusting it into the nearest man's groin. In the next instant, Ammon's blade sliced through the elbow joint of the second man. Both dropped to the ground and rolled in pain, moaning.

Ammon panted hard but felt a rush of energy surging through him while other robbers closed in. He blinked in disbelief at their persistence, but there was only time to react. Ammon raised his sword and grunted as another came at him. His side step let him avoid the bash, and a quick, powerful swipe dropped the foe's arm. And then another. A few more tried to lift their weapons against Ammon, and more limbs fell at his feet.

Movement slowed as the remaining men paused, the air thick with indecision. They locked their eyes on Ammon, who readied his blade above his shoulder. Suddenly one man bolted for the trees; others followed. Their leader was dead, and every man acted for himself. When it appeared no one else would challenge him, Ammon lowered his sword, letting the tip sink into the ground. He leaned on his weapon, his breath coming hard.

Several of his fellow servants ran to his side to make certain he was all right. They checked and saw that the only blood came from the splatter and what trickled onto his hands from the sword and not from a wound. Surrounding him, their faces were set with awe.

"We thank you for our lives," Gilgah said, his eyes wide. "Such skill with a sling and sword I have never seen."

The men chorused their appreciation and amazement before stunned silence fell again.

A tall servant broke the uncomfortable hush. "After Rimlaki fell, you gave the rest of the men their lives, taking only their limbs. Why?"

Ammon looked him squarely in the eyes. "These are our brethren. Shedding blood unnecessarily is wasteful and wrong. At times we must fight against wickedness, but we should never let it cloud our judgment of what is right," Ammon huffed, his voice growing in passion. "Leaving Enos hanging from a tree warned us that our lives meant nothing to them. They did not feel the same way when *their* lives were threatened." Then his voice softened. "As to those with clubs, they were only following an angry leader. I did not wish to send them out of this world with such wickedness as their final act." Ammon dropped his gaze to the ground.

No one spoke.

Ammon lifted his head. "I am sorry it ended this way, but they left us little choice. We had to defend ourselves and King Lamoni's sheep."

"Yes, of course," one man quickly put in. "But how is it you are not wounded—one man against so many?"

"God protected me." Ammon's smile grew stronger. He waited for the questions to arise, but his companions stared at him with blank expressions.

Why don't they take this opportunity? Do they not know of God and His power? Ammon shifted his weight in the silence. Maybe they were feeling badly about how they had treated him. If so, it was progress. He took a tentative step, and the circle opened before him.

"Well," Gilgah said, "I believe we should return Enos's body and report to the king as soon as possible. He will want to know of this before his trip to the high king's feast."

Heads nodded.

As the servants returned to the sheep, Ammon went over to the shade canopy, untied the knots, yanked it down, and used the canvas to carefully wipe his sword clean.

Gilgah and three others approached. They cut the rope holding Enos's body, laid it on the canvas, then picked up every appendage lying about and tossed it onto the canvas next to the body.

Ammon wondered if this was an odd custom of theirs or if they were simply cleaning up, but he said nothing. The family would want Enos's body, but the arms weren't exactly spoils of war. Maybe they would later bury them. The four corners were brought together and the bundle dragged behind the men.

The journey back was uneventful. The only noises were of bleating sheep, an occasional cracking branch underfoot, and the drag of the heavy canopy. Most of the men stayed back from Ammon, who wondered how far he had overstepped his approachability. Only Ahabi dared grin at him with admiration. The scene filled Ammon's mind over and over, and he still did not see another way to have prevented these deaths. He bobbed his head, satisfied with the outcome.

In that moment, gratitude overwhelmed Ammon along with a need to give credit where it belonged. His eyes glistened. Ammon prayed silently as he walked. *Thank you, Lord, for the protection of our lives and that I could be an instrument in Thy hands.* He recalled his prayer from early that morning, pushing aside the accompanying image of the king's lovely daughter, and knew God had mercifully granted his cries. He had found favor in the eyes of his fellowservants on the very day it had been asked. Such an amazing blessing! He felt certain he could strengthen his new alliance with these men and become their friend.

The day had cooled somewhat by the time the group returned to the house of the king. Ammon set his sword and pack next to his bed. A growl in his stomach tempted him to visit the cooking room to see what offering he could snatch, but he remembered the king's desire that they also feed his horses. His stomach could wait, but the horses needed care. They must be prepared for the royal family's trip in the morning, and the stables might need mucking out.

He hoped the other servants would join him as soon as they disposed of the canopy full of arms.

***

Gilgah spoke to one of the guards outside the front door of King Lamoni's large house. "The servants over the king's sheep request an audience with the king."

"What kind of mess are you bringing?" one guard answered as they both studied the bloodied material at the servants' feet. His gruff tone sounded as menacing as his overall look. The thickset man had his head shorn down to the skin, a dyed marking of red in the center of his forehead, and a stony expression. He wore a loin skirt and sandals. Bands of gold ringed the muscular biceps folded across his expansive chest.

Gilgah swallowed hard. "We have an amazing tale that the king will want to know about."

The guard checked inside the canvas. "So it appears. I'll ask him, but I hope you won't be upsetting the king. He's expecting visitors." The guard stepped inside to face the errand boy in the vestibule before inclining his head toward the throne room. "Deliver the message."

A moment later, the boy returned. "The king says he will see them if they are quick."

"Follow me," the guard told Gilgah; then he turned to wag a warning finger to the group. "And don't spoil his mood. He's getting ready for his father's feast."

A dozen servants lifted the bag high enough so as not to soil the hall as they walked. When it drooped once, it left a red splotch on the floor. The servants were led to an arched opening on which hung a heavy woven cloth that muffled sound. More guards stood stiffly on either side. They hid any emotion at the sight of the bloodied bag.

One guard asked for the name of the spokesman then said, "Wait here until I announce you."

All at once the formality of standing before the king, the ill end-of-the-day timing, and the king's fateful edict over the flocks struck him. Gilgah's knees quaked as the guard parted the curtain and he and his group entered the throne room.

Chapter Ten

"FATHER WILL NOT BE HAPPY if you make us late for his guests." Hepka frowned and stamped her foot. She watched as Abish quietly continued plaiting Karlinah's hair.

"You mean *you* will not be happy," Karlinah said. She didn't care to socialize with Father's friends who would accompany them to Grandfather's tomorrow, nor with Japethihah, who had been invited to the evening meal tonight. It was enough to destroy her appetite.

The two sisters had made a truce after their father's announcement of Karlinah's betrothal. Hepka couldn't stay mad with events progressing. They still didn't know who had spread the lies about her, but as long as Jaros's father acted pacified, Hepka had decided to go on as if nothing had happened.

Hepka bit at her fingernail. Karlinah smiled at her sister's anxiousness. It was easy to see why Hepka would be excited for tonight's guests and the festivities tomorrow. Karlinah didn't begrudge the celebrations. The festivities in Jerusalem had been grand affairs that would have given gratification if not for Masoni's taste for free-flowing wine.

Besides the abundance of delicacies and sweets, Hepka could gossip with other girls about her betrothal. She would be the center of attention since Karlinah didn't wish to discuss her own upcoming marriage. Glad they would not join in the dance of available girls surrounded by men who whooped and clapped to the tambourine and drumbeat, she shook her head. A fleeting image of a quiet, humble stone artisan rippled through her mind, and she noted the contrast. *I wonder what that craftsman is doing now.* It was a silly thought, and she tossed it aside.

Abish finished the fancy braid and tied off the end with a silky ribbon instead of the cloth and clay bead ties Karlinah usually wore. She wound the braid around Karlinah's head. Turning to Hepka, Abish asked, "What do you think—on top or at the back?"

Hepka circled her sister. "At the back."

Karlinah waved a hand as if it didn't matter but felt glad to gain affable attention from Hepka. She hoped she wouldn't encounter Ammon before they left and have him see her in her finery. She didn't want him changing his mind, and until the ceremony, anything could happen. Anything? Like if a better match than the dreadful high priest could be found in her grandfather's land? Hmm. What if there was a respectable but humble noble there—like that stone artisan—who took an interest in her without probing eyes? Would Father say the gods now favored him having contacts in other lands more than they favored Japethihah? A corner of her mouth lifted.

Abish fashioned the long braid into a coil at the back of Karlinah's head and fastened it with seashell combs. Next, Abish went to the basket of peacock plumes and selected three fine ones to adorn the plait. Karlinah thanked Abish and told the woman she preferred to dress herself.

Abish bobbed her head. "Your overnight things are all packed and ready for the early start tomorrow. Come safely back to me."

"We will," Karlinah said with a smile.

Hepka paced back and forth as soon as Abish closed the door.

"Don't worry," Karlinah said. "I'll be dressed before Mother comes to check on us. I have an idea." Karlinah's voice grew playful. "How about a little eye liner? This is a special occasion."

Hepka seemed both excited and uneasy at the prospect. "What will Mother say?"

Karlinah shrugged. "Maybe she will say you look grown up enough for marriage. Maybe she will say how nice it looks on you. Maybe it will be too late for her to say you have to wash it off." With that, they both laughed.

Karlinah dipped a feather into her wash basin, rolled the tip between her fingers to a fine point, and then swirled it through a small pot of ash paste. As she applied it to Hepka's eyelids, she remembered how others had adorned her like this and more. A twinge of guilt flooded her mind. *This is nothing like that,* she told herself.

Masoni had wanted to enhance her beauty with some of the trends of noble families. Two of his sisters had marked their faces with beauty scars in carefully carved designs, and Masoni himself had tattoos on his left arm. Karlinah hated seeing blood, especially her own, and had successfully put him off.

The prince could not stay pacified for long. He turned to having her teeth sharpened or encrusted with jade or shiny iron pyrite. She didn't necessarily oppose this demand, but he saw her hesitation as disobedience. As his bride she was Masoni's property, but it seemed he wanted to control how she looked and play with her as a child would a doll. Then what? Would he tie boards around their future baby's head to achieve the newly popular flattened look? She had shuddered, and Masoni took it for her answer. He flew into a rage, shouting that he was the master and she would obey him.

That night she had received her first beating.

Hepka's voice brought Karlinah to the present. "Don't forget the other eye," she reminded, her eyes still closed.

Karlinah banished the memory and applied a thin, dark line across her sister's other lid. She stepped back to appraise her effort. "Oh yes, that's what you needed to draw attention to your beautiful eyes!"

Hepka fluttered her lashes. "Jaros should see me like this."

Even with a round face, Hepka now looked all of her fourteen and a half years. She had inherited her father's features—average build; small eyes; a wide, flat nose; and near-perfect teeth. Karlinah took more after her mother, with a slight figure, a face more oval than her mother's heart-shaped one but sharing high cheekbones and a pointed chin. Her teeth lay in slightly crowded rows but shone as brightly as Hepka's. Large eyes with long lashes and a delicate arch to her brow were Karlinah's most striking feature.

Karlinah slipped her indigo tunic over a long, patterned skirt. The color accented the plumes in her hair. The royal family regularly wore more clothing and longer skirts than common citizens, but tonight's festivities demanded extra jewelry. Hepka helped her fasten the shiny, gold collar at the back of her neck. Gold bracelets and a colorful girdle at her waist finished the look.

Karlinah grabbed the sandals Abish had set out, slipping them onto her feet, when Ishmael burst into the room. She opened her mouth to lecture her younger brother about barging in, but his news tumbled out too fast.

"The Nephite is in the throne room talking with Father," Ishmael rushed his words in excitement. "They brought Father a pile of bloody arms." He slowed and pointed his thumb at his chest. "*I* saw the cloth they were wrapped in." A smirk settled on his face.

"Arms from bodies?" Hepka asked in horror.

"What are you talking about?" Karlinah shuddered, certain she didn't want to hear about blood and body parts.

The eleven-year-old huffed, bobbing his shaved head as he spoke. "The arms the Nephite chopped off with his sword!"

Hepka shrieked and put a hand to her mouth.

Taking Ishmael's chin in one hand, Karlinah looked into his eyes. "Slow down," she ordered. "Start at the beginning and tell me what you know."

"I went to get ready for the feast when I heard a crowd of men in the vestibule, so I stopped to look. They dragged a big cloth bundle with blood soaked through it. Lots of blood!" He paused to grin. "One of the guards told me to turn around and wouldn't let me get closer. I wish I could've seen inside the bundle."

Swallowing, Karlinah shook the image from her head. Ishmael loved action and wished to be an army captain. Mother had recently let him shave his head like the soldiers but wouldn't go as far as letting him put the red warrior mark on his forehead. How much of this tale came from her brother's imagination?

"How do you know the cloth held arms?" Hepka asked.

"I tiptoed back after washing my feet and dressing. I heard the guards talking before they could see me. They said something about finding the brave Nephite who protected the king's sheep so Father could speak with him. They talked about the great strength he possessed to slice through so many arms by himself."

"Arms of the servants?" Karlinah asked warily.

"I guess." Ishmael shrugged. He raised one hand holding an imaginary sword and cut through the air, making a whooshing noise. "Now he's in there talking to Father."

Karlinah creased her forehead. How could the Nephite be a great protector of the sheep if he wounded the king's servants? They were the only ones protecting the sheep, and Ammon had been among them, so it must have been their arms in the bundle. She ground her teeth thinking that this Nephite would pretend helpfulness and then use his sword against her father's servants.

Apparently Karlinah's thinking did not measure up to Ishmael's hoped-for reaction. He stamped his foot at his sisters. "I'm going to go find Jarom and tell him. I know *he'll* think the bloody cloth was remarkable." Ishmael ran out the door in a flash.

Karlinah clenched her jaw. She hoped Ammon would be tortured before her father had him killed.

Chapter Eleven

King Lamoni sat on his throne of chiseled stone, leaning wearily to one side. He propped his elbow on the armrest and let his rounded chin settle in one hand, the other hand holding his staff. A cushion on his seat and behind his back added needed comfort. Lamoni's large, feathered headdress tilted slightly but still covered the balding circle on the top of his head. He grew tired, anxious to get this last audience over with and join Mierah to greet their guests.

The slap of Gilgah's leather sandals against the colorful tiles echoed off the high-ceilinged throne room, thundering in the king's ears. Lamoni straightened in his chair, watching with small, dark eyes while the servant bowed low before him. Lamoni put forth his hand as if to raise Gilgah from the ground, as was their custom of peace. The serious-minded shepherd trembled before him. It pleased Lamoni yet served as an irritating reminder that he would soon give submission to the one person who held higher authority—his father, the high king.

"Oh, Great King," Gilgah said, "as a hu-humble servant over your flock, I bring a report of mighty miracles showing unto the king the, uh, strength and power of our new fellowservant and friend to the king, Ammon, in preserving your sheep."

At the mention of Ammon's name, Lamoni leaned forward with interest. What would his guests think if they saw a Nephite in his house? It might further elevate their opinion of him that a Nephite had chosen to serve him. "Go on," he encouraged.

Gilgah visibly relaxed at the king's favorable mood. Wiping away the moisture from his hairline, he related the details of the day without interruption, ending with, "And now, Great King, your servants have brought back the arms of those men who lifted their clubs against Ammon as a witness of the great things he has done for thee this day."

"Bring them forth," Lamoni said to his guards, his curiosity piqued.

They parted the curtain, and eight servants carried the awkward bundle with ease. The remaining three servants, all but Ammon, trailed behind. They laid the canvas at the feet of the king, stretching out the four corners to show the contents.

The metallic smell of blood and moldering body thrust its way into the king's nostrils. He instantly recoiled. Severed limbs covered the body of Enos. Though smeared with blood, Lamoni could see the dark Lamanite skin. There were some appendages with elbows, some without. The flesh had shrunk back from the jagged edges of fractured bone. The king stared long enough to make a rough estimate of a score of limbs. He swallowed hard, composed himself, then looked up at the eight. "All of you were witnesses and agree with the testimony given?"

Heads nodded, anxious to please the king, whether or not they had heard Gilgah's words. It was just as well; Lamoni did not wish to sit through multiple recitations. He should be seeing to his guests' arrival, but he pushed the priority aside, unable to let the astonishing account leave his mind.

Lamoni desired to hear Ammon's side of the events. He turned to a guard. "Find Ammon, and send him to me." The guard went out.

Lamoni put both elbows on the armrests of his throne and tapped his fingers together, pondering Ammon's actions. The servant had shown courage, no doubt, but why would anyone want to single-handedly take on such odds? The Nephite must have believed he could come out on top or he wouldn't have tried. That or he had a death wish. The king wagged his head. Never had a servant shown such valor in his duties. Never. And such strength! Lamoni didn't think any warrior in his army matched the strength of Ammon. "Surely this is more than a man. Could he be the Great Spirit punishing this people because of their murders?"

The servants looked wide-eyed from one to another and then back to their leader. Finally Gilgah spoke. "Whether he is the Great Spirit or a man is not for me to judge. But this I know—your enemies could not slay him. And because of his expertise and great strength, no one could scatter your flock. You may be assured that Ammon is a friend to the king."

Lamoni let out a slow breath of relief. If a king's actions could be wrong, pondering punishment from a superior being proved unpleasant.

He needed Ammon on his side. The king dipped his head once and met the eyes of the simple shepherd whose gaze showed growing self-assurance.

Gilgah glanced at his brethren again and continued more boldly. "And now, O King, we don't believe a man has such great power as to avoid the aim of every stone and remain unharmed by the attacks of so many against one. We, as faithful servants in all that the king has asked of us, witness unto you that Ammon cannot be slain." The servants vigorously nodded.

King Lamoni tapped at his mouth with trembling fingers. Their respect for Ammon appeared greater than their fear of him as king. He might have gotten angry with them if his own mind had not been troubled. He swallowed hard. "Ammon must be the Great Spirit of whom our fathers have spoken. He has come down at this time to preserve your lives, so that I will not slay you as I did your brothers."

Fear struck Lamoni's heart like a bolt of pain. Though the Lamanites believed in a higher being, they supposed that whatever they did was right. Had he offended the Great Spirit with the many murders he had caused? Would it make Ammon angry that the king had sent for him? He blinked several times, feeling tears threatening to form. This would never do.

The guard returned and warily watched the servants in the room as he approached the king. He likely sensed the contemplative mood and bowed before the king.

Lamoni cleared his throat before the guard could speak. "Where is this man who has such great power?"

"He is feeding your horses and those of your guests who have just arrived. He shall arrive shortly."

The king raised his eyebrows. "Surely there has not been any among all my servants as faithful as this man. He remembers and executes all my commands!" He slammed a fist onto the arm of his throne. "Now I know that this is the Great Spirit." *I desire him to come unto me. But what shall I say?*

Sighing, Lamoni settled into his seat. What a strange day. He opened his mouth to speak when a guard at the entrance lifted the curtain and Japethihah entered. His billowing scarlet robe swished about him as he drew nearer, silently demanding everyone's attention.

"Forgive me, My King," the priest said with a bow, ignoring all others and moving closer as he spoke. "I have come to learn the reason for the trail of blood on the floor. The guards claim to know little, and I am concerned your guests will see it. Is everything all right?"

"Yes. No. Well . . ." The king cringed at being flustered. "We were discussing the Nephite servant's amazing strength in defending my sheep at the waters of Sebus today."

Japethihah's face contorted. "Discussing with these?" He gestured toward Gilgah's men. His face grew more unpleasant as his gaze caught the pile at their feet. His hand touched his throat. "What on earth?"

King Lamoni explained, "The evidence of Ammon cutting off the arms of his attackers as he defended my flocks. His strength and obedience to my commands leaves me pondering whether he is more than a man."

The priest made a noise in his throat, sending him into a coughing fit. When he recovered, he said, "Surely you cannot seriously consider such a thing. The man is a deceiving Nephite. Need I say more?"

Gilgah took a step forward. "We have already testified to the king what we have seen with our own eyes. This is the work of one man—Ammon."

"Silence," Japethihah hissed. "No one asked you to speak, but since you wish to be so *helpful,* clear away this mess." Japethihah turned back to the king. "The gods will be angry indeed. I shall appease them through sacrificing the offending Nephite, who has pulled this deception over you. The offering might also entertain your guests."

Lamoni noted Gilgah's restraint as he opened his mouth then clamped it shut and folded his arms. "No," the king said. "I am curious to hear the Nephite give a recounting of his actions."

"Beware. He will only speak lies to his advantage."

Thick silence followed the priest's claim. Lamoni glanced around the room, perceiving apprehensive faces. He saw Gilgah press his lips into a thin line. "Nevertheless." The king's voice was controlled yet firm.

Japethihah drew a strong breath through his nostrils and let it out. "Let my warning be remembered. No good will come from this Nephite." He glanced once more around the room. With a flip of his garment, the priest strode away.

Within minutes, Ammon entered through the same arch which Japethihah had departed from. He took a few steps forward, stared at the silent, somber group, and turned to leave.

The servant closest to Ammon told him in a low voice, "Rabbanah, Great and Powerful One, the king desires that you stay."

Ammon stopped abruptly and slowly pivoted. A few more strides, and he arrived halfway into the room. "Here I am. What will you have me do for you, O King?"

Lamoni caught the scent of the stable upon Ammon's muddied sandals, and for once it seemed sweet to him. He marveled at the Nephite's faithfulness while not daring to meet Ammon's eyes for more than an instant; he stared at the floor while the silence stretched on. An awful recognition of how many scores he had killed over petty grievances filled his mind. Shameful horror and guilt weighed on his heart, pressing and squeezing until his eyes were drawn to a subtle movement. Ammon had turned to take in the scene. The king watched as Ammon's gaze fell upon the red limbs on the floor and then back at him. At least these deaths were not his to claim.

Still the king held his tongue. *What can I say to one stronger and more powerful than I, than my father? Will he strike me for my evil deeds?* Beads of sweat formed on Lamoni's brow.

"What do you desire of me?" Ammon prompted, his uneasiness showing in the slump of his shoulders, his head down while he waited.

Gilgah licked his lips. The king noticed but ignored him and everyone else. Over and over in his mind, Lamoni questioned what he should say. He felt disturbingly small but in a different way than his father made him feel.

It seemed an hour had gone by when the king saw a change come over Ammon's patient stance. His body straightened to full height, his face seemed to shine, and he gazed toward the ceiling. Lamoni swallowed against his tightening throat.

Ammon spoke softly yet boldly. "Is it because you heard that I defended your servants and flocks, slaying seven of their brethren with the sling and the sword, and smiting off the arms of others in defense? Is this the cause of your marvelings?"

The king's intake of air could be heard in the hushed room. He locked his eyes on Ammon's. Still he could make no other sound.

"Why is your marveling so great, O King? Behold, I am a man who is your servant. Whatever you desire of me that is right, I will do."

A man? How could that be? "Who are you? Are you that Great Spirit who knows all things?" The king's voice barely reached Ammon.

"I am not."

King Lamoni leaned forward. "Then how do you know the thoughts of my heart? Please, speak boldly and tell me concerning these things. And also, tell me by what power you could do all this."

The servants and guards blinked in anticipation, but King Lamoni disregarded them. The tingle of something important prickled at his spine.

"If you will tell me concerning these things," Lamoni added, "I will give unto you whatsoever you desire. And if it were needed, I would guard you with my armies, but I know you are more powerful than all they. Nevertheless, I will grant whatever you desire."

Did Ammon struggle to hide a smile? King Lamoni felt a tightening in his gut. After causing such wonder and stirrings within, this better not have been a trick. Ammon had refused the offer of taking one of Lamoni's daughters to marry, but would he take advantage this time? *Does he want my kingdom?* Loathing giving so much up, Lamoni knew he must stay true to his word. He straightened and waited to hear the request of this great being.

"Will you hear and believe my words if I tell you by what power I do these things? This is all I desire of you."

The king had to close his slackened mouth. He could see amazement on the servant's faces, and one scratched his head. The king eagerly answered. "Yes, I will believe all your words."

"Do you believe there is a God?"

"I do not know what that means."

Gilgah's gaze bounced from Ammon's to the king's. The servants seemed as eager to learn as Lamoni. Though their presence was somewhat annoying and intrusive, the king did not dismiss them. It might be good to have them here as witnesses to Ammon's message.

"Do you believe there is a Great Spirit?"

"Yes."

"This is God." Ammon continued with everyone's full attention, "Do you believe that this Great Spirit, who is God, created all things in heaven and in the earth?"

"I believe that He created the things of the earth, but I do not know the heavens," the king admitted.

"The heavens are the place where God and His holy angels dwell."

"Is it above the earth?" King Lamoni asked.

"Yes, and God looks down upon the children of men. He loves all His children and knows the thoughts and intents of the heart, for by His hand they were created."

"I believe what you have spoken." Lamoni meant it as if he'd spoken an oath.

Ammon paused, touching a hand to his chest, and the king looked into his glistening eyes. He waited for Ammon to regain his composure, thirsty for more.

"Are you sent from God?" the king prompted.

"I am a man," Ammon said, "and man, in the beginning, was created after the image of God. I am called by His Holy Spirit to teach these things to this people that you may be brought to a knowledge of that which is just and true. A portion of this Spirit dwells in me. It gives me knowledge and power according to my desires and faith in God."

Ammon looked around the room and spoke to all. "I would like to teach you from the beginning about the Creation of the world and the creation of Adam, the first man on earth."

Lamoni nodded both his interest and his permission. No one but Ammon moved. The servants looked to their king with fear that he might dismiss them. For some strange reason, Lamoni wanted them to stay and told them so.

Ammon taught from the Fall of man in the Garden of Eden down to the time their ancestor, Lehi, left Jerusalem. Then Ammon rehearsed from memory the history concerning the rebellions and journeys of Laman, Lemuel, and the sons of Ishmael. Lamoni recognized that it was this same Ishmael for whom this region, as well as one of his sons, had been named.

The words were spellbinding, and Lamoni lost all track of time as the scriptures were explained down to the present day. It saddened him to think that they had followed those incorrect traditions with vehemence. He felt cheated and blinded by the traditions he'd carried on without question. Now he questioned everything. Was his governing existence one great falsehood? He felt responsible to make changes in the lives of his people.

"My heart pounds within me," Gilgah dared to state during a pause.

Ammon gave a gentle response. "Yes, my friend. You are feeling the Spirit of the Lord here among us." He smiled at each man.

The prominent smell of cooked onions and spices wafted into the room, hinting that the meal for the king and his guests would soon be ready, but food seemed too frivolous to deter them from Ammon's preaching. If their stomachs were empty, none seemed to care.

Finally, Ammon expounded to them the plan of redemption, prepared from the foundation of the world, where Christ would save all men who would repent and come unto Him.

This was the answer Lamoni sought. This is what his people needed to know. He licked his lips, growing excited that there was something strong and powerful enough to cause a break in tradition with his people. Lamoni's eyes were moist, and the thudding of his beating heart reached his ears. He thought of his own need to repent and of his desire to give up his sins for something greater, and these thoughts sent peace to his soul. Glorious warmth filled him, and he wanted to shout it from the mountaintops.

Without warning, he stood and affirmed before the men, "I believe all these teachings to be true. I want to be forgiven." He looked upward, clasped his hands together, and said, "O Lord, according to thy abundant mercy which shines upon the people of Nephi, have mercy upon me and my people."

All the strength seemed to go out of Lamoni's body, and he slumped to the ground as if he were dead.

Chapter Twelve

ANNOYED BY HEPKA'S PACING IN her bedchamber, Karlinah cried, "Would you stop?"

Hepka halted, and deep silence filled the air. She went over to a hand-hewn stool next to her sister, sat, and slipped her fingers under her thighs to avoid chewing her nails. More than an hour had passed since Ishmael's visit, and still no one summoned them to meet with their visitors.

"It must be that Nephite's doing." Karlinah squeezed her hands into fists.

"He is showing off to Father and the guests without us," Hepka said.

"Maybe Father already executed Ammon, and that is what is taking so long." Karlinah's stomach growled, sending her into motion. She stood and paced the floor.

Hepka laughed out loud, and Karlinah realized she'd been caught performing the same annoying practice. Rolling her eyes, Karlinah grabbed Hepka's hand. "Come on. Let's find out what's happening or at least grab a bite to eat from the cookery. I'm starving."

Karlinah led the way to their mother's bedchamber. They rounded a corner and saw a gathering of servants outside her doorway. Something was wrong. Karlinah could feel it in the pit of her stomach. Dropping Hepka's hand, she rushed to the door with her sister in close pursuit. Servants parted to let them enter.

There upon the queen's bed of silk pillows lay the body of their father. Their mother sat near his head and looked up at her daughters with tears streaming down her cheeks. Karlinah gasped, feeling like a fist had punched her stomach. Hepka gave a gargled exclamation. Three nervous-looking dignitaries and their wives stared at the sisters, whispering and wringing their hands from the back of the room where the queen's clothing hung from wall pegs and baskets.

"Is he . . . ?" Karlinah couldn't finish. She did not smell death, only the scent of flowers in a vase next to the washbasin. Did any hope exist?

Their mother gave a slow nod, and Hepka's knees buckled. A servant quickly supported her.

Karlinah's breath caught as a sharp pain stabbed her heart. She stood in shock, eyes glued on the stiff body. For a moment she reminisced the similar image at her husband's funeral with his body laid out on a bier, only this time she loved the person who had died.

The queen gulped air through choking sobs. "They carried him in to me like this"—her hand passed across her husband's body—"with no warning." She shrank back down upon her abalone-decorated chair, appearing small and fragile, like a frightened child.

This was too personal for the three couples lining the back wall. They looked as uncomfortable as Karlinah felt. It fell to her to release them from the awkward situation. She approached them with composure she did not feel. "I apologize for the difficulty of the situation and beg your understanding. My mother will be unavailable for the rest of the evening. Our servants will see to your comfort until you return home tomorrow."

The compliant guests backed out of the room, leaving a few consoling words on their way out. The servants also left the queen to grieve alone.

Karlinah knelt by her mother's side and put an arm around her, shaking her head in disbelief. In a strange way, she felt glad to know her mother had tears for her father. This proved that her parents' relationship differed from hers with Masoni. Maybe time was all it took. It gave her hope that she could eventually accept or at least tolerate Japethihah. Was happiness possible for her?

Hepka's sniffles brought Karlinah's attention around; she forced other thoughts away.

"How?" Karlinah wanted to know. No blood or marks could be seen. Through blurred tears, an image came to her of a knife sticking out of Masoni's side and the memory of her hand seeming to burn after she released her grip on its handle.

The queen shook her head, her voice barely reaching above Hepka's sobs. "Japethihah says that evil has come upon our house because of the Nephite. I am told the white man was speaking with Lamoni when it happened. There are no indications on his body. Maybe his heart gave out.

He merely sat on his throne, speaking . . ." She let her words trail off. "His guests were waiting, and I was left to entertain until his business finished. Thank you for getting rid of them." Mierah glanced at her daughter. "Now to get rid of this Nephite. I can't do this." She covered her eyes with her hands.

Karlinah patted her mother's back as a vision convened in her mind of the Nephite standing before her father's throne, a pile of arms strewn at his feet. *Did he upset my father enough to kill him? Did the white man administer some kind of poison?* Her eyes flashed in anger. Who saw what this Nephite did? He must own up to his blame! Her fists balled. Bile crept up her throat and, just as suddenly, choked back down. *Had Masoni's father felt anger like this?* The only reason he could have treated her as kindly as he did was his lack of suspicion. Guilt crept into her mind, but she told herself to ignore it. Others had done things much worse than she. It was time to confirm her suspicions and make certain the Nephite got the punishment he deserved.

"Stay with mother, Hepka." Karlinah gulped air, rose, and marched out of the room, storming past the queen's doorway servant, who looked up in surprise. She wanted to find the menservants who might know something.

Turning the corner, Karlinah spied Lamonihah down the hallway, speaking with a few men. She slipped back out of sight and listened. The answers reaching her ears were not as she expected.

"He stood several paces back from the king," a man's voice said. "Ammon never touched him."

Karlinah wished she could see the faces gathered. She listened carefully.

"Ammon's eyes shone, and he spoke with power," another said. "His message pierced us to the center."

Karlinah ground her teeth, breathing deeply through flared nostrils. Such nonsense they fed her brother. They were all in it together. Japethihah was right. The Nephite brought evil and violence. The bloody arms proved it. But what of the conversation had she missed?

"What was this message from the Nephite?" Lamonihah questioned.

The first speaker took over again. "He taught us about the creations of the Great Spirit, who is God. He then explained the scriptures from Father Lehi's time down to ours, showing us of the incorrect traditions of our fathers."

"Nephite lies," Karlinah rasped then put a hand over her mouth, sorry to have betrayed herself so early. Too late now, she strode right for them, arms swinging and chin held high until she stopped abruptly next to her brother. Karlinah's forcefulness gave them little choice but to open up the tight circle.

One of the younger servants with a shaved head straightened and faced her directly. "Forgive my boldness, princess, but if you were there to hear Ammon speak of these things, you would have believed too."

Karlinah blinked at the audacious youth, opened her mouth, and closed it. Had he lost his senses? And how could he presume to know what she would think? Gilgah should reprimand his charge, and Lamonihah shouldn't let a servant talk to her that way, but they overlooked it. She wanted to protest, but words didn't come.

"And my father believed in the preaching of Ammon?" Lamonihah asked, ignoring his sister's sputtering.

"He did," the youth confirmed. "And he cried out to the Lord asking for mercy upon him and his people. That was when he was overcome and fell to the earth."

Lamonihah's eyes narrowed. "Overcome?"

The servant thumped his chest. "The feelings that came into our hearts were strong—powerful enough that we now only want to do good." He lowered his eyes. "Perhaps the heavy burden of the past murders of the king's servants troubled his mind to the point of collapse."

"Ha!" Karlinah burst out. That didn't sound like her father one bit. He was king and could do whatever he liked. If Lamonihah didn't put an end to this foolishness soon, she would.

Gilgah cleared his throat. "I do not believe the king is dead but that he sleeps under the protection of the Great Spirit."

Karlinah and Lamonihah stared at him incredulously, open-mouthed. Karlinah remembered seeing Gilgah at the entrance to her mother's room. Hadn't he helped carry the still body? How could he say such a thing? Now she knew his mind was not clear.

"Ammon preached of life—not death," Gilgah continued. "Christ shall come and do mighty works upon the earth. Why not show a mighty miracle unto—or through—our king?" He stroked his chin. "Something tells me to wait and see." The man's tone remained serious, calm. No one spoke.

Wonder pricked at Karlinah's mind. Lamonihah slowly shook his head in bewilderment. He excused himself from the circle, took Karlinah by the arm, and escorted her back to their mother's bedchamber, where they found the rest of their siblings. Ishmael, Jarom, and Hepka softly cried, but little Tobias played contentedly with a ball at his mother's feet. Mother seemed to have gained control of her emotions for the moment, but she appeared to be in some sort of stupor; her eyes stared through them. Karlinah noted Evah's absence, likely troubled with the sickness of women in the early stage of being with child.

Japethihah was there, praying over her father's body. She tightened her lips then relaxed. His presence could be soothing her mother. When he finished the words, he nodded at the new arrivals and left the room. Karlinah felt glad not to have to speak with him.

A healer had placed a poultice on their father's forehead to draw out impurities. It would either stimulate circulation if he lived or allow him to become clean for burial. Then the priest had done his part with chanting and incense. Bloodletting might be considered next. An involuntary shudder coiled down her spine.

Karlinah watched as Lamonihah touched his father's cheek. By the astonished look on his face, her brother must have felt warmth. He lifted a finger of his father's hand, and the joint flexed. Lamonihah's fingers tried to find life in his father's neck, but Lamonihah said he couldn't tell if the faint throb was his own. Karlinah couldn't forget the lack of color in Masoni's face nor his horrified stare, but her father's color remained, his features peaceful. Was it too soon for his body to be cold? Or did their father really sleep in the Great Spirit's protection? This seemed such a strange concept, though she wanted to believe it. She closed her eyes hopefully but found no answers. Would the gods give Japethihah some sign that her father would live? She decided to ask him and slipped out the way the priest had gone.

Finding him kneeling before three different idols at the front porch altar, Karlinah paused. He must have heard her, for he turned his head in her direction.

"Excuse me," she said, her question suddenly vanishing as he looked at her with a stony face. This mask she knew all too well. *He's displeased with me and won't give away any of his thoughts until I share first.* She would play his game this time. "Noble Priest, I, uh, hoped the gods could tell you what is happening with my father."

"I am seeking inspiration even as we speak." He kept his voice even, but his face softened. "And please call me Japethihah. I am your betrothed, after all."

Karlinah wouldn't let that last part seep into her mind, didn't think of him that way. She needed to know about her father. "Then you don't know what will become of him?"

"No, not yet." His eyes held hers until she looked away.

The king's condition would undoubtedly put off their marriage, and now her father could never recant his pronouncement by finding another more suitable match at the feast. It seemed senseless to ask, but a lack of communication—she had learned through Masoni—bred undesirable surprise.

"Obviously our . . . marriage must be delayed. No one can think of anything but our king. My wedding clothes have not been procured. Neither have the servants been instructed concerning the arrangements." She shrugged as she held out questioning hands.

Japethihah took a step toward her. "The last message I received from the gods pertained to our inevitable betrothal. I am expecting the ceremony to take place in eleven days when the stars are favorable," the lilt to his voice returning, "with or without King Lamoni. Your brother can represent your father if need be, and I don't care what you wear. On this, the gods have spoken, and we *shall* obey."

Karlinah glowered, hot pressure building in her throat. If this indicated his attitude once they were married . . . she'd better let him know now that his prize would not be a docile one. She might be forced to marry, but he would know what kind of woman he was getting.

"How dare you demand such a thing with my father in this condition!" Her breaths came faster as she seethed. "You'd prefer a grief-stricken wife on your honeymoon? I don't care about the stars. Let the gods wait." She folded her arms and stared back at him. Unlike Masoni's household, she could be herself here. Japethihah had better get used to it because she wasn't about to relinquish her passions.

Half of the priest's mouth curled upward. "You are quite right. Our honeymoon should be filled with pleasure, not grief. I am certain the gods would be satisfied to wait until"—he rested a finger on his chin—"a respectful seven days after the king's burial."

Karlinah flushed with heat. He'd turned her words to his favor. *This cunning, conniving, selfish old man will be just like Masoni!* With no response and tears threatening, she spun toward the exit. A soft chuckle pursued her.

Karlinah could hardly think. She paced the hall, fists tight, not sure whether her knotted stomach would welcome food or if she should go to bed hungry. The sight of Abish rounding the corner sent a sigh through Karlinah's body, and she unclenched her hands. "Abish!" The woman opened her arms, and Karlinah welcomed her embrace.

"There, there," Abish cooed, patting Karlinah's back. "Things are not as bad as they seem."

Karlinah broke away to look at Abish. Instead of the placated look she expected, Karlinah found unyielding features that could almost make promises to her. Before she could ponder on it, Abish took her hand and led Karlinah down the hall.

"You get a good night's rest," Abish said, "and we'll speak more tomorrow. Things will become clearer soon. It will be all right."

Alone in her bedchamber, the weight of enduring too much at once caved in on her. Karlinah let the tears fall, emotion washing down her cheeks. She finally grasped at the hope that if Lamonihah became king sooner than later, it might work in her favor. Though he liked the match, her brother did not share the same bond or loyalty to the high priest that her father had. Persuading him about a different arrangement might be possible. But Japethihah had a greater gift with speech than she and would also try to sway the new king. Whatever she talked Lamonihah into, Japethihah would talk him out of. Pulling the feathers from her hair, Karlinah let them fall to the ground.

One certainty lingered—there would be no celebration feast tonight or on the morrow.

Chapter Thirteen

KARLINAH AWOKE IN HER BED the next morning with a dull ache in her head and an empty stomach. A dream of a drunken Masoni coming at her with his knife burned in her mind until last night's events flooded back to her, replacing the knife's awful image. Her father's body and the servants that caused doubt seemed surreal. She was grateful for Abish, who had walked her back to her room, patted her hand, and told her everything would turn out right. She'd seemed so certain. Sitting up in bed, Karlinah recalled the hope in Abish's and Gilgah's voices from last night and let it build. What if Father had awakened on this new day from whatever state his body was in? What if he were alive?

Rising too quickly, Karlinah swooned then caught her balance. She stepped to her clothing baskets and noticed a food tray left for her by Abish. Though ravenous, the greater longing prevailed. She quickly put on her rabbit-skin robe, girded it around her, and threw open the door.

Sounds at the front entrance told Karlinah their guests were leaving. She must have slept late. A familiar squeal turned her head in the other direction. She saw Tobias running from the servant who chased him. No doubt her duties consisted of entertaining him and keeping him away from their sorrowful mother.

Karlinah knocked at her mother's door and heard nothing. She tried once more before gingerly opening the door. No one, not even the body of her father remained in the room. Believing they would not take his body to the sepulchre without the people of Ishmael being allowed to pay their respects, she tried her father's room next and then, finding it empty, rushed to the throne room. Wouldn't it be marvelous to find her father sitting on his throne? Her heartbeat quickened as she stepped through one of the arched openings into the spacious room.

Incense, intended to mask the smell of death, filled Karlinah's nostrils. There in the middle of the room, the still body of King Lamoni lay on a raised bed. A guard stood near each corner of the bed. Her mother slept in a chair next to the bed, wearing the same long dress as last night, her head resting on her husband's arm. Nothing had changed. Nothing. Instantly, fresh tears spilled onto her cheeks. Karlinah backed out of the room.

She raced down the hall to her chamber, not wanting to talk to anyone. The tray of food no longer held appeal. She threw herself on her cushions and sobbed. After a time, she sat up, ready to nibble some fruit while questions filled her mind. She tried to imagine how the land of Ishmael would function without its king. Was Lamonihah ready to take charge? What would she have to face? It became hard to breathe. A troubling uncertainty forced Karlinah back to the throne room. It felt cavernous and suffocating at the same time. Her lungs seemed to find more air when she saw her mother awake, her arms outstretched. The embrace offered comfort.

In the afternoon, Japethihah came to freshen the incense and pray with the family. He gave a kindly smile and took two steps toward her. She stiffened. He raised an eyebrow at her and turned to face the queen. He asked Queen Mierah about burial arrangements, but she would not discuss it. Perhaps her mother had unsettling questions as well or her reasons included a headache as she rubbed at her temples. Once more, Japethihah begged the queen to allow wailers in to frighten away the god of death and the underworld.

"Go pray at one of the altars," the queen suggested, dismissing him.

Karlinah managed to keep a straight face. Japethihah cast one long glance Karlinah's way as he strode away. She couldn't tear her eyes from him, fearing he might come back, but he never turned around.

Not long after, Queen Mierah allowed household servants to drift in and out, paying their respects. Most bowed silently before their king, lingering briefly with their own memories of him before returning to their chores. It gave Karlinah something new to watch while they waited. *Waited for what?* That was the unspoken question.

When two of the guards came in together, Karlinah caught something of their whisperings.

"So he still sleeps?" The larger man nudged the other.

The second guard shrugged. He lowered his voice, but Karlinah made out the word *prophet* before they went silent. She watched them through narrowed dark eyes until they glanced her way. She shifted her gaze and walked over to Lamonihah, Evah, and Hepka. She waited until the guards were gone, hating the feeling that they might know more than she did about her father's condition.

The queen turned to her older children and whispered, "Do you know this prophet of whom they speak?"

So her mother had been listening too.

Mierah's voice rushed on. "Is this the Nephite who slew the arms of those who would scatter the king's flock? I have heard from the servants that the arms were brought as a witness of marvelous loyalty to the king."

Understanding dawned, and Karlinah closed her eyes, letting out a soft groan. "Ammon . . . protected the flocks?" She shook her head. She had been so wrong and could no longer blame him.

Lamonihah gave his sister a sideways glance before answering his mother. "I do not know if he is a prophet, but he is familiar with the records of Nephite prophets and expounded them before Father fell to the earth."

"So he witnessed my husband's . . . death?"

Lamonihah nodded. "Yes, along with a score of servants and guards who heard the Nephite preach." He placed a hand on Mierah's arm. "Mother, I do not wish to upset you or give you false hope." He paused.

Karlinah ignored her feeling of stupidity and held her breath. It was time to put aside her prejudice and listen. Hepka also leaned in to listen while Evah stood calmly next to her husband.

Mierah looked around. The guards were on the other side of the room in their own conversation. "Speak freely, my son."

Lamonihah licked his lips. "There are servants—Gilgah for one—who say Father is not dead but sleeps in the Great Spirit's care. I don't know what to make of it. Father is as still as stone, but I do not think his body stinks, as some have suggested."

"I too have been troubled by the warmth and softness I feel when I touch him." Tears glistened in Mierah's eyes, and she went over to touch her husband's cheek.

The sisters did the same and verified the warmth. His skin felt pliable, his color rich with flowing blood. Karlinah almost expected him to wake any second and speak to her.

If she could only will it to be so. She bit at her lip.

"It was not like this," their mother said, rubbing Lamoni's hand, "when our little Ammarish died five years ago. I felt her warmth in my arms while she struggled for breath—warmth that instantly left her body when she died." She choked on her next words. "I . . . stroked her tiny cheek for a moment and could . . . feel the soft skin tighten and turn gray. Before we buried my baby, her little body was stiff and hard." Mierah's body shook with sobs.

Karlinah put an arm around her mother's shoulders as tears sprang to her own eyes. Hepka noisily sobbed, and Evah wiped silent tears. After a moment, their mother straightened, her jawline resolute.

"I will not allow my husband's body to be put in the sepulchre while it still has warmth. We will not yet sound these events beyond this household."

Wide-eyed, Karlinah listened, her heart stilling.

The queen stood firm for a moment before collapsing into a chair, a more relaxed look coming to her face. She sighed. Her eyes went to the nearby food tray, and Evah brought it to her. Mierah chewed and made soft noises, telling Karlinah her mother actually tasted this meal. The flat maize cake topped with fried quail eggs surrounded by green peppers and onions looked appetizing, and Karlinah suddenly realized that what little she'd eaten wasn't enough. As she left for the cooking room, she saw her mother rise from her chair to speak, renewed strength shining through her eyes.

"I want to see this Nephite."

Chapter Fourteen

AMMON NOTICED THE SERVANT BOY coming his way as soon as he entered the king's house.

"Ammon, the queen summons you. She's waiting in her bedchamber. Follow me."

Stopping first at the servant quarters to wash his hands and face, Ammon followed the boy, who led him down the corridors on the family side of the vestibule. Two guards at the queen's doorway accepted him without question. The boy left him to step inside alone.

Ammon couldn't help but notice the fine things in her room. A dozen pillows sat on the silky bed cushion. Wooden pegs mortared between the stonework held a score of embroidered robes and dresses. Baskets of jewelry, combs, and feathered headdresses sat on the dirt floor below them. A mosaic-tiled table held a painted water jar and wash basin; a vase of hibiscus flowers left a light, delicious scent in the air. Next to the small table sat a chair with the seat and back inlaid with abalone shell. He quickly took it all in and faced the mistress.

"My Queen." He bowed. "I am here at your command. What would you have me do?"

Large, jade earrings framed the queen's heart-shaped face, a face lacking the pain of a woman in grief. She stood gracefully with her hands interlaced in front of her. Silver bracelets rested at both wrists. A hopeful look filled her dark eyes. Her voice sounded gentle, humble.

"The servants of my husband have made it known to me that you are a prophet of a holy God and have power to do many mighty works in His name." She paused to study him, and he dipped his head once.

"If this is the case, I wish for you to go into the throne room and see my husband. He has lain upon his bed for the space of two days. Some say he is not dead, but others disagree and say he ought to be placed in the sepulchre. As for myself, to me he does not stink."

An opportunity presented itself that didn't often come along. Ammon curtailed a smile lest she think him arrogant over the praise. Here stood a woman who trusted in him with hope for her husband's life at the word of servants. Servants. If that wasn't humility, he didn't know what was.

Ammon bobbed his head again, his heart swelling. "I shall do as you bid."

Queen Mierah walked with Ammon to the doorway and commanded a guard to escort Ammon to the king's body and then back to her room, according to however long Ammon wished to take.

Once he reached the royal body, he appreciated her prudence in this regard, especially with the king's two daughters in the throne room scrutinizing his every movement. They watched with guarded eyes but spoke no words to him. He thought it best to take no notice of them, especially the oldest, spirited one.

Ammon placed a hand on the king's forehead and then took his limp, pliant hand in his own. He closed his eyes, striving to ignore the glares, to feel the Spirit of the Lord. He took in a deep breath and waited for the calm he knew would come. Soft words floated into his mind: *Tomorrow Lamoni shall rise.* The strong beat of a drum hammered against his heart, threatening to burst open the warmth swelling inside. When the feeling faded, Ammon opened his eyes and turned, allowing the guard to escort him back to the queen.

The bedchamber door remained open, and Ammon clapped his hands to signal his entrance, bowing once more. Queen Mierah took a step toward him, her eyes bright and wide in expectation.

"I have done as you bid and can tell you with certainty that your husband is not dead but sleeps in God." She beamed, and he continued, "His natural frame was overcome with joy from the light of the glory of God. The dark veil of unbelief is being cast away from the king's mind. Tomorrow he shall rise again."

Visible relief washed over the queen's face before her lip quivered as if she might cry.

"Do you believe this?" It seemed obvious, but it furthered Ammon's purpose to ask.

"I've had no witness except your word and the word of our servants; nevertheless, I believe it will be as you have said."

Ammon's heart pounded again at the power of her words. Could it be that simple for her? "There has not been such great faith among all the Nephites." His voice held awe.

The queen put a hand to her mouth, her eyes glistening. Ammon could see her struggle to find her voice. She blinked and swallowed. "The Great Spirit has chosen to make Himself known to us," she managed in a whisper. "Thank you. Do you know your way out?"

"Yes." Ammon bowed and quietly left the room. Glancing back at a sound, he wasn't surprised to see her follow him out and turn in the direction of the throne room. This graceful woman of faith would watch over the body of her husband from that time forward, expecting to see King Lamoni wake.

***

The golden sun of a new day filtered from the inner courtyard through the stone archways of the throne room. The light stretched onto Queen Mierah's face; she opened her eyes and squinted. Chiding herself for dozing off in her chair, Mierah found instant reassurance, expressed in a sigh, at the presence of her husband's still body. She had not missed the miracle.

The chief servant over the sheep entered through the curtained doorway from the vestibule and bowed before the queen. Whatever he wanted would wait. She stood impatiently and clicked her tongue. "Do not bother me now, Gilgah."

"Forgive me, O Queen. I require nothing from you. I . . . a sensation came over me to check the condition of the king."

Mierah cleared her throat and spoke louder. "Not now." She waved the back of her hand in dismissal and returned her eyes to her husband.

With words of, "As you wish, my Queen," Gilgah lingered to glimpse at the king on his way out. Mierah found it briefly irritating but didn't care to focus on it. The servant slowly backed away as another figure caught her eye. Ammon. His intrusion annoyed her less, but she wished to remain alone.

The curious Gilgah lingered inside an archway at one edge of the large throne room. Mierah shot him a disapproving look, wishing she could match her husband's commanding presence, but she became distracted by Ammon's expression. He stared in wonder at her husband.

The creeping golden light made its way across the king's face, and he opened his eyes. The queen took in a sharp breath as King Lamoni sat up and then rose from his bed. The miracle! Queen Mierah rushed to her husband, and he stretched forth his hand to her. Love, relief, and joy all flooded her heart; she cried an indistinguishable sound. His smile sent an unspoken message that warmed her throughout.

A strangled gasp from the back of the room heightened Mierah's awareness that Gilgah and the guards had also witnessed the miracle, though this fact became insignificant compared to the joy filling her entire body.

"Blessed be the name of God, and blessed are you," Lamoni said in a strong voice.

Happy tears streamed as she clasped her husband's hand. Their eyes locked.

"As sure as you are standing here, I have seen my Redeemer!" he continued. "He will be born of a woman, and He will redeem all mankind who believe on His name."

Questions filled her mind. She wanted to drink in all that he could tell her, and it wouldn't come fast enough. This energy built to a tingling sensation, a heady dizzying that intensified until it seemed too much to bear. All at once, the thrill seemed to burst her heart, and the floor rose to meet her.

***

He had been right to come. The feeling that he would witness something marvelous had driven Gilgah toward the body of his king. Then a glorious light seemed to awaken him. Awe held Gilgah's feet in place. Warmth filled him to the very center of his being as his king spoke words of truth.

Then the miracle turned into something alarming.

Gilgah and the guards gaped as both the king and queen sunk down and lay on the floor. Two guards seemed unable to move, and another shrunk back in fear while the fourth took a tentative step toward the royal couple, stopping when Ammon fell to his knees. The Nephite's voice carried through the stillness.

"O God, I thank thee for blessing these Lamanites and turning them from iniquity. Be with and protect this king and queen until they receive strength according to Thy will. May these events bear witness of Thy love and may this people accept Thy tender mercies. Amen."

Instantly Ammon collapsed to the earth near the bodies of the king and queen.

If it weren't for that gnawing feeling to check on the king, Gilgah would have missed this great wonder. A sensation of gratitude that could have melted the marrow in his bones warmed him. His knees quaked and buckled, but the uncontrollable sensation held reverence rather than fear. From the floor, he could see four guards crumble to the tile. They cried out to the Lord in both fear and awe. Gilgah felt compelled to join their voices in prayer and praise.

A maidservant came in with a tray of food for the queen. Startled at the sight, she dropped the tray with a clatter and ran back to the cookery.

"Come see what has happened!" Gilgah heard her call.

Even as homage flowed from his lips, he saw six maidservants rush into the throne room from the cooking room. At that moment, a man called his name. Ahabi and his fellowservants had come looking for Gilgah and heard the commotion.

The curious sight of the king, the queen, and Ammon lying prostrate on the ground beckoned the new arrivals cautiously closer. A holy power must have compelled them to join Gilgah on their knees. They began crying out with all their might, acknowledging God's existence. The women's reverent voices blended with theirs. A light-headed sensation was the last thing he remembered before everything went black.

Chapter Fifteen

Noticing that the other voices had ceased to call upon God, Abish opened her eyes to see the others lying, rather than kneeling, on the floor. It didn't occur to her to feel afraid. Her heart pounded furiously, yet peace permeated the room. A trembling smile creased Abish's cheeks as emotion flooded her heart. Soon she would be free of her secret.

She stood with her hands clasped to her chest, looking at but not seeing the figures on the tile. Her mind filled with the face of her father when she, at eleven years of age, heard him tell her family of his own remarkable vision from the Lord. They became believers in God and tried to follow His teachings as best they could. Following the illness and subsequent death of her parents not long afterward, she entered the household of the king as a servant.

Already having learned that, in her culture, it meant her life to keep these beliefs to herself, Abish tried to be an example of goodness, which had earned her the responsibilities with the queen's baby daughter at the age of twelve. Keeping a measure of faith within her heart, she never dreamed circumstances would change. Now she thrilled at the prospect of sharing this miracle. If the people could see this scene with their own eyes, it would convince them of the power of God.

Abish ran down the hall knocking on doors and calling out to wake any of the household still sleeping. "Come see! Come to the throne room!" She ran down the steps of the front entrance toward the nearest house and pounded on the door until a woman opened it. Abish could smell the morning meal cooking.

"Come and see for yourselves. Great things have happened to King Lamoni and his household. Come quickly!"

Before the woman at the door could open her mouth to ask more, Abish raced off to the next house. A great store of energy fueled Abish as she went from house to house to make the miracle known to the people. A few workers were already in fields behind the huts or out feeding animals, and she shouted to them, attracting attention and motioning with her arms. The clamor sent curious citizens to the king's house. Out of breath, Abish returned to see the fruits of her efforts.

The crowd spilled out onto the front steps. Abish pushed past the people and made her way into the throne room. Coming from the fresh air, the smell of incense and body odor assaulted her nose. The servants lying on the floor took up much of the central space. She found the royal children Jarom and Ishmael in their bedclothes, with perplexed looks on their faces, standing between bodies of servants. Hepka held on to a fussing Tobias, who wanted his mother, and Karlinah stood beside her, looking helpless. Abish caught her eye, nodded reassuringly, and mouthed to Karlinah that everything would be fine, but it did not change her look of worry and annoyance at the noise. Lamonihah crouched beside a guard, touching him for signs of life. He went to a servant next. Abish supposed he had checked his parents first.

Many pressed into the edges of the room through the arches to have a glimpse. Others filled the vestibule leading to the throne room where the thick curtain separating them lay torn underfoot. A great rumbling of voices echoed through the hall with cries of "What has happened?" and "Let me see." Those with a view of the throne room were pushed back for others to have a turn. Shoulders squeezed their way through cracks in the crowd. Abish saw a short man jumping for a look from behind others. Small children perched on their fathers' shoulders. By now, many had inspected the throne room, and a commotion of opinions arose.

"What is this great evil that has come upon the house of the king?" someone cried.

"It is because the king suffered that this Nephite"—a man pointed to Ammon—"should come into our land." There were shouts of agreement.

Abish could believe neither her ears nor her eyes. She saw Karlinah's head bob along with the others. She moved closer to the center.

"No," a voice rebuked the last remark. "This evil is because the king slew his servants who could not keep his flock from being scattered."

"The Nephite has done this iniquity," a recognizable voice insisted. "This is punishment from the gods for the king allowing him into our land."

Abish glared at Japethihah. His influence could sway many with the mention of his gods.

"Do not be so quick to call it evil. It is not certain any of these are dead," Lamonihah shouted. "But I do know that the Nephite has been a protector of the king. He saved our sheep from being scattered."

Abish watched as Karlinah's chin dropped. Clearly, Lamonihah's opinion surprised her.

"Can you not see the bodies on the floor?" a man called out.

A roar of shouting plumed into the air. Lamonihah tried to answer, but his words drowned into the cacophony. Heated discussion erupted throughout the room, and Abish wasn't sure what to do. The chaos lasted for some time and seemed to grow in intensity. Only when the figure of a man pushed through the crowd did the noise die down.

"He slew my brother!" a man with a shaved head spit out fiercely while stepping between bodies on the floor. He moved closer to Ammon and drew his sword.

Time seemed to slow. The glint of the man's sword caught her eye. Beyond the sword, Karlinah's terrified look came into focus. Hepka screamed and whirled little Tobias away from the scene. He started crying, and Karlinah took him in her arms. Gasps and shouts of "No!" echoed through the air. Someone started chanting, "Death to the Nephite," and it grew into a turbulent pitch. Abish could not think what to do. She stared at Lamonihah, willing him to take charge of this madness.

The chanting ceased, and the crowd grew still. The shaved-headed man had paused with a wicked smirk to look at faces around him, seeming to enjoy the attention.

"Give the Nephite what he deserves," Japethihah pronounced with finality.

The enraged man raised the blade in both hands above his head while onlookers stared in shock. Abish shut her eyes, wishing she had never brought on the crowd.

"No!" It was the voice of the eldest prince.

Abish opened her eyes to see Lamonihah pulling his sword from its sheath, preparing to deflect the blow, but he was too late. The man suddenly fell dead to the earth, his sword clanging to the floor.

A collective gasp reverberated. Several shrank from their proximity to the prostrated bodies as if harm would come upon them, but they could go nowhere for the press of the crowd.

Thick silence filled the air while Lamonihah reached to feel if life throbbed in the man's neck. He stood and shook his head. "Without a doubt, this one is dead."

A woman voiced her wonder. "Why can't the Nephite be slain? What is the meaning of this great power?" New hope awakened within Abish.

"He is the Great Spirit," another suggested.

"A Nephite cannot be the Great Spirit. Maybe the Great Spirit sent him."

The companion of the man who now lay dead on the floor said, "He is a monster sent by the Nephites to torment us."

Loud murmurings for and against followed. Not again! Clenched fists bobbed in the air. Abish would have covered her ears if it would have done any good. Tears welled in her eyes. *Stop it. Stop it,* her mind shouted in vain.

"The Great Spirit has sent this Nephite to afflict us because of our iniquities."

A man from out in the vestibule scoffed, "We have no iniquities! It's the Great Spirit that helps the Nephites destroy our people out of jealousy."

The shouting volleyed into sharp contention. Abish frowned. This perfect opportunity had turned sour. Her lip quivered, and tears leaked out as she closed her eyes. *You can do something about it, Abish.* Her eyes flew open, and she twirled to see who had spoken to her. There was no indication. Her head drooped as she pushed the thought aside. *Who am I to gain their ears?* Yes, she had gotten the people here, but now they wanted Ammon dead.

A soft voice filled her mind again, blocking out the clamor and surging her confidence. *Lift the queen by the hand.*

She blinked. A slow smile spread across her wet cheeks as she understood. With squared shoulders, Abish stepped between the servants' bodies and made her way to the queen. The shouting tapered off as several watched her with interest. Voices from the back asked what was happening.

"Stop! They are unclean, and the Nephite's evil will spread to you," Japethihah called through the low murmur. "Do you want to die as well?"

Ignoring the priest, Abish bent and took the queen by the hand. She heard gasps as the queen arose to her feet. Tobias called out with delight to his mother. Abish dared not take her eyes from the queen, though she could hear sobs of relief choking in Hepka's throat, or was it Karlinah? A rumble momentarily rose and fell as curious eyes gazed at the queen.

Her voice pierced through the room. "O blessed Jesus, who has saved me from an awful hell! O blessed God, have mercy on this people!" Then she clasped her hands with joy and spoke in tongues, many words which were not understood. This brought on a volcano of whispers among the people and strange looks of confusion on many faces.

"A magician's trick," a woman called out and stormed from the room. Several followed with murmurs of doubt and rage.

The queen took her husband by the hand and tugged. He rose to stand on his feet.

Surely these miracles would be enough to convince the remaining crowd of God's power. Turning about, Abish found that not all the faces were filled with wonder. Confused and angry voices stirred from this corner or that, implying the display had been set up under false pretenses.

The king must have noticed too. Abish saw him raise his arms to hush those gathered, but the buzz continued. The urgency to draw their attention back to him increased. If the mob got out of control . . . .

"Let the king speak!" Abish was surprised to hear her voice ringing in the air.

Karlinah arched an eyebrow her way. Abish could only return a lopsided grin.

"Listen to your king!" Lamonihah shouted. The volume quickly died down as attention turned to the king.

Lamoni spread his arms out in front of him. "Do not doubt the goodness of God in this matter. I, your king, tell you that I have seen my Redeemer, and He has shown me mercy."

"The king is deceived!" the high priest cried. Abish wanted to sew his lips shut. "He speaks of a white man's invisible god. Your gods stand upon altars and in your houses where all can see them. They protect your crops and your children. Listen to this foolishness no more. Follow me." He jerked his flowing robe with both hands and dramatically marched from the room. A small following trailed behind him. *Good riddance*, Abish thought.

Lamoni continued strongly as if oblivious to the outburst. "I truly have seen the Christ, who shall come to earth and be born of a virgin. His mercy is available to all who repent of their wicked ways. Listen to my words, O people of my kingdom, as taught to me by the Lord's servant, Ammon."

At the mention of the Nephite, there were some who would listen no more and turned to flee the king's house. Abish watched them go, her heart aching.

The queen's children gathered for hugs from her while their father preached. His words centered on repentance and God's love for His children. Many stood transfixed by the king's teachings; others settled comfortably on the tile. The message appeared as joyous to them as it was to Abish. Her father had also seen in a vision that Christ should come to earth. He had taught her a portion of the same things that King Lamoni now spoke—that through Christ's Atonement all could become clean. She yearned these long years to know more than what her father had taught, but she'd never hoped anything as glorious as this could happen. Thankfulness swelled in her bosom. Her eyes scanned the crowd, observing that Ammon had risen and helped the remaining servants to their feet.

It wasn't long before the king motioned for Ammon to come and stand next to him. With his hand on Ammon's shoulder, the king said, "My people, this is a true man of God. Give ear to his words, for I would like Ammon to teach us the gospel of Christ."

Ammon then taught more words from the Lord to the attentive audience. Time passed without notice. Abish learned that she was created by God as His spirit child and she could return to dwell with Him after death if she was made clean by partaking of the gift of the Atonement through repentance. She thrilled to know that her parents' lives existed beyond the grave. Lastly, Ammon spoke of baptism. She wanted to become a member of Christ's true Church and witness that she believed; she wanted to follow His ways and be saved from eternal damnation.

Servants mingled with citizens, declaring that their hearts had been changed. They no longer desired to hurt or offend or do any manner of evil. Some witnessed to having conversed with angels, learning the things of God and His righteousness.

Abish wondered what it would be like to talk with an angel. She thought of her parents, who had gone to heaven. Did they speak with angels? Just then, Hepka approached with hands clutched to her bosom. She reached for Abish, and the two embraced.

"I've never felt like this before," Hepka confided. "Such joy fills me! All of us are children of God. You are no longer my servant—you are my friend, my equal."

"We should serve one another," Abish replied.

"I can't wait for baptism, as Ammon says we must accept."

Abish beamed at Hepka for a moment before turning toward the eyes she felt penetrating her. There stood Karlinah with arms crossed. Her head tilted to one side, and the familiar skeptical twisting of her rosebud mouth appeared. Abish's heart sank.

Her favorite member of the king's household had not been converted.

Chapter Sixteen

KARLINAH PEERED INTO THE THRONE room. The curtain had not yet been replaced from yesterday's commotion, and she could see her father speaking with Ammon. She withdrew a few steps into the hall, pacing back and forth while the guards pretended she was invisible. Hearing footsteps, she peeked into the room and saw Ammon exit another way. Karlinah caught her father's eye with a wave, and he gave her a broad smile as she stepped inside.

"Do you have a moment?" she asked.

"For you, my Karlinah, always." He stretched out his arm, and she came close for a hug. She smiled at his newfound gentleness while her father's excited voice raced on.

"Ammon told me how he and his brethren desire to preach to Lamanites in other lands." The king grinned broadly. "In fact, Ammon and I will go tomorrow to the land of Nephi to preach to your grandfather. I told Ammon I want our masons to build sanctuaries where we can worship and be taught. Won't that be wonderful?"

"Of course, but do you think Grandfather will listen to this Nephite?" Karlinah pursed her lips to one side.

"That is why I am going with him." Her father laughed. "If I can change, I am hoping he can too. Now, what is bothering you?"

There were so many thoughts tumbling in her head that Karlinah didn't know where to start.

She could never reveal her primary concern. Her father would be crestfallen that she was not more remorseful for killing her husband. Her main concerns were avoiding discovery and subsequent punishment. It might be selfish, but she valued her life. No angelic experiences had changed her like they had him, and in a way, she felt a tinge of jealousy that he had been worthy while she was not.

Her father waited with patience.

"Why does everyone understand these things you teach but me?" she blurted. "Even Jarom says he believes Jesus will come. How can they be certain without seeing?" It frustrated Karlinah that her inexperienced nine-year-old brother could make more sense of what happened than she could.

Lamoni stood, placing his hands on his daughter's shoulders, and looked into her eyes. "When I testified I had seen the Savior, many felt the certainty in their hearts. When the Spirit witnesses the truth, it is easy to believe if one's heart is not hardened. Your witness will come when your heart is ready." His eyes shone with kindness, but hers filled with sadness. It was hard being different from everyone in the household.

As far as her heart being ready, she would have to pry off the satisfying fingers of vengeance that clenched tightly around it before that would happen. She blew out a breath. "Apparently I am the only one in this household whose heart is not ready. I don't understand what you mean by a witness."

"What did you feel, Karlinah?" Her father's gentle voice soothed. He tapped his heart. "In here."

She pursed her lips, thinking. "I caught some of what you said, but Tobias became a distraction, and I worried how my betrothed's response would affect me. Japethihah announced that you were deceived, remember? Everything seemed so strange and conflicting. I'm not sure that anything that felt good was more than just happiness to have you and Mother back. I was happy for your joy and those around me who found joy in what they were learning."

"See?" Lamoni's smile widened. "You *did* feel something good."

"I know you had a remarkable experience, but it wasn't *my* experience. It seemed too distant, too hard to comprehend. It's not that I don't believe you, it's . . . I don't know."

Ammon's teachings had pricked uncomfortably at her heart. Did she feel unworthy because she was glad Masoni was dead? It bothered Karlinah that Masoni's father had called what happened to his son "murder." She didn't feel she had a murderous heart, but something prevented her from feeling that the message applied to her. The barrier between her father's words and her heart remained. She skipped to another concern. "When Ammon spoke about things in the future, it made me angry."

"Angry?"

Karlinah exhaled. "Ammon isn't any better than us. How can he know things in the future that none of us can? Why did a Nephite have to come here and shake things up? We were content before all this. If the Great Spirit wanted us to learn more of Him, why through a Nephite? The Nephites hate us." Karlinah shuddered. *And I hate them.*

"Hmm." The king stroked his chin. "Just because there are wars between our two peoples doesn't make either side bad. Ammon doesn't hate us. He came to live among us. I am thankful he came to preach the truth so we can find happiness."

"Our ways have been happy enough for me."

Her father sighed. "The tradition of hatred for Nephites is strong within you. You have hardened your heart against Ammon." He took her hand and patted it. "You cannot feel the Spirit testify to your heart if you are not willing. Observe Ammon and learn to trust him."

Trust. She had once trusted that Masoni would be a good match for her, but she quickly learned strong wine turned him into a monster. At least she could see this coming. Ammon seemed unpredictable. Karlinah dropped her hand.

"How can the power of his sword and a pile of arms be something I can trust?" Her voice rose. "Nephites are killers. It could be our necks he cuts next!"

"Karlinah, Karlinah," Lamoni soothed. "All men carry weapons, but Ammon has not used his except in defending my flocks. Ammon is filled with the Spirit of the Lord. He would never harm us. Look at the good he has done."

Masoni had done a few good things too. "It doesn't matter. He still killed and cut off men's arms. I'm not convinced a man who does these things is filled with goodness."

"What about me? Can't you tell I've changed?"

"*You* I can trust. I've known you all my life. And you're not a Nephite." Her father held his hands up and shook his head. "It shouldn't matter."

Hot tears filled Karlinah's eyes. She had come for comfort, for understanding, but her father had only confirmed she would never believe the words of Ammon. As one who couldn't trust the Nephite, she was doomed to be an outcast, pitted against so many believers in her household and community. Karlinah turned and ran from the room, going until she found herself outside beating her fists against the rough trunk of an old oak in the public courtyard.

"Dear princess, what is wrong?" a gentle voice asked with concern.

This voice she knew well. She turned to see a tall, blurry figure through her watery eyes. Karlinah wiped her tears and sniffled, not trusting her voice.

"It can't be that bad." His voice sounded kind, his eyes soft, and the tilt of his head reassuring. Japethihah stretched forth both arms. "Come here and tell me all about it."

She paused. Maybe she had been wrong about him. Maybe she should start practicing that better attitude she wanted concerning her future husband. Visible comfort waited, and she needed it. Karlinah stepped into his arms and placed a wet cheek against his chest. His arms felt warm and soothing around her, but hers remained at her sides. He stroked her soft hair and cooed encouragement while she got a measure of control. She pushed a step backward, regretting she had surrendered easily but feeling better.

"My father is no help." She sniffed. "I don't understand why everyone believes this Nephite."

"Not everyone."

Karlinah remembered having seen him leave the throne room with a band of followers.

"I don't trust him." Japethihah shook his head. "He speaks of foolish traditions and a future he cannot know."

Karlinah lifted her eyebrows. He validated her confusion on this very point.

Japethihah explained, "He's too friendly with your father. He must want something he has not yet revealed."

"Like what?" Did Japethihah know something she didn't? Karlinah realized how little she knew about Japethihah. Or Ammon, for that matter.

Japethihah casually waved his hand in a circle as he listed possibilities. "Power. Position. Wealth. He has already been lifted from servant to preacher in only a few days, and I don't think he will settle there."

Karlinah's face puckered with skepticism. If Ammon wanted power, he would have accepted marriage when offered the king's daughter. Maybe Japethihah feared Ammon would replace him as high priest.

The smooth voice went on. "Or he could have been sent as a spy. Many things could come from that—all to the gain of the Nephites." Japethihah clicked his tongue twice.

This made sense. She should track Ammon's preaching as a protection to her people. She could play spy too.

Japethihah's dark, beady eyes stared hard at her. Karlinah swallowed and stared back until it became uncomfortable. She didn't know how to respond.

"All I'm saying is I wouldn't be too quick to trust this Nephite. The gods are getting angry." He took a step toward her. "No matter what happens, I will be here to protect you. You and I are alike. Allies. We don't fall easily for the traps of the cunning. We must unite for the good of your father's kingdom, as the gods have sanctioned."

She blinked and went rigid as Japethihah bent his face to hers. Her mind rejected his intentions until the last moment when she clamped her mouth shut. His lips met hers, but Karlinah didn't give in to the touch, so he kept it brief. When her surprise melted, she wiped the back of her hand across her mouth.

"What was that for?" she asked angrily, feeling he had taken advantage of her attempt at a better attitude. She considered slapping him, but he'd already moved two paces back.

Japethihah chuckled softly. "To unity."

"Don't you dare do anything like that again! I'm not yours yet."

"Soon enough, my dear. The time has come for you to accept that the gods have determined your fate." He gave a slight bow.

Karlinah watched through narrowed eyes as Japethihah slipped away.

Chapter Seventeen

AMMON THOUGHT CAREFULLY ABOUT WHAT he would say when he met Lamoni that morning. It would probably be best not to mention the Lord's warning that Ammon needed to avoid Lamoni's father because he would seek Ammon's life.

After greetings were exchanged, Ammon divulged his plans. "I shall not go with you to visit the high king today; I need to go to the land of Middoni to seek the release of my brothers from prison."

Lamoni tilted his head to one side. "How do you know your brethren are in prison?"

"The voice of the Lord told me."

"Ah," Lamoni said, unruffled at this new development. "I know that in the strength of the Lord you can do anything, but since King Antiomno of Middoni is a friend of mine, I will go with you. I will flatter the king, and he will cast your brethren out of prison." A confident smile creased his face.

It didn't take long for Ammon to see the wisdom in this. He nodded.

The horses and chariots had been prepared; it didn't matter that their destination had changed. Once on the way, a gentle breeze swept past as the horses pulled the two chariots along the dirt highway. Three guards followed on horseback. Ammon drew a swallow from the water skin at his side. A sword rested at his other hip. Blackbirds, wrens, and toucanets chattered in the trees alongside the riders, who conversed easily together. After a while, Lamoni's voice took on a serious note.

"I am afraid my eldest daughter doesn't see your good intentions. She is caught up with the fact that you are a Nephite."

"I am sorry to hear that. The tradition against Nephites is stronger for some than others."

"She has not attentively listened to your preaching." Lamoni frowned. "I fear something else is disturbing her."

Ammon strained for balance as the wheel hit a rut. "Your daughter and I didn't get off to the best start. I hope eventually to earn her trust so that she may listen."

This put Lamoni into quiet contemplation for a time, and Ammon respected his silence. He thought about the beautiful daughter whose demeanor had turned frosty during their brief encounters. Was she as hardened as she appeared? Ammon had learned of her betrothal to the high priest and knew this might make it even harder for her to come around.

An hour later, they spotted dust from a chariot and horses making their way toward them from the opposite direction.

"Perhaps this is King Antiomno and our journey will be shortened," Lamoni hoped aloud.

As they neared, the feathered headdress of the chariot rider and the eight guards straddling horses sharpened into focus. Lamoni revealed the mystery. "You will get to meet my father sooner than I thought."

Lamoni's voice sounded anxious, and Ammon tried to read his face. A hint of concern rested there, though nothing had been mentioned of last night's warning. Did Lamoni fear his powerful father? They slowed the horses until they came to a stop, side by side. Both Lamoni's and his father's guards stayed at a respectful distance. Ammon stiffened when he saw the mighty king press his eyebrows together into a hard glower.

"Why did you not come to the great feast I made for you and your brothers? The entire gathering noticed your absence. Not showing up rivaled a slap in my face." Before Lamoni could respond, the king's angry voice rushed on. "And where are you going with this Nephite, this child of a liar?" His black eyes rapidly shifted back and forth from Lamoni to Ammon.

"O Great King, my father, we travel to Middoni to free Ammon's brethren from prison," he said, pointing a shaky finger at his companion. "Do not be angry. I was under the power of God and incapacitated with a lack of strength."

Ammon watched Lamoni's grasp on the chariot tighten, turning his knuckles white. He rushed on with hardly a breath while Ammon's senses heightened in alert. Could that warning also have meaning of danger to Lamoni?

"You see, Ammon protected my flock from being scattered by robbers. He smote off the arms of the men who lifted their swords against him—without any help. My servants brought the evidence to me as a witness that Ammon has power from the Great Spirit, who is God."

The high king's eyes held fast to his son's, unrelenting. Ammon wondered if any of this explanation made sense to him.

"The wonder of a Savior who could redeem me held such power that I was caught up in the Spirit of the Lord and fell to the earth as if dead for two days and two nights. My body had been drained of all energy. This, O King, was the cause of my absence."

The older king stepped down from his chariot, pushed his flat palm toward his guards to signal them to stay where they were, and marched over with clenched fists. "Lamoni, where are your senses?" he bellowed. "You shall have nothing to do with those prisoners. Nephites continue to deceive us with their lying and cunning that they may govern us and rob us of our property."

It was as if the old king hadn't heard Lamoni's explanation, but Ammon understood the man's prejudice. Hatred toward the Nephites had been planted in each Lamanite since Lehi's family left Jerusalem to cross the ocean. Laman grew jealous of Nephi's preaching to direct the people toward righteousness. When the sons of Lehi divided, Nephi's people were blessed by their industry and righteous living. With bitterness, Laman's followers taught their sons that they had been cheated out of the choicest lands, their right to the government, and the records.

Lamoni gazed at his feet and shook his head. His father's next words brought his head up fast.

"I command you, Lamoni, to slay this Nephite with your sword! You shall not go to the land of Middoni but shall return with me to the land of Ishmael." The king stood firm.

A prickle ran down Ammon's spine, and the hairs on the back of his neck stood out. Sweat ran into his eyes, and he blinked away the sting.

Lamoni's mouth fell open before he clamped it shut. He dropped from the chariot and closed the distance to his father, stopping with his feet wide apart. They were now eye to eye; the king's anger simmered while Lamoni exuded confidence.

"I will not slay Ammon, neither will I return to the land of Ishmael, but I will go to Middoni to release the brethren of Ammon, for I know they are just men and holy prophets of a true God."

The high king reached for the hilt of his sword. The shrill sound of the blade sliding from its sheath pierced the silence. Two of his horsemen rushed to his side, as did Lamoni's guards. Ammon jumped from his chariot, drew his sword, and stood next to Lamoni. Two more of the elder king's guards dismounted and rushed to Ammon, grabbing his arms, twisting them behind his back, and wrenching the sword from his grasp. A third guard on horseback touched a sword to Ammon's stomach. Lamoni's men drew their weapons on the guards surrounding Ammon. It was three against three, but the high king had five more who waited at hand.

The high king spoke to his guards. "Stand down. If this becomes my fight, I can take this stinking Nephite alone." His eyes trained on Lamoni's. "But my quarrel is with my son. I will give him another chance to obey the king of all the land of Nephi."

Ammon had seen that vile, eager look too many times. As the guards backed away, Ammon retrieved his sword, letting it hang unthreateningly from his hand. "You will not slay your son," he said, "though it is better he should fall than you, for he has repented of his sins. If you should die with such anger, your soul could not be saved. His innocent blood would cry from the ground for vengeance."

The king shook with rage and raised his sword high. "I know if I should slay my son, I would shed innocent blood, for it is *you* that have sought to destroy him."

When the king pivoted and took a couple steps toward Ammon, the missionary was ready. The blade sliced down, thudding against small stones in the dirt as the Nephite leapt to the side. Eight guards moved to obstruct Lamoni's three from interfering. Clangs rang out as Ammon blocked every strike. Their sandaled feet scuffed up clouds of dust while all the guards watched the duel, weapons ready.

"Father, stop!" Lamoni called out.

"Stay back," he exclaimed to the group.

The high king grunted with each forceful swing Ammon deflected. Ringing swords clashed as the king attacked. Ammon only protected himself. Not until he heard his opponent's breath growing heavy did Ammon attempt more than defense. Surely his mission on earth would not end here today. Ammon had faith in the Lord's promise that he and his brethren would be protected as strongly as he knew that the previous night's warning was currently being fulfilled. The Lord could not lie. The notion garnered further strength.

Though fueled with anger, the tiring high king was no match for Ammon. He placed an accurate blow to the king's weapon-holding arm, leaving him with a disabling wound. His eyes grew wide as Ammon pointed the sword at his heart. The guards quickly surrounded Ammon with drawn swords. The old man collapsed to his knees in pain. He dropped his sword and pressed a hand to his wounded arm.

It seemed Lamoni could only stare at the standoff. His guards hovered at the edge of the circle, restrained but looking ready for action.

The high king spoke first. "You surprise me, Nephite."

"Tell them to back away." Ammon motioned to the remaining threat.

The high king huffed. "My men could run you through before you know it."

The previous warning fluttered behind Ammon's eyes. He licked his lips. "Not in time to prevent my blade from doing the same." Ammon pushed the tip closer to the king's heart, and the guards leaned in at his back.

"Spare me! I beg you to spare me."

"Call your men off," Ammon insisted.

The high king signaled his men, who sheathed their swords and stepped back.

Ammon took the tip of his sword off the king's chest and raised his weapon in both hands. He heard the guards draw their weapons again and Lamoni's guards scuffling in retaliation. Ammon's commanding voice penetrated the sound. "I will smite you except you grant my brothers be cast from prison."

The king stared at the blade above his head. It gleamed in the sun, and terror filled his eyes. "If you will spare me, I will grant unto you whatsoever you ask . . . even to half the kingdom."

Ammon held his stance. "If you will free my brothers from prison and let Lamoni retain his kingdom according to his own desires, then I will spare you. Otherwise, I will cut you to the earth."

"This is all you ask?" The old king blinked rapidly, relief settling on his face. "I grant that my son may retain his kingdom from this time forth. I will govern him no more. Your brethren shall be cast out of prison."

Ammon waited for the king to add his oath and the guards to relax before returning his sword to its sheath.

Lamoni picked up his father's sword, tossed it in the chariot, and checked his father's wound under the head guard's watchful eye. He took his girdle and bandaged his father's arm.

The dust-covered king stood and spoke to Ammon. "You are not greedy like other Nephites. Do you not realize you could have been richer than my son Lamoni?"

"I know how many cities you control. Power and riches are not my objective. My brethren and I have come to serve and preach the ways of the Great Spirit, who is God."

Lamoni put a hand on Ammon's shoulder. "He has proved to be my most valiant and faithful servant in Ishmael."

The high king looked from one man to the other. "Never would I have believed a Nephite could have such love for my son."

Apparently encouraged, Lamoni said, "Ammon has brought joy into my life through his preaching. My mind has been enlightened to the ways of righteousness, and my heart has changed."

The high king's chin trembled. "Will you and your brethren come to my land to teach me?"

Ammon knew how hard this request must be for such a powerful king. Gratitude and love flooded his heart. He nodded his head. Not only was he under the Lord's protection, but this king had humbled himself enough to accept missionaries from what Lamoni called "just men and holy prophets of a true God." Ammon could envision the great potential for missionary work in the land of Nephi. Already his joy was full unto bursting.

Chapter Eighteen

AFTER A FEW DAYS' ABSENCE from the judgment seat, the upcoming cases should more than fill King Lamoni's day. He sat fidgeting on his throne in the empty room. Knowing his people still needed someone to lead and direct them didn't make his concerns any lighter, but judgment using the Spirit as a guideline could prove consistently powerful. He pondered all the things needing changes. Would he need to dismantle the class system that yoked the slaves and the poor beneath the commoners and the merchants beneath the noble, or would these things dissolve on their own? It would take time, he realized, for equality to weave its way through the city. The good news was spreading among the citizens, yet Ammon had a lot of preaching to do to convert the minority that so far had rejected or refused to hear his words.

Lamoni had already freed his slaves. The family had accepted they would now join in the work with the staff—all but Karlinah, who grudgingly made her bed and missed Abish bringing a morning tray of food. It would be an adjustment for her. He sent up a silent prayer on her behalf.

Two guards approached, bringing the list of cases to be tried. He chuckled to learn several cases had already been crossed off. Good. The people's grudges and differences were already taking on a new perspective. A glance at the first name caused him to frown. He hoped it wouldn't be too unpleasant.

"Send in the high priest." He sensed a strange quality to his voice, more polite than commanding, and he cleared his throat.

"Yes, O King." The guard's feet padded away.

Japethihah approached the throne, head held high, his silk robe swishing as he walked. He bowed into a soft puddle of indigo folds on the floor.

"Gracious King, I am pleased to see you restored to health."

Lamoni smiled at the priest's interpretation but offered only a polite, "Thank you."

"I am grateful that the gods have given such a great leader another chance to show the king's obedience to them."

"My obedience now lies with the one true God. I am afraid this will mean some changes that concern you, Japethihah."

The priest gave a nervous laugh before the king continued, "Not all is as it once was. First, I must question your reception of the word of God through Ammon. Have you a desire to become a believer?"

Japethihah's face fell. "I . . . uh . . . nothing has changed with the coming of Ammon. I am in tune with many gods, not just one. We almost lost you. My desire to serve and provide guidance is more intensified, if that were possible." A quick smile returned. "The gods are troubled over Ammon. I advise extreme caution. It might be best to banish him from our borders. Let me consult the stars and see if the gods require a sacrifice."

"There is no need for that, Japethihah. I know of a surety that this is not the method by which truth is revealed. I should like to teach you all that I have learned."

A look of horror settled on the face of the priest. "You're going to throw away generations of religious belief at the word of one deceitfully clever Nephite?"

"No, at the word of the Great Spirit, who is the one true God. Our incorrect traditions shall be set aside and replaced by revealed truth. Those who embrace and follow these truths receive His blessings and mercy."

Japethihah touched his throat. "You can't be serious!"

The king hardly blinked. "I have been shown the Lord's way, and I cannot go against it lest I face His wrath rather than mercy."

"This is a dangerous mind-set. The gods will be angry. Our crops will fail by scorching heat or relentless rain. Sickness and infertility will abound. Only submission and sacrifice will soothe them."

Lamoni snorted. "Enough about the gods. You must listen to me. There is but one true and living God. I am sorry, Japethihah, but you must understand that these old beliefs and your position as high priest have become obsolete. The Lord abhors such things as human sacrifice."

"Obsolete?" Japethihah tightened his fists, and his eyes twitched with anger. He opened his mouth then snapped it shut.

"I do not intend to simply throw you into the streets. You will receive a handsome compensation for your faithful service and be taught the ways of the Lord if you are willing."

"Me, become a commoner?" His eyes rolled wildly. "Have you gone mad?"

"Some may call it that, but I assure you I have never been in better spirits. Take some time to ponder what you will do. I will see to it you receive three months' compensation by the end of the day." Lamoni watched a lump travel down Japethihah's long neck.

"What about Karlinah—our betrothal?" At that Lamoni pressed his lips together, and Japethihah continued with sarcasm, "Surely you do not think to revoke the perfect match?" The priest's voice turned to pleading. "You know I would take good care of her."

"Circumstances have changed, Japethihah. I no longer wish to require my children to be forced into marriage. The tradition that requires Karlinah to marry first is a foolish one, without sound reason. Her title as princess will remain simply that—a title, one as obsolete as that of high priest. She will be free to choose whoever makes her happy."

"Even if she chooses a commoner?"

The king dipped his head. "All are God's children."

"Outrageous!" A sly smirk came over the former priest's lips. "And if she chooses me?"

King Lamoni's heart skipped a beat, and he had no response.

A soft chuckle started deep in Japethihah's throat as he turned and walked away.

***

Brushing away dust and particles from the crevices he'd just created, Cumroth admired his work on the stone pillar at the entrance to the army captain's office. He liked being here in Shilom where citizens said hello or gave him compliments. He had been practically invisible in Jerusalem. He also liked the words he heard carried through the adjacent street.

Yesterday a man came to the city who was far from being invisible—a Nephite. He came to preach boldly his gospel message. Cumroth and his father worked on the pillar while admiring Aaron's attempts at conversing with strangers in the street. He greeted all with apparent ease in his polite language and friendly manner that hinted at genuine interest. Cumroth found himself studying the expertness of the missionary's social skills. It reminded him of his mother before she and his younger sister were taken by fevers. Too bad he hadn't had her example to guide him once he gained an interest in females. Perhaps she could have made a difference in his awkwardness.

Soon Cumroth's interest had turned to the missionary's message rather than his manner. The words sank into his heart and that of his father's. It gave cause for their lively discussion last night. Now Aaron had moved farther down the street, and his words no longer filled the sculptors' ears. Cumroth's father, Corianthem, immediately set down his tools to run after Aaron.

***

Karlinah strolled onto the front porch and noticed a small gathering out in the dirt courtyard where Ammon preached. She rolled her eyes, certain she didn't want to be upset by hearing the words of the Nephite. She turned to go back inside, thinking the interior courtyard would have better privacy, when a thought pricked her mind. Hadn't she wanted to listen to the missionary—to play the spy? Why not now?

She gazed at the crowd, and movement caught her eye. The group surrounding Ammon opened up, spreading out, as a tall form pushed his way in from the back. Japethihah. A shiver of revulsion crawled down her skin, but she quickly gained control, knowing it would not be her with whom he would contend. She chuckled to herself and sat on the porch steps, ready to be entertained. Karlinah sat transfixed as Japethihah closed in on Ammon like a hawk on a rodent. He circled from a rod away, eyes trained only on the teacher.

Ammon quickly finished his point and stopped to stare at the disruptive newcomer. "Your name is Japethihah, is it not?"

"It is."

"Do you have a question?"

Japethihah twirled his hand in the air dramatically. "Oh, where to start? Where to start?"

Karlinah got up and moved closer. It struck her as odd that she was torn between which man she wanted to win the impending competition. Could Ammon hold his own against Japethihah's skill? She couldn't help feeling sorry for the talented former priest who had been dismissed by her father. No more flattering messages to do whatever made one happy. Now there were God's laws and new priests and teachers consecrated to spread God's word. Karlinah still hadn't taken the time to find out more, but the sight in the courtyard piqued her interest.

Japethihah stroked his chin. "This plan of redemption, of saving our souls, you say it was prepared for mankind before we came to earth?"

"Yes, because of God's love for us."

"How is it the Great Spirit—or God, as you call Him—knew what bad things we would do in this life before our birth? Are we doomed to such failure and displeasure from our Maker, who is supposed to love us as His children?" He raised an eyebrow expectantly.

Bad things like taking pleasure in the death of one's own husband? Karlinah wondered.

All eyes turned from Japethihah to Ammon. Only the twittering of a distant flock of toucanets sounded as the crowd awaited Ammon's response.

"It is not hard to understand that the natural man will sometimes succumb to the temptations of Satan, the evil one. God gave us the gift of agency that we may choose right from wrong. As none of us is perfect, we will not choose right every time. Justice demands each will have his or her reward or punishment accordingly. This is why the mercy of repentance is so important."

Karlinah frowned. *Punishment? What kind of punishment?*

Japethihah crossed his arms and lifted his chin. "I suppose you will tell us next that the Lamanites will be greatly punished while the Nephites have chosen better and will receive a greater reward. You call this justice?"

"All men, regardless of skin color, will be judged according to their knowledge of the laws of God and what they do with that knowledge. A man who has never been taught these laws will not be judged the same as one who has. I am in Lamanite lands today to share God's laws that ye may abide by them and come unto Him."

I'm to be judged for what I did? Will everyone know? Karlinah's breath came heavy.

Japethihah laughed dryly. "But God didn't love my father or his father, who never received these laws? Are there only certain times the Lamanites are worthy of hearing God's laws—this from a fair God who loves us equally?"

"The word of the Lord comes to men, whatever '-ite' they may be, whenever there are those willing to listen to his word. The prophecies and warnings have been handed down through prophets and recorded in scripture that men may search them." Ammon's voice remained calm. "As I have explained, men will be measured using their own knowledge. It is worse for a man who rebels against his knowledge of God than for one who never had the knowledge in the first place."

I may not have had knowledge of God, but I knew what I wanted once Masoni tripped and fell on his own knife. I wanted him dead.

Karlinah closed her eyes, remembering his wild eyes and his anger that she wouldn't perform her wifely duties with him in such an angry, drunken state. He had rushed at her, knife in hand. That was when he tripped and the knife entered his abdomen. She had never seen him so furious. It was either kill or be killed, so she had pushed the knife in farther to stop her own pain and prevent her death. But he still lived, mouthing strangled words, one hand clawing at her. Karlinah shuddered at the memory. One of his stupid stone idols crashing on his head had ended all her misery. That terrifying moment had brought amazing relief.

Japethihah's voice saved her from further reliving the image. "You have taught that this Christ who is to come will appear after His Resurrection. No doubt you will say He appears to the favored Nephites. Am I right? Are the Lamanites again shunned and treated as dogs?"

Karlinah was surprised by how much Japethihah knew of Ammon's teachings, probably so he could debate or mock the points of doctrine.

"You ask good questions," Ammon said. "You have been listening. The thing you must do, that all must do when they hear the word of God, is to open your heart to feel the witness of the Holy Spirit testify of its truth."

That's what her father had said. Karlinah doubted Japethihah's heart was open to feeling such a witness. What about her own? She shuddered, not wanting to compare herself to Japethihah, but didn't she also want to see Ammon proved wrong? She watched as Japethihah's chest rose and fell, seething in silence. Ammon had silenced him but not by callous measures. The kind but firm voice of the missionary shifted her attention.

"But to answer your question, I do not know the location, only that Christ will appear to the more righteous part of the people. He will receive all those who come unto Him." Ammon spread his arm out in front of the crowd. "The majority of Ishmaelite citizens, who are Lamanites, are counted among the righteous and will enjoy the Lord's blessings if they continue to follow Him. I commend you for your choices. Those of you contemplating whether to join yourselves to the people of God, open your hearts. God will give you answers if you seek them."

The crowd dispersed while Karlinah pondered Ammon's message about being counted with the righteous. How could she join their numbers unless they knew of the evil thing she had done and forgave her for it? But in their judging, they might not deem her worthy of forgiveness, and her secret would have been told in vain. The murder of a prince was no small thing. They could insist she be punished. No. She couldn't risk it. The secret must remain hidden.

Chapter Nineteen

KARLINAH ARRIVED AT THE LARGE oak tree to see Helami waiting for her. She noticed he hadn't brought flowers for her like he had when she first returned to Ishmael. His foot shuffled back and forth in the dirt, and he struggled to meet her eyes. *This can't be good,* she thought.

When Karlinah learned that Helami wanted to meet her at the tree in the courtyard, her heart leapt with excitement. His previous interest in her had been brief, cut short by her father choosing Japethihah. Word of their severed betrothal had spread, and Helami was once again free to court her. She liked his tender nature and looked forward to spending time with him. But this meeting wasn't turning out at all as she'd hoped. She nervously fingered the beads dangling from the tie at the end of her long braid while she greeted him.

"Hello, Karlinah. I've been . . . avoiding you, and I don't want to do that anymore," the young man with short-cropped hair began. When she didn't answer, he looked up at her with round eyes.

Karlinah felt a muscle twitch under her eye, and she concentrated on controlling it. *Stay calm.* She gave a slight nod and let Helami speak.

"I want to be honest by telling you myself."

"Telling me what?" Karlinah felt her lips pinch as she anticipated what he might say.

"I'm so ashamed." He glanced at his feet again. "I sought to gain favor and a position of power through marriage to one of the king's daughters. I was too late with your sister. It seemed a gift from the gods when you came back to Ishmael unwed. That man I used to be—the one who sought power—he no longer exists. I've changed."

Karlinah arched her brow, stuck on one thought. "My sister?" He had tried to court Hepka?

Helami went on. "You are beautiful, but I now look for other things in a wife. I'm sorry. I didn't want to feel awkward around you or leave you wondering."

All because there was no position to seek anymore. Karlinah breathed deeply, not certain how to take the news. Part of her wanted to cry and part was incensed. Did he prefer Hepka over her, or would any princess do? Her value as someone's potential wife had crumbled like the positions in her father's court. Would all believers shun her? She folded her arms. This was what Ammon had done!

Realization dawned, sending more anger through her veins. She thrust an accusatory finger at him. "You're the one who spread lies to stop Hepka's wedding so you could marry her instead."

"Well, yes. I . . . thought you knew."

"How would I know that?"

"Uh, I apologized to Jaros. I just thought . . ." He furrowed his brow. "It was Japethihah's idea. He said the gods had chosen you for him and I had a better chance with Hepka. He said you told him of Hepka's fear of the dark."

"That presumptuous parasite!"

"You mean she doesn't fear the dark?"

No words would come through her gritted teeth.

"Then I apologize for hurting her as well. Please tell her for me, will you?"

She let out a dry laugh. "Apologies. Your confession is supposed to make me feel better? Tell her yourself."

Helami tugged at the neck of his tunic. "I just . . . didn't want to lie to you."

Karlinah threw her hands in the air before placing them on her hips. "Suddenly you're interested in honesty now that my father's court is dissolved. Is this all in the name of repentance? Does Ammon have everyone confessing their sins so they can feel better? Where does your apology leave *me*?"

"I'm sorry." Helami blinked and took a couple steps backward. "I was selfish, but I've changed. I hope you can forgive me."

Karlinah stared at the pain on the young man's face. It seemed greater than hers, but it didn't excuse his treatment of her and Hepka. He had caused the strain between them. She felt tears forming. Before they could fall, Helami turned and quickly walked away. She watched him through blurry eyes, the hurt surpassing the anger.

She stood there alone for a moment, wallowing in pity. No solution came, and it got her indignation up. Marching with heavy steps back to her house, she rounded a corner too fast in the hallway and nearly collided with Ammon coming the other way. She let out a startled cry.

"Good evening to you too," Ammon said with a smile.

Here stood the root of her new trouble with men. Well, that wasn't completely fair, and she knew it. Karlinah wasn't in the mood for apologizing, yet she knew the collision was mostly her fault. "I'm sorry," she said with a huff.

He gave a dubious look. "Well, don't worry about it. We're not hurt."

Karlinah folded her arms and grimaced. "Do you want something?"

"Food," Ammon said evenly. "I'm starving—haven't eaten all day."

This response made Karlinah drop her arms and take a step back. Was he so committed to preaching he hadn't found time to eat? This was not like any man she knew. His face looked so harmless and human. His body, on the other hand . . . A weak smile curled onto one side of her mouth, and she slowly shook her head.

"So you do know how to smile," Ammon said. "And a beautiful smile it is."

Karlinah quickly sobered her face.

Ammon held out both hands before she could utter a word. "Don't worry. I'm just expressing an observation, not my feelings for you." His voice turned gentle. "I can see you are upset. Want to talk about it?"

"No!" Karlinah realized how harsh it sounded. His concern seemed genuine, so she shouldn't punish him for her displeasure with Helami. She added a softened, "Thank you. I'm giving it some time to sort itself out."

He waited, eyes fixed on hers. "I'm a good listener," he prompted.

Karlinah was reminded of her mother's gentleness. She exhaled, feeling lighter, like a snake shedding a layer of skin. Not ready to expose a softer layer, she laughed it off. "Another time. You go find something to eat."

"Have it your way," Ammon said with a smile. "But may I suggest you fast about it—this struggle in your mind? That is what I do when I have a problem—and why I have not eaten. Fasting humbles me before God. I can leave my problems in His hands. With God, all things are possible."

The words rang true to Karlinah the instant she heard them, but since they had come from his Nephite mouth, she swiftly dismissed the feeling. *Hypocrite*, she scolded herself. *You're no better than Helami.* This self-revelation startled her. She was every bit as narrow-minded toward Ammon as his converted young men seemed to be toward her.

Looking at the ground, she wondered what sort of problems Ammon had. He always seemed so self-assured. Yes, there were many who hadn't changed, but she couldn't deny delighting in seeing more smiling faces and people who helped and cared for one another rather than cheating and insulting them. It was hard to give a Nephite the credit, but the proof remained. Ammon wasn't what she had expected. But sometimes his followers took their blatant honesty too far. Helami had asked for her forgiveness. If she couldn't grant his simple request, how could she expect others to forgive her greater sin?

She didn't want to ask Ammon any questions right now. She wanted to be left alone. But too much filled her head, and one of those thoughts leapt from her mouth. "Ever since you came, people are obsessed with repentance and honesty. Can't we just live together in peace?"

Ammon had a confused look on his face. "Doesn't repentance lead to peace?"

She blinked, letting the words sink in. Repentance seemed a way to find peace—as it had for Helami and Karlinah's family—but it wasn't worth letting out *her* secret. Others could repent of lesser sins—even murders carried out by the king's order, but no one had challenged their base, indolent ways before Ammon's preaching. She had caused the death of a king's son who had not disobeyed any law. No law existed about how a man treated his wife.

Ammon continued, "If you were truly honest with yourself, you would see that letting the Lord into your life would give you the peace of mind to dispel this cloud hanging over you. Fasting will help you find your answers."

"Cloud?" she snapped. That did it! Karlinah huffed and stomped away. Ammon telling her a cloud hung over her head, presuming to know what she needed, and telling her what to do went too far. Who did he think he was?

When she arrived at her bedchamber, Karlinah splashed water on her face from the bowl on the table and wiped it dry with a cloth. Ammon meant well, and as much as she hated to admit it, he had a kind way about him, but he talked too much; he said the wrong things.

So why did everyone else savor his wisdom like children with sticks of sugar cane? Why weren't his words delicious to *her*? Something must be wrong with her.

Helami had rejected her because she hadn't been baptized, yet these Christian men were the kind who appealed to her. Humble men—like that stone artisan in Jerusalem. Where had *that* thought slipped in? She blinked and rocked her head from side to side. Would all suitors reject her even without knowing her secret? *Not everyone.* Karlinah shuddered at the thought of Japethihah. It gave no comfort. Time slipped by, and the young men were charming other girls. Once again, the lonesome burden felt like a stone in a sack of grain, weighing her down.

***

"What are we going to do about Karlinah?" Lamoni asked his wife. He sat beside her on the bed cushion and gently took her hand.

Mierah sighed. She had been thinking about Karlinah's impenetrable heart for several weeks now. "I thought service would do her good," she shook her head, "but she enjoys cooking so that she can increase her talents. She takes more pleasure in coming up with something tasty than in feeling compassion for others."

The king put a hand to his chin. "Her life has been too easy. She would be a lot more humble if she had to struggle for things."

"Well, we can't deprive her into believing."

Lamoni's chuckle brought a smile to Mierah's lips. She gazed into his eyes and saw the worry behind them. Mierah touched her husband's cheek, warmed by his tenderness. She reflected on her first weeks as a scared bride of this man, then a stranger, trying to learn what would please him and what wouldn't. Now they shared a deep connection from the greatest experience of all—seeing their Savior.

"Karlinah sees the contrast between herself and the believers, and it scares her," she said.

The king tapped at his lip. "She's afraid of Ammon as well. And Japethihah is no help. He keeps her confused with his subtle lies."

"That snake! I've seen the way he publicly challenges doctrine by twisting meanings."

"He's been a real disappointment to me. I used to trust and confide in him. Do you know he still believes he can win Karlinah's affection?"

Mierah growled softly through her teeth. "I hope she can see through him because I'd hate to see her make such a big mistake. I wish she would listen to those who have her welfare in mind more than to the likes of him. Those with whom one keeps company make all the difference."

"You may be on to something, my dear," Lamoni said. "If she would mingle with the right sort of fellows . . . but so many are put off by her lack of commitment to become a Christian."

"And Hepka will soon be married, leaving Karlinah feeling like a dried maize husk." Mierah frowned.

"If we don't do something about it, she just might live with us for the rest of her life."

Mierah smiled at his joke and then turned serious. "Something terrible must have occurred with Masoni, but she won't speak of it. I believe she is getting over his death, though, and starting to look at men again. She just needs prodding in the right direction."

"I will not force Karlinah to marry against her wishes, but maybe we can guide her a little—invite a few young men over to socialize?"

"That is wise, my dear." Mierah patted his hand. "Karlinah needs to be the owner of her conversion, not follow someone else's say-so because she is married to him or because her parents wish it. She has to stay true to herself. You know how passionate she can be. Once the doctrine takes root in her heart, she will dedicate herself to being a devoted follower."

"So how do we get it to take root?"

Mierah lifted her shoulders. "We don't. *She* does. But we never give up. We keep exposing her to doctrine, surrounding her with good people, being examples. Someday it will sink in. I just worry that it will be later rather than sooner."

Chapter Twenty

THE STONE STEPS RUNNING ALONG the front of the king's house felt cool in the morning shade. Karlinah sat, leaning back on her hands, ankles crossed, as a group of young people filled in the prime places next to her. The steps provided the nearest seating to hear the king's speech. Latecomers would be standing far back in the courtyard or side streets. Karlinah tucked her legs in to allow more room for the newcomers.

"Thank you," said a girl with smooth skin over cheeks that plumped when she smiled. "I'm Esha."

"Karlinah."

The girl giggled. "I know who you are."

It felt good to be acknowledged, even if briefly. Others said hello and then talked amongst themselves while more citizens arrived. Karlinah missed the days of a basketful of friends, but too many had entered the circles of betrothed or married couples. She looked at these youths and suddenly felt old. It should be Hepka with this group, but she was off with Jaros. Karlinah was nearly seventeen and unmarried. It burned in the back of her mind that she was no longer the most desirable maiden in the land, as had been her right. Eager at this chance for friendship, she leaned in and turned her head toward their conversation.

Genuine kindness permeated even while they bantered. Mesmerized by his smile, she stared at a young man telling Esha he would help her milk the goats again if he could keep from tripping over them. She laughed, but Karlinah could only smile at the image.

"Have you ever milked a goat?" Esha asked, turning to her.

Karlinah shuddered. "Never. Is it hard?"

"Not once you get one in its milking stand," the young man said. "It's the loose ones you have to worry about. A few of them like to butt their heads at you." He laughed, and his buttermilk teeth shone against a dark spot where a tooth was missing. It was still a welcome smile. "I'm Ammosiah."

She looked into his rare, honey-brown eyes and found them captivating. She soaked up the feeling of inclusion, starved for socialization. A few others asked her a question or two, but Ammosiah and Esha dominated her attention.

The time for King Lamoni's speech drew near, and families strode together up the dirt street to listen. Karlinah sighed and watched the gathering crowd for a moment until she felt those golden eyes on her. She blushed.

Ammosiah leaned closer. "What's it like having Ammon in your household?"

"I hardly ever see him," she said. "He's only there to sleep, and then he's off preaching all day. Sometimes he's gone for several days in a row." She never took her eyes from his face.

He nodded. "I wish I could go with him sometime."

"You do?" Karlinah drew out the question with rising intonation. Why had so many readily accepted Ammon? She wanted to hear his story if he would tell it.

"His words satisfy the hunger in my soul."

Karlinah noticed her heart beating stronger, and she truly wanted to know what made Ammosiah feel this way. What could satisfy her soul? His mesmerizing stare and the color of his eyes captivated her attention. She felt a tingle of pleasure. Could Ammosiah see her goodness and find her alluring just as she was? Could others? She hoped so. These new acquaintances, former commoners, were refreshing to be around. She'd had too large a dose of living with egotistical royalty already.

Just then the hum of voices hushed as King Lamoni walked out onto the porch. Lamoni gazed at the crowd lining the steps and filling the dirt courtyard before him. He raised his gold-cuffed forearms, the only form of jewelry he still wore, in a shushing motion. Gone was the feathered headdress of superiority. A long purple cape draped over his shoulders showed the only evidence of King Lamoni's leadership. He wore a knee-length loin skirt, and his broad chest was left bare.

"I bid you all welcome and thank you for coming at my request." The king flashed his perfect teeth. Small, dark eyes glanced around.

Karlinah enjoyed this gentleness from her father. She gave Ammosiah another glance. His broad smile and full attention were trained on the king. He turned his eyes on her as if he noticed her movement. Warmth flooded her face, and she promptly turned her attention to her father and his deep, resonating voice.

"I have assembled you this day to tell you my cause for rejoicing." He beamed. "Again, I wish to testify that I have seen my Redeemer." Lamoni's voice choked up, but he continued in strength. "Christ shall come forth and be born of a woman and redeem all mankind who believe on His name." His voice raised another notch. "This is the legacy I leave for my people. This knowledge is what I wish to hand down to the generations that come after me."

Several heads nodded their understanding, and Karlinah swallowed away a creeping uneasiness. She felt her heart beat more quickly at her father's words and dismissed it as embarrassment. How could she participate in her own father's legacy without becoming a believer? Karlinah picked at a loose thread on her skirt.

"I want you to know that the people in the land of Ishmael are a separate and free people, with no oppression from the government of my father, the high king. You have the liberty of worshipping anywhere within my reign."

Murmurs of approval sounded through the crowd.

"I want to build a place of worship in the land of Ishmael," Lamoni continued. "Along with my masons, we will organize the rotation of men to more quickly build a synagogue. Women will provide food or clothing to the workers. Households will take turns. My largest cooking room will be used to prepare and serve their food. My servants and family will assist. Let us work together. We will supply the builders' basic needs while they provide a place of worship for us."

Lamoni paused as discussions broke out among the crowd. This concept of common sharing and all working appeared favorable until a tall man wearing a girdled, scarlet robe shouted a question. Karlinah groaned inwardly. *Not Japethihah.*

"And if I don't wish to worship in your synagogue? Will I still be required to work on it?"

The courtyard buzzed once more before settling to hear more from Japethihah.

"Not all of us have chosen to put our trust in the religion of a Nephite. I cannot support a building allowing only one belief of worship—unless, of course, it becomes hazardous to the health of a citizen to freely express himself. But I trust, Good King, you will not harm your citizens, as was not the case a short time ago."

Karlinah cringed, and her stomach twisted uncomfortably. She brushed a strand of hair from her face and stole a glance to see Ammosiah's reaction. The whole group of youth had fastened their attention on the exchange.

As rational as Japethihah sounded, she felt the attack. She looked at her father and saw one cheek twitch. She wondered if he recalled with pain the servants whom he had ordered beheaded. His face set calmly again with a smile, and she let out the breath she hadn't realized she'd held. Could she likewise ignore the past and join her father's legacy?

Not while thick guilt bubbled inside her.

The king answered with strength. "No man will be forced to do anything against his beliefs. You and everyone here will have their choice, Japethihah. However, let it be known that this synagogue will not be desecrated with idols or anything opposing the one true God. What you do within your own home is a private matter. The synagogue will be for the public."

"You mean, the majority." Japethihah folded his arms, a smirk on his face, his point clearly made.

Karlinah thought it a bold thing her father wanted to do—having the people work cooperatively without wages to build a meeting place. It would be nice having a building large enough to hold this group for Father's speeches instead of standing in the wind, rain, or hot sun, but she could envision Japethihah causing more trouble during the construction.

"Lastly," the king said, ignoring Japethihah's remark, "I have assembled you to hear the proclamation of my father, the king, for he and his household have been taught by Ammon's brethren and are converted unto the Lord."

Gasps of shock and delight erupted from the crowd. Karlinah already knew of this information, but it struck her now how it affected the people of Ishmael. Had her grandfather given up his sins, his secrets? He must have serious secrets too. Now that his manner was more approachable, she wished he lived close enough to speak to about this. She desired to learn more about what repentance meant from someone closer to her own situation—one who had killed but had not had a vision.

"This proclamation states that none should lay their hands upon Ammon, Aaron, Omner, or Himni, or any of their brethren who go forth preaching the word of God in any lands of the king. They shall not be bound nor imprisoned; neither should they be smitten, spit upon, cast out, or suffer any obstruction to their preaching. They are to have free access to the houses, temples, and sanctuaries of the people. This is by the high king's decree.

"Know that I wholeheartedly agree with and will enforce this proclamation in our land." He rolled up the parchment and shook it in the air. "A sorrowful sight met us when Ammon and I went to deliver his brethren from prison. We found them naked, thirsty, and hungry. Their skin had worn raw where the cords bound them. Nevertheless, they were patient in their sufferings. Never again will such afflictions occur in any lands of the king."

When Lamoni dismissed the assembly, Ammosiah came to sit next to Karlinah. It was easy to smile at him. His amber eyes were a refreshing change from so many dark ones. It warmed her to look into them.

"What did you think of your father's speech?" Ammosiah asked. He pulled his knees up and leaned his elbows on them.

"Nice and short." She chuckled. "I am happy to have a free land, and the synagogue will be wonderful."

"Yes." Ammosiah stared straight ahead, smiling. "I'm happy the missionaries can preach in safety. Now Japethihah and his associates can rant all they want, but they can't hurt Ammon." He turned to fix his eyes on Karlinah's. "I also liked the idea of a legacy to leave the next generation. I look forward to my own children having these truths to make them happy."

Karlinah drew in a deep breath, wishing for more air.

"I hear you have learned to cook," Ammosiah softly said. "Perhaps you would also like to learn how to milk goats. Or you could invite me to supper sometime."

Karlinah didn't know if she felt self-conscious about Ammosiah's bold hints and religious beliefs or irritated that so many mistrusted Japethihah when he was no more vocal than Ammon. This was not the time to analyze. Her chest tightened; she wanted to get away.

Karlinah got to her feet. "Yes, well, I have to go now. Good-bye, Ammosiah." She ran into her house, certain those golden eyes followed her.

Chapter Twenty-One

HORSES PULLING CARTS, MEN YELLING orders, and hammers pounding log and stone usually prevented Karlinah from sleeping in after sunup as work on the synagogue progressed. But not today; today was the Sabbath, when all heavy work ceased. She lay in bed, approving of this day-of-rest concept Ammon had instigated.

Karlinah knew he would be in the courtyard today, preaching to all who wished to hear. Hepka and Abish had nudged her with chidings of, "Don't take our word for it—listen to the man. Don't you want to know for yourself?" She supposed she did but didn't know if her heart was ready for change or ever would be. She would like to get some answers about how repentance worked—if Japethihah wasn't around.

He had become a pest lately, like an insect that appeared suddenly to buzz in her ear before disappearing, saying derogatory things about Ammon and telling her she must not work like a servant. In his honey-sweet voice, he had told her, "There are still a few of us who would honor royalty if given the chance. *I* could treat you as a queen with the pampering you deserve. Think about it, my dear."

Ammon, on the other hand, had proven himself a friend to her people, and Karlinah supposed she could trust him. So many citizens had found the happiness she yearned to feel. Masoni shouldn't have made her feel like nothing, but she now realized that his behavior was not the common way.

Karlinah dressed in a long sheath with simple ornamentation. She slipped a bracelet above her elbow—her favorite of hammered gold, polished to a shine—and combed her ebony hair. Not taking the time to plait her long tresses, Karlinah grabbed some strawberries and a piece of leavened bread from the cooking room on her way outside.

The strong voice in the courtyard told her Ammon was already preaching. She moved to a spot at the back where she would be least noticed. More than a hundred listeners encircled him. It reminded her of when Japethihah used to draw a crowd. Karlinah watched Ammon's face to see if he enjoyed the attention. He seemed different somehow. Were his words smooth like Japethihah's?

"None of us is perfect," Ammon said, "even when we try to be good."

Flattery indeed. At least she didn't have to be perfect to become a believer.

"This is the beauty of repentance. It makes us clean through the blood of the Lamb of God."

Blood. Karlinah's face scrunched up. What's he talking about that for?

"Christ will sacrifice himself, atoning for our sins with His own blood. An infinite Atonement where . . ."

Karlinah shook her head and blocked out the rest. He's talking about blood and sacrifice.

She remembered inflicting the final blow to Masoni's head, backing away as red blood streamed down his forehead and into one eye. She'd run from his bedchamber, dropping the crimson knife she had twisted deeper into his abdomen. Worst of all was scrubbing the sticky blood from her hands—knowing whose it was and what she had done.

Now Ammon spoke of the blood of a lamb, sacrificial blood, sins—it turned Karlinah's stomach. What did these people see in his preaching? She wanted nothing to do with it.

***

In the afternoon, Abish found Karlinah in her bedchamber. "You have a visitor." There was a twinkle in her eye.

"Who?" she wanted to know, putting down her embroidery.

"A handsome lad with yellow-brown eyes who said his name was—"

"Ammosiah!" Karlinah said at the same time as Abish.

"He's waiting in the vestibule."

Karlinah strode down the hallway. She stopped to smooth her dress and turned the corner to see Ammosiah sitting on a bench. He rose, and the two closed the distance.

"Are you all right, Karlinah?" Ammosiah's brow wrinkled.

"I'm fine. Why?"

"I saw you this morning listening to Ammon, but then you left so quickly. You looked like you might be ill."

Karlinah grinned. "So sweet of you, Ammosiah. I was troubled, but I'm fine now."

"Troubled? How?" Concern again creased his brow.

"Let's go into the garden courtyard, and I'll tell you all about it." Karlinah showed Ammosiah to the interior courtyard, where they sat on a stone bench encroached upon by passion-flower vines. The flowery scent filled their noses, and a butterfly flitted past. The grass felt soft beneath Karlinah's bare feet.

"It seems silly now." Karlinah reached to pick a blade of grass and rolled it between her fingers. "I have a sensitive stomach when it comes to blood."

Ammosiah's face showed confusion. "Were you bleeding?"

"No." She gave a weak smile and blinked her lashes at him. "Ammon was talking about the blood of the lamb when I got there. I don't remember his wording, but I found it unpleasant."

Ammosiah's forehead relaxed. "Oh. Now I know what you heard."

Karlinah was glad not to have to explain further.

"Ammon was talking about Christ as a sacrificial lamb, not the blood of an animal." Ammosiah crinkled up his face.

Is he laughing at me? Karlinah pushed away her annoyance.

"Christ will shed his blood for us after He takes our sins upon Him." Ammosiah continued with a grin. "If that's when you left, you missed the point of Ammon's message. We can be forgiven of our sins as we change our hearts to follow Christ. He will lead us on the right path, and we can be exalted in His kingdom when we repent and follow Jesus Christ."

Ammosiah was looking at her like it was the simplest concept in the world. The trouble was she didn't understand most of it. Karlinah folded her arms. "I don't want Christ to lose blood for me. If anyone offers me their blood, I don't want it."

"You haven't heard about the Atonement?" His voice was kind.

Karlinah looked at the ground. "Not really. My youngest brother took much of my attention when my father and Ammon first preached in the throne room." That and witnessing her parents recover. It had been a lot to take in at the time. Her mind had swirled with distracting thoughts of distrust for the new Nephite and concern about what Japethihah would do, to visualizing Masoni rise from the dead like her father had. She hadn't concentrated on much else.

Ammosiah took his time to explain the doctrinal message in greater detail, and Karlinah asked a few questions along the way. By the time he was finished, it made sense. Finally!

Repentance meant being clean from sins by giving them up and following the doctrines the prophets preached, not by revealing sins to everyone. Could she leave her secret in the past? Would the blood of Christ be enough to wash her greatest sin away? Karlinah felt warmth and calm consuming her doubt as her heart pounded within her chest. Contentment surrounded her. Surely these were romantic feelings that stirred within her, though they didn't make her feel any more affection toward him. Perhaps the subject matter wasn't conducive to romance.

"Thank you." Karlinah smiled at her friend, glad her misconceptions about Ammon's preaching were cleared up. "Now I know why everyone has such hope—it's a great message. Wouldn't it be wonderful if it were true?"

Ammosiah stared. "You don't believe it?"

"I didn't say that." Karlinah kept her voice calm. "I want it to be true, I just don't know with surety yet. Give me time to think about it, to let it soak in. Christ hasn't come yet to atone for our sins. It's not something anyone can verify."

"The Spirit verifies it to you." His eyes bulged. "Didn't I explain it well enough?"

"You did an admirable job. Don't take it personally."

Ammosiah huffed impatiently. "It's not something you see to believe. You feel it in your heart, your soul. Wasn't there anything?"

Karlinah shrugged. She wasn't about to mention romantic inclinations if he didn't share them. "I've always judged with my mind, not my heart. This is all so new to me. I need to fast and pray about it as Ammon says."

"Ammon says," Ammosiah muttered. "Everyone listens to what Ammon's says. What about *my* words?" He stared at the ground while shaking his head. "I thought I was cut out to be a missionary too. You were the perfect challenge. I thought *I* could be the one to bring you the message of happiness."

"Ammosiah . . ." But Karlinah didn't know what to say. Why was he acting like this? The hair on the back of her neck prickled, and her breathing deepened. All the good feelings in her heart dissipated. Maybe she should change the subject. "Would you like to go for a walk?"

Ammosiah got to his feet and blew out a breath. "I don't have time for that. I'm preparing for missionary service."

Karlinah's forehead creased. "Missionary service? What are you talking about?" Did he want to join Ammon's band of missionaries? The words "the perfect challenge" echoed in her mind. So *that* was why he wanted to spend time with her. Veins bulged at her temples. He wouldn't give time to let her explore her feelings? She stood and set her clenched fists onto a familiar spot on her hips and leaned close to his face. "Am I just a missionary challenge to you?" Ammon had never been as officious as this. "Get out." Karlinah worked hard to keep her voice under control.

Without another word, Ammosiah turned and retraced his steps the way he had come.

Karlinah's lips pressed together as she watched him retreat. One more man disappeared out of her life. Not that she wanted him back, but she feared the dull ache in her heart might never find love that could fill it.

Chapter Twenty-Two

THE TWO PRINCESSES MADE CONVERSATION on their way to offer refreshment to the construction workers. They looked upward at the walls of stone that would become the synagogue.

"How tall do you think it will be?" Hepka asked her sister.

Karlinah twisted her mouth and shifted her water jug to the other shoulder. "Hard to say, but I hope they're ready for the roof soon. I wish they'd used the stair-step design. It's more interesting."

"Most of the laborers are not trained masons, Karlinah. But a few artisans have been hired." Hepka shrugged. "The shape may be ordinary, but have you seen the small decorative rocks placed in the mortar between the stones? They've done a beautiful job."

Karlinah gazed at the dots of dark lava rock accented against lime mortar, breaking up the overall gray color. She frowned. "I guess I'm just anxious to have the synagogue finished. It's been a lot of extra noise."

Hepka snorted in agreement. "I won't miss that part. It would have been nice to get married in the synagogue, but I'm glad we didn't wait."

Karlinah recalled her sister's wedding in the meadow and how beautiful she had looked. Hepka's braid, interwoven with ribbon, had been coiled on top of her head and flowers neatly tucked in. She could hardly take her eyes off Jaros to listen to the king's words of advice. Karlinah stumbled on a rock, calling her attention to where they walked.

They approached the next set of workers. Two men kneeling upon mats were chiseling a design into a large stone. Their muscular backs shone with sweat. They were among the majority of the workers who preferred the cool loincloths as their sole clothing for labor.

Hepka spoke first. "Care for a cool drink and a cake of bread, sir?" She held out her basket. Karlinah set her jug down and dipped out a cupful, certain the men would fetch their own cups.

Both men got up from their knees and turned toward the girls. When Karlinah looked to whom she poured the water for, her breath caught. Her hand wobbled. Here stood a ruggedly handsome young man with the deepest pools of dark eyes she ever saw. His shoulder-length hair was tethered back out of his way, revealing ears that stuck out slightly. The stone artisan from Jerusalem? She could hardly believe it!

A smile begged to come out, and she let it go all the way to her eyes. He returned the gaze, unblinking, while he took the cup. Karlinah shifted her eyes downward in embarrassment for a moment before bringing her gaze up. It reminded her of the time he had bowed his head in respect of her position. Had he actually seen her then? Did he know her now? She didn't think so. The feeling of his watchful eyes penetrated her soul while she shakily dipped and poured water for the older man.

Karlinah felt an awkward silence while the two drank. Her skin prickled, and she rubbed her arms, her senses heightened. Her eyes went to his chest and shoulders when his head tipped back to drain the cup. His muscles were firm and toned. A tingle ran through her. *No, men cause trouble.* She lifted her lashes for another glance at his face. This didn't *feel* like trouble.

The younger one wiped his mouth with the back of his hand while his eyes locked on to hers. Karlinah felt her face grow hot but held his gaze.

"My son and I thank you," the elder said, putting away his cup.

Hepka squinted at the stone from several angles. "What is it supposed to be?"

The elder clutched both hands to his heart, groaned, and pulled out an imagined knife. Hepka grimaced and Karlinah stiffened. His son laughed heartily as if having seen such antics before.

"I am only teasing," the father said. "We are stone artisans who take pride in our work, but not to worry. You shouldn't be able to tell what it is at this stage. Come back in a few days. Then you will see."

Such an invitation showed his satisfaction in their work, and Karlinah found her respect for both of them growing. "We shall do that," she committed, receiving the younger man's huge grin that showed a full set of teeth with a crumb of golden bread wedged between two of them. She stifled a giggle.

Karlinah bent to pick up the jug then slowly flipped her long hair behind one shoulder. *I can tease too.* Flashing a smile, she was on her way. Just before disappearing around the next corner, Karlinah paused to glance back. The young man was rooted to the spot, watching her. She heard his father make a sound in his throat to call him back to work.

That night, Karlinah dreamed of the handsome stone artisan. She awoke remembering his high cheekbones, strong jawline, and dark eyes, and wishing she had heard his voice. She couldn't remember the tone or pitch when he had spoken in Jerusalem—only that his few words exuded both submission and self-respect. Then she covered her head with her pillow. *No, Karlinah, no!* It had been fun to sport with him, but she didn't want to get her hopes up over a man. They always disappointed her.

Quit thinking about him, Karlinah scolded herself throughout the next day. *You hardly know him.* Another voice inside her head told her not to worry over harmless flirting. There was plenty of time to find out the stone worker's disposition. She could allow herself a few daydreams. The first voice reminded her Masoni had also once set his eyes upon her in such a way. Then she shook her head in disgust.

She was tired of comparing every young man she met with Masoni.

How could she keep his memory from cropping up? She *had* to get rid of this guilt. Telling herself that any comparison bested Masoni, she let her mind linger on the craftsman.

Beautiful eyes, nice teeth—why did she find nice teeth so appealing?—and a well-honed body were not supposed to be criteria for capturing so much of her attention. Even his funny ears were endearing. She told herself a stone artisan must have qualities such as patience, creativity, and industry with his skilled work. And hadn't she found him humble and polite on their first encounter? He must be a far cry from an arrogant, selfish prince. The notion intrigued her more.

Comparisons to Helami, Ammosiah, even Japethihah entertained her thoughts. A man worth pursuing would have to be more sincere and mature than they. She wanted to know more about this man—the sooner the better.

Now that King Lamoni practiced a gentler rule and believed all men were equal, he told her she was free to choose in the matter of marriage. He would not arrange a betrothal for any of his children. Karlinah knew her father only wanted her to be happy with someone she could learn to love. At nearly seventeen, she felt old. Time did young women no favors.

Could this artisan be what she wanted? She shook her head, feeling silly over the question. But serious questions kept inviting themselves into her thoughts. She should simply make the decision for the both of them.

A traveling artisan who worked in various cities needed some help. No playing games, less painful. She grinned.

Could she be what *he* might want?

Working on the synagogue implied that he was a Christian. Would he be able to accept her as she was? She considered herself no different than the believers, learning to serve and acquiring new skills, but they didn't always see it that way. She could be an agreeable wife. And pleasant to the eye. All this should be enough for any man, shouldn't it?

***

It was midafternoon when Karlinah finished crushing the handfuls of dried maize kernels into tiny granules inside the worn stone's concave indentation. Her hands were tired, but it felt good to complete the task. Now maybe she could dismiss the thoughts accompanying a repetitive, stationary chore. Thoughts of a certain craftsman.

Was he excited to visit different lands, as she assumed he must, or was it lonely for this quiet man to be a stranger everywhere he went? At least he had his father. Perhaps a mother waited somewhere for their return. Or a girl of special interest.

Humph. Too bad if there is. She's out of reach, but I am not. Karlinah bounced down the porch steps and into the sunshine.

Walking absently down the street, she could smell cooking fires and hear children's mirth amongst the construction noise. Her mind played a game of what if. What if she should be so bold as to walk up to this captivating man and invite him to dinner? What would he do if she explained as they ate that she had a mutually beneficial proposal which fit their cultural expectations?

It was time he should marry, as much for himself as for her, and since he traveled and worked so much and had little time to go about such things, she could solve his problem for him, do him a favor. It would be the perfect arrangement. He could finally quit traveling; there was plenty of work in Ishmael, and they had a place to live in the large family compound behind the king's house. She would take care of everything else so he could live a quiet life of luxury in the company of a beautiful woman who allowed him to follow the teachings of Ammon.

He would be a fool to refuse such an offer. Did she possess the courage to make it? Getting him to believe it was his idea would be much better.

The grin slid off Karlinah's face as she spotted this man heading toward the path to the river. She stood still and blinked. He carried a drying cloth, indicating he intended to bathe. An idea forming, she returned to her bedchamber to get her tools to gather clay for some new beads, giving him a head start toward the riverbank. It was the place where the potters got their clay and the perfect cover for a happenchance meeting.

Sauntering along the familiar path to the river, Karlinah took little notice of the green foliage, the shadows created by twisting vines and ferns, or the hum of insects. She passed two girls coming her way, each with a jar of water on one shoulder. There was little other foot traffic today.

Before too long, the path opened up to a grassy area alongside the riverbank. She stopped in her tracks. There was the artisan, sunning himself on a large, flat boulder. Though she had expected him, the sight of his rippling muscles made her legs wobbly. His eyes were closed, and he looked like he might be asleep, except she knew he couldn't have been there long enough. His wet hair and skin glistened with fresh beads of water.

"Hello there," she called.

He opened his eyes and sat up on one elbow. "Hello."

She loved how his face brightened as he gazed at her. "No, don't get up. You look so comfortable I might have to join you." She gave a chuckle to show he didn't have to take her seriously.

"I—I've dripped all over the place, but there's plenty of room." His was a pleasant, midrange voice—not too deep or high and not sickeningly sweet like Japethihah's.

"I don't think it would be proper," Karlinah teased. "I don't even know your name."

A look of horror came over his face as if he had just realized the impropriety of their situation.

"Don't worry. I don't believe you'd harm a mosquito." She scrambled up to sit two arm's lengths away. "I'm Karlinah."

"Cumroth." A shy smile came to his lips.

Cumroth. She returned the smile. "You could have had a hot bath, you know. There are public times available in the king's bathhouse."

"I know, but no one would want a bath right after mine. I was covered with so much granite dust. Scrubbing it away hurts." He made a pained face, and Karlinah laughed.

They lapsed into a comfortable silence until Cumroth said, "Oh, did you come for a bath?" He moved, and she put out a hand, gesturing for him to stay.

"Not at all. I'm here to collect a little clay."

"You mean that stuff I slipped on over there?" He pointed. His smirk told her he knew all about clay. He likely used it in his work.

Karlinah put a hand to her mouth, playing along. "You didn't. Were you hurt?"

He shook his head. "Do you . . . need any help?"

"I might, if it's as slippery as you say."

Karlinah slid off the boulder after Cumroth and took hold of his arm. She let him guide her and clasped her hand over his while she knelt down. She opened her bag and removed a scraping tool. It only took a moment to select a handful. He watched as she kneaded it on a rock to remove air bubbles and rolled it into a ball. Then she dipped a cloth into the water and wrapped the clay ball with it before putting it in her bag.

She stood and looked toward the stone cutter, who swatted at an insect rather than be caught watching her. She hid a grin. "Well, I have what I need." She paused to let her intentions sink in. "It's been nice talking with you."

"Uh, you're . . . leaving already?"

Karlinah tilted her head to the side and smiled innocently. "I have to get back to my tools before this clay dries."

He put a tunic over his still-wet body. "I could walk you back. One never knows what could be lurking in the jungle."

The smile on her face broadened. Good. It was *his* idea now. "That would be nice. Thank you."

The two walked along the path talking about such inconsequential things as the beautiful jungle and how hungry he was getting. Karlinah asked about his father and how the stone designs were coming along. At places where the trail narrowed, he took the protective lead. By the time they reached the courtyard, Karlinah was convinced of Cumroth's pleasant personality, though she had done most of the talking. The match, if she could get him to propose it, would be more than acceptable.

They stopped in front of the synagogue. "I know you need to go," he said, "but I would like to see the beads when you finish."

She dipped her head. "And after seeing you lounge on that rock today, I'd better make sure some serious progress is going on with that stone."

His eyes widened, and he opened his mouth.

She laughed and saw his face relax. "I know the workers need a break once in a while."

"And a bath." His smile came easily.

"Thank you for walking with me," Karlinah said.

"Thank you for protecting me from all those wild animals." They both laughed easily.

Saying good-bye, Cumroth turned into the synagogue.

Her hips swayed as she made her way home. Like bees after honey.

Chapter Twenty-Three

THE NEXT MORNING, ABISH APPROACHED with little Tobias snuggled in her arms.

"The queen is not feeling well. Can you watch over Tobias this morning until I come back from helping Evah?"

"Certainly." Then Karlinah hid a frown. Her plans to meet Cumroth would have to wait until later.

Abish set the boy on his feet and retraced her steps.

Karlinah sighed resignedly and took Tobias by the hand.

"Have you eaten this morning?"

Tobias nodded.

"What do you want to do today?"

"Go outside; go outside. No more maize mush."

"Hmm," Karlinah said, ignoring the sound of her own stomach. "I think going outside is a good idea."

Picking up Tobias, she touched her nose to his in a side to side motion. She continued in a higher, childish voice, "Would you like that, my little iguana lizard? Want to go on a walk with Karlinah?"

Tobias giggled. "I not a 'guana." He scrambled to get out of her arms, so she set him down. Forgiving the offense, Tobias jumped up and down and repeated in a singsong voice, "Go outside with Linah."

Karlinah took his hand, and they headed for the sunshine. The sound of hammers clanking and men calling out instructions filled the humid air. Tobias wanted to run everywhere, and Karlinah continually reined him in.

"Be careful," she said. "You can't get so close. Take my hand."

"What's that?" his little voice asked over and over, as he pointed.

Karlinah told Tobias all about whatever they saw. The ropes pulling pallets of stones to another side of the building were his favorite. Smooth logs used as wheels were placed in front of a pallet so it could roll upon the logs with greater ease. Workers followed behind, hurrying to catch logs that no longer held weight and then racing to place them ahead of the pallet. Once, a log rolled away from the men down the road. Tobias squealed in delight. The operation went smoothly for several minutes, and Tobias became bored.

"Let's go find the hammer-and-chisel men," Karlinah suggested.

"Hammuh and chizo," Tobias repeated.

Karlinah laughed and took his hand. "Ham*mer*," she emphasized.

Tobias copied the intonation. "Ham*muh*."

Karlinah giggled, scooped Tobias into her arms, and tickled him until he screamed. After she set him down, he skipped toward the sound of pounding.

"What doing?" Tobias could barely see over the huge stone block on the ground.

The older man chuckled. "Well, little man, to whom do you belong?" Then he looked up to see Karlinah approaching, and they recognized each other at the same moment. "Hello again," he called with a wave.

Karlinah managed a greeting while her eyes searched for Cumroth.

"Cumroth will return shortly. He just went to get—ah, here he comes."

Karlinah liked hearing the son's name. *Strong, like his body.* Her eyes followed his to see Cumroth coming with a satchel over his shoulder.

He brightened at the sight of Karlinah and spoke with animation. "Ah, you came to make certain we are working."

"Perhaps. We were out for a walk and decided to see what improvements you've made."

He noticed little Tobias at his father's feet, and his voice grew sober. "Is this your son?"

"My little brother, Tobias. I am not married."

A twinkle sprang into Cumroth's eyes. He stooped to clasp Tobias's shoulder. "Hello, Tobias. I am Cumroth."

"Coom-woth."

They all laughed, and Tobias hid his face in his hands. Cumroth ruffled the boy's hair, and Tobias peeked up at him with a shy smile. Karlinah thought Masoni or Japethihah would have ignored the child. *Stop comparing.*

The flash of teeth and sparkling eyes made her knees weak. She turned to Cumroth's father. "I'm Karlinah."

Cumroth's father took a step forward. "And I am Corianthem."

Karlinah's eyebrows shot up. "*The* Corianthem? Of Corianthem and"—she looked to Cumroth—"Son fame? Of course!" *Why did I not realize this?* She beamed, reflecting on the improved status of her intended future husband. The match fit better than expected.

Cumroth shrugged, showing a half grin, while his father said matter-of-factly, "King Lamoni wanted the best." Then Corianthem turned to Tobias. "Would you like to see what we have been working on?"

Tobias jiggled his head up and down. Corianthem gently lifted Tobias so he could get a better view of the top of the stone.

"It's a jungle cat!"

"Yes. A jaguar," Corianthem answered in a satisfied tone. "We will stain the shadows with charcoal paste, and he will come to life!"

Tobias frowned. "I can't say *jagwah*."

"Do not worry, my little friend." Corianthem set Tobias on the ground. "You will be all grown up before you know it."

Tobias's face brightened, and Karlinah was pleased by her youngest brother's trust in these men. Somehow it verified her choice. She shifted her eyes between them. "It is truly a masterful work."

"I am happy you think so," Cumroth said. "Would you and Tobias like to watch?"

Karlinah noticed Corianthem giving his son a sideways glance. Tobias jumped up and down asking her for permission, which she easily gave. Corianthem gave a commentary while Cumroth made gentle taps and digs into the stone. It was painstakingly slow to get the desired results, though Tobias did not appear bored. He must have liked the tapping sound, blinking hard each time the hammer hit the chisel or pounding his fist onto his other palm to keep time with Cumroth.

Karlinah slowly shook her head. "I don't think I could have the patience for such work."

Cumroth reached out and took hold of the end of Karlinah's plaited hair. "And yet you take time to groom all of this lovely hair, to walk with your little brother, and to answer his endless questions. Is this not patience?"

Karlinah stared, mesmerized by his subtle insight. This felt more like truth than one of Japethihah's shallow compliments about her outer beauty.

His large, rough hands found the strips of woven cloth tying her braid in place. He fingered a bead the size of his thumb, dangling at the knotted end of the cloth, and he studied the designs scratched into the clay. "This is what you make with the clay?"

"Yes, but there is no comparison to your work." Karlinah looked at her feet, remembering how Masoni had yanked the ties from her hair, forbidding her to wear something so childish.

"It is a finished work nonetheless. Simple and beautiful."

A shiver of pleasure tingled through her body as Karlinah looked up at him. She found herself liking the way an artist noticed things. His honesty came through without pretense, the compliment sincere. Did criticism ever slip from his lips? This was maturity Japethihah and Masoni never showed.

"Would you like to try?" Corianthem suggested, holding out his chisel.

She put her hands up and took a step backward. "Oh no, I would only ruin it."

Corianthem chuckled and reached into the satchel to pull out another chisel. He stretched the tools out toward her and said, "Here. No work of art will be ruined. We have some excess pieces you can practice on."

"Oh, I should have realized."

Tobias called out, "Me do it."

Corianthem laughed. "Come over here, my little friend, while Cumroth shows your sister what to do."

Corianthem placed a waste piece on the block table for Tobias. He set the mat down then motioned for Karlinah to kneel on it. Kneeling beside her, he propped Tobias on one knee. Next, the older man put his hands over Tobias's small ones and helped him to tap with the chisel.

Karlinah watched them for a moment. "How do I hold it?" she asked Cumroth.

"It will be easier if you let me guide you." He bent over her shoulder from behind and touched his hands to hers. Their cheeks were less than a hand span apart. It sent a shiver through her. She tried to stay steady while Cumroth seemed intent on the task.

"This is what my father did when I first learned. Now loosen your grip on the chisel just a bit. That's better." Karlinah willed herself to follow the instructions. "Give a few gentle taps. Yes. Do not let your head get too close—the particles may fly. Now place the chisel in the opposite direction and tap some more."

A small notch of stone soon chipped out, and Cumroth took out a horsetail brush to clear the debris. "You did it," he exclaimed, turning his head toward her. Karlinah took her eyes off the stone and turned toward him at the same moment. Suddenly aware of how close they were, he cleared his throat and straightened, avoiding her steady gaze.

"Try one more chip next to it on your own."

Karlinah could feel him move back a pace. She gave a few taps, increasing the force with each one. Hitting the chisel too hard, a large chunk broke loose. "I told you I do not have the patience for this. I'm afraid the closest I will ever get to be an artisan is making my beads. I'll leave the masterpieces to you."

They locked eyes while she spoke. "You have a gift. I did better when you were guiding me, Cumroth." Did she detect a flush from him as she said his name?

"You should have seen my first attempts. Or should I say it's a good thing you did not?"

They both laughed and fell into comfortable silence.

"We should let you get back to your work," Karlinah said. "Thank you for the lesson." She waited to see what else he might say.

"It was my pleasure. Come back for another anytime."

Karlinah lowered her lashes and then looked at him. "Maybe you would like a lesson in sculpturing clay?"

His smile widened at the invitation. "One lesson for another?"

She inclined her head and then held out her hand to her little brother. "Come, Tobias. It's time to go home."

Corianthem chuckled a moment later, and Karlinah looked back to see why. Cumroth stared after them like a sunflower to the sun. Another glance a few steps later showed his smile slipping from his face as they crossed the courtyard toward her house. Karlinah hoped he was sad to see them go. She gave one last wave, which Cumroth dazedly returned. He seemed frozen in place as they turned to climb the porch steps. It hadn't occurred to Karlinah that Cumroth might be horror-struck to learn she was the daughter of the king.

Chapter Twenty-Four

THE SHADE OF THE COURTYARD's large oak was just what Cumroth needed for a midafternoon break. He sat and leaned against the trunk with a cloth between his back and the rough bark. He closed his eyes, ignoring the sounds of construction. Again, Karlinah's sweet face appeared in his mind. Her image sent a thrill within him before he winced and groaned. *Why did she have to be a princess?* Everything he knew of her seemed desirable—her manner, her kindness to others, the way he could talk to her with ease. That, Cumroth realized, was his best measuring stick. Any girl with whom he felt comfortable talking was a rare find. Too bad he wasn't worthy of such a prize.

He possessed the rough edges of chipped granite while many around him were polished smooth. But a princess? He shook his head. She was marble. Cumroth picked up a pebble, tossed it in the air, and caught it in his palm. Roughness and simplicity couldn't match with refinement and royalty. He would have to put her out of his mind. He stared at the smooth rock and threw it hard at the ground.

Just then, a handful of men walked through the courtyard. Cumroth caught a few words of their conversation. One word—Karlinah—sent his head up, and the tall one must have noticed. The man caught his eye, and Cumroth quickly looked away, not wanting to be caught eavesdropping. He closed his eyes and leaned his head against the tree, listening to their indistinct, fading words.

Minutes later a voice sounded so closely that Cumroth opened his eyes with a jerk.

"Good day, sir. Are you new here?"

Cumroth answered affirmatively and got to his feet. Apparently this man knew enough of the citizens to recognize a new face. He carried himself with dignity, was a few years older, and dressed more elaborately than most. Who was he?

"I am Japethihah."

He inclined his head. "Cumroth, the stone artisan."

"Ah. The synagogue. Adding to its exquisiteness, are you?"

Detecting sarcasm, Cumroth said nothing.

Japethihah interlaced his fingers and rested them across his midsection. "Forgive me, I am a master at observation and couldn't help but see your interest at the mention of the princess. I take it you have noticed her beauty?"

Cumroth bobbed his head, trying to appear indifferent. "Who wouldn't?"

"Of course." A sly smile curled one side of the man's mouth. "With your being new here, perhaps I can save you some trouble by passing along a warning—not that you would concern yourself with her, but one never knows what *she* might do. You see, she is a heartbreaker." He let these words sink in before continuing effortlessly. "She has a dozen men at her fingertips until she decides to discard one or pick up another. She thrives on the attention of men, giving false hope while preferring not to marry any of them."

Cumroth pressed his brows together. This didn't sound like the girl he had met. He wondered at the man's truthfulness or possible jealousy. "Are you a suitor?"

"Oh no." Japethihah showed little emotion. "She thinks me too dull, even when I was the high priest." His chin lifted, and his eyes held a faraway look before returning. "The princess has a certain level of taste. As a stone artisan, perhaps she will find you worthy of her attention."

If a high priest was too dull . . . Cumroth's neck grew hot. "I am a simple man." He had worked in too many kingdoms not to recognize his lowliness, even though his craft was sought after. It was his only claim. She was royal born regardless of newly accepted equality.

Japethihah's grin broadened momentarily. "Well, then you have nothing to fear." A serious visage replaced the grin, and Japethihah lowered his voice. "Whatever you do, if you should speak to her, do not mention Ammon. Sadly, her temperament toward him is downright hostile."

"What do you mean? I thought the king's household supported Ammon."

"All but Karlinah. Ammon steals all the attention, and she hates Nephites. She refuses to be baptized." Japethihah lowered his head and shook it. "It's such a shame not to count her among the believers."

"That *is* a shame. I had no idea." Cumroth looked down, his heart sinking. He wasn't sure about Karlinah seeking so much attention, but he assumed she had been baptized. Doubt stabbed at him. How much did Cumroth really know about her?

"Well, consider yourself warned. Anything else I can help you with, brother?" Japethihah lifted one brow.

"Thank you, no. I appreciate you speaking with me."

Japethihah smiled. "Anytime, my friend. Anytime."

***

A cool breeze greeted Karlinah and Abish as they descended the steps of the king's house. Gray clouds gathered in the distance. Abish set her basket down to tie a shawl around her shoulders. The smell of ripe fruit and fresh maize cakes filled their noses. Karlinah bounced on her toes, ignoring the temperature drop, and stepped hurriedly when Abish was ready.

"Slow down," Abish said.

"Come on. It's going to rain. The workers don't want soggy cakes."

Abish glanced at the sky and flashed a dubious look. "The storm is hours away."

Karlinah slowed to avoid more suspicion, but she couldn't help feeling anxious to see Cumroth again. Before long, she spotted a certain young man and his father and pranced over to them. "Hello there. Need a morning snack?" her cheery voice rang.

Abish gave her a wary glance.

"We have maize cakes, cheese curds, papayas, mangoes, and plums." She held out her basket to Cumroth, smiling sweetly.

Cumroth gave a stiff incline of the head and reached for a mango. "Thank you."

Karlinah blinked her long lashes at him, but he looked away. She supposed he felt uncomfortable in front of Abish.

"Beautiful fruit from beautiful girls," the older man said. He reached into Abish's basket.

Karlinah was encouraged by Corianthem's warmth. "I see you have finished the jaguar." She fingered the stone, tracing the outline of the animal's back. "It appeared lifelike as we approached, but the detail up close is exquisite. No wonder your work is singled out."

Brightness momentarily flickered in Cumroth's eyes. "My father and I thank you." He took a knife from its sheath at his waist and started peeling his mango. "So Ammon is staying at your house?" He glanced at her.

"That's right, but I hardly ever see him with his preaching and all."

Cumroth bobbed his head, his chin jutting out. "What do you think of his preaching?"

"I haven't listened to him much." Encouraged by his attempts at conversation, she plodded on. "Once I heard Ammon talking about blood and felt sick to my stomach because of it." Karlinah laughed. "It had to do with the Atonement, but it was confusing at the time. Someone later explained it to me." She shrugged.

"I see." He sliced a piece of orange flesh as the silence grew thick.

Corianthem gazed at his son with a creased brow. Abish stood in silence. Karlinah tried again. "So what is the next design you'll work on?"

"Just filler blocks." Cumroth turned away at a slight angle, popping the slice into his mouth. Juice trickled onto his chin.

Karlinah scowled. *He's not acting shy; he's avoiding me. Why? Does he think I like Ammon?*

Corianthem swallowed a bite of maize cake. "We're trimming with grooves of squared spirals in alternating patterns—an attractive design— the last to be finished. You must come again and see it."

Karlinah brightened. "I would love . . . to." She hesitated uncomfortably as Cumroth's head twisted toward his father in a glare of disapproval. Such rudeness! What was going on? "Well, I can see you are busy," she said. Hurt and annoyance laced through her voice. She turned on her heels. "Let's go, Abish."

"Good-bye," Corianthem called out cheerfully. "Say hello to my little friend Tobias."

As they moved on, the girls could hear Corianthem chiding Cumroth before his voice faded.

"Anything you want to tell me?" Abish asked.

"What's to tell? Workers get in bad moods."

"Workers? What about their 'little friend Tobias'?"

Karlinah cracked a sad smile. "We talked a few days ago, and he was pleasant. Apparently he has changed his mind about me. It's not the first time, you know."

"Humph. It's his loss. We should have given him a lemon to go with his sour disposition."

Karlinah sniffled then laughed, but the empty ache remained in her chest. She wouldn't have the heart to mention the possibility of their betrothal if this became Cumroth's permanent attitude. Her plan was failing. What had she done wrong?

Days later, her experience with Cumroth still bothered her. He continued to captivate her interest while he had clearly lost interest. Why the change? She pressed her lips together, hoping for answers. When none came, she sighed.

Quick judgment often got her into trouble. He deserved another chance. She closed her eyes, remembering the touch of his hands on hers, his rippling muscles, the coolness of his moist skin so close to hers, the twinkle in his eyes. She would make certain their next meeting went better.

Chapter Twenty-Five

ON THE NEXT CLEAR DAY after several rainy ones, Karlinah and Hepka, each with a basket of soiled clothing in hand, crossed the dirt courtyard to the path leading to the river. As they passed the synagogue, Karlinah stopped, her heart skipping a beat. Cumroth knelt with three girls surrounding him, watching him work. *Three!* He said something, and she heard giggles. Setting off with a stiff march alongside her sister, she worked her jaw the rest of the way to the river. She had never rubbed her laundry so hard against a wet rock.

"Ready to talk about it?" Hepka softly asked after a while.

"No!" It was all Karlinah needed to release a dam of tears.

Hepka waited for her sister to gain control.

"I'll never get married. Everyone I care for has rejected me," Karlinah said.

Hepka moved closer and put a hand on her sister's shoulder. "What are you talking about?"

Karlinah's bottom lip drooped in a pout. "I've tried, Hepka, believe me, but no one that I want wants me. I don't know how you and Jaros did it. It's hopeless. I'll never get married."

"Give yourself some time. You just haven't found the right man," Hepka soothed. "I hate to see you so miserable." She paused. "Jaros has a cousin who will be coming—"

"I thought I had found the one, but he doesn't care for me." Karlinah sniffed. "I can't get him off my mind. It breaks my heart."

Hepka tilted her round head. "What?"

"Remember the father and son stone artisans we met working on the synagogue?"

Hepka nodded, her eyes opening wide. "Him? When did this happen?"

"His name is Cumroth. We spoke a few times, and something connected for both of us. I know it did. Then he suddenly starts acting like he hates me." Her lip quivered. "I don't know what could have happened unless he found another girl." The image of the three girls surrounding him burned in her mind.

"Hmm. Well, he doesn't know what he's missing." Hepka firmly dipped her chin. "For a moment there, I feared you were going to tell me you were pining for Japethihah."

Karlinah groaned. "Can you see us together? He's a dried-up maize stalk, and I'm a little flower."

They giggled and continued scrubbing and dipping clothing into the cool water.

"Don't ever settle for someone like Japethihah," Hepka said. "He's not good enough for you."

"Right. I'll take a liking to Ammon instead." The sarcasm was thick.

"I mean it, Karlinah. Japethihah has an evil heart. I feel it when he is near. I can see it in his eyes."

"Is that why he doesn't appeal to me?" Her voice lightened. She wasn't about to mention Japethihah's similarity to Masoni. Karlinah stood to ring out her wet garments. "Then what does it say about me that Ammon isn't appealing either?"

"Nothing. But it goes much better when the two share like-mindedness. I don't know what I would have done if Jaros had not been converted."

Hands stilled, Karlinah stared into the water. "That's the other reason men don't want me," she whispered. "Cumroth probably found out I haven't been baptized, and now I'm not good enough for him."

Hepka placed one hand on her hip. "What's that about, anyway? You *are* a good person. It's time to get baptized. Haven't you had witnesses enough from Father and Ammon? Have you ignored the scriptures? The earth and your very life denote there is a God. Are you waiting for a lightning bolt to hit?"

An exasperated, wounded-sounding exhale came from Karlinah's mouth. She couldn't believe her younger sister would speak to her like this. "Maybe it's not that simple for some of us. Ammon talking about Christ doesn't mean *I* know He exists. And even if He does, aren't there many gods?" She bit her lip, stalling. Of course her sister would think she was good, but if God could look into her heart, would He see a murderer? Better to avoid that confrontation.

Hepka looked thoughtful. "It's like waking yourself up in the night because you heard yourself snore."

"What?" Karlinah wrinkled her forehead. What kind of an answer was this?

"Haven't you ever done that?"

"No." But Karlinah heard the hint of doubt in her own voice and added more firmly, "I don't snore." *Unless I'm on my back*, she added silently.

Hepka raised an eyebrow. "See. That's denial. I could get Abish to corroborate."

"Never mind." Karlinah's voice showed irritation. What did snoring have to do with anything?

"You wake yourself up because you were snoring too loudly, and it hits you that you were snoring. No more denying it. You know. That's what it's going to be like for you, Karlinah."

"What what's going to be like?"

"Your witness. You're going to wake up and have it hit you that you believed all along, but now you can come to terms with it. Suddenly you accept it. No denying."

Karlinah stared hard at her sister. This actually made sense. She shook her head, smiling. Could Hepka be right? Would she suddenly know? Didn't she almost know now? Almost.

"It takes faith, Karlinah. Move past your doubt. You've seen our parents raised from the earth with a miraculous change of heart. You've heard witnesses from them and from a prophet, but you don't let it penetrate your soul." Hepka let out a deep breath, searching for a gentler emotion. "It takes desire and effort to open your heart and let the seeds of faith have a place to grow. It's not in Ammon we put our trust. Trust in the Lord, Karlinah. The Great Spirit is the one true God. Pray to Him. He has done His part many times over. It is your turn now."

Karlinah blinked. The challenge hit hard, yet she thrilled in setting out to meet it. In the stillness, she felt her heart beating powerfully from Hepka's words. She remembered feeling this way before—listening as her father retold his experiences and when Ammosiah explained the Atonement. Hadn't she mistaken that feeling in her heart for romance? With cold feet and water dripping from her elbows, the sun warmed her from the inside out. Karlinah opened her mouth in realization. This was not the sun. Had she been denying the witness inside her all this time because of the secret she guarded?

Her father said the same thing. *Your witness will come when your heart is right.* Maybe it *was* time to make her heart right—time to give up this troublesome secret.

***

Karlinah sat on the porch steps, waiting for Ammon to finish speaking to citizens in the courtyard. She knew he would head this way sooner or later. The man should be starving by now. Moments later the young missionary did as expected. She stood to catch his attention. "Ammon?"

He lifted his eyebrows with surprise. "Yes?"

"After you have eaten, would you have some time for a few private questions?" His smiling eyes struck her as handsome, even for a Nephite. It's funny how time can change one's mind of things.

"I am in no hurry. We can converse now if you would like."

She returned the smile. "I'd like that. Can we walk outside, away from the house?"

"And from listening ears?" he guessed. She nodded.

They started around the corner of the house, passing family-owned huts and a vegetable garden. The yard looked empty. Ammon held his hands together behind him and let Karlinah speak first.

She got straight to the matter. "Could a good, warm feeling within me be a witness this gospel is true?" She searched his eyes.

"It might be."

She snapped her head back. What—no sure answer? Didn't he want an easy convert?

Ammon's smile remained strong. "But I would not measure such a feeling all by itself."

"What do you mean?"

"Feasting makes me feel good, but I should not do it all the time. A blanket warms me, but it is no indication of a higher power."

She laughed.

"A measure of wisdom to go with your feelings is best. You know— heart and mind together. You certainly should not join yourself to something with a *bad* feeling about it."

She crossed her arms, giving him a crooked smile, and he continued.

"A good feeling is only a start—like a seed that gets planted. Neglected seeds do not prove useful. You won't know if it grows into something desirable unless you give it nourishment and time to see what kind of fruits come forth. Then you will know if it was a good seed"—he held out one cupped hand and then the other as if there were something in them to compare—"or a bad seed."

"I've seen so much caring and helping one another from the Christians. Is this the kind of fruits you mean?"

Ammon nodded. "Following Christ makes them want to do good, to be charitable. I know little of what you were like before, but I have seen your service to others, Karlinah. Has your heart not changed for good?"

"Maybe not as much as others, but yes, I believe so." Her smile brightened. "The seed *is* good." *It's just my shame fighting against it.*

"Then nourish it with faith until it becomes sweet above all that is sweet and fills your whole soul. The Lord will hear your earnest prayers and give you answers in His own good time." His light eyes bore into her dark ones. "All is possible with God."

Karlinah nibbled her lip. "Even forgiveness? I mean, I heard you talking about repentance and forgiveness once. How does it work?"

"Repentance is a change of heart that often comes after the pain of suffering consequences for wrong choices. Hopefully this pain leads to feelings of sorrow about disobeying God's commandments and a desire to change. One promises to leave those mistakes or wicked ways behind and follow God. We are cleansed from the stain of sin through the Atonement of Jesus Christ that we may be worthy to enter the kingdom of heaven. Christ will suffer for us that we might not suffer eternally."

Karlinah's voice grew animated. "After one is sorry, it's a promise to change—that's all repentance is?" She narrowed her eyes. "What about forgiveness?"

"When we do our best to follow God's ways, He will forgive our sins if we give them up and confess them to Him. We obtain forgiveness through confessing to God." Ammon swatted at an insect on his neck.

Karlinah looked at the ground momentarily. "Confessing to only God?"

Ammon bobbed his head. "Unless it is a public sin that should be confessed publicly. If the sin is against a person, you should also confess to him or her. It is like an apology, a peace offering showing your change of heart."

"I can't do that." She frowned. "He's dead."

"Would you like to tell me about it?" Ammon's eyes were kind.

Tears formed in her eyes as she nodded. By the time Karlinah explained that she had started out protecting herself from her abusive husband and ended up wanting to kill him, her head rested in her hands. "I wanted him dead, wanted it all to stop." Sobs choked her words.

Ammon touched her shoulder. His voice brought her wet eyes up. "You killed him to stay alive."

"Yes, but I *wanted* my husband dead. The king called what happened *murder*." She looked down and whispered, "I believed him."

"He was wrong. You acted in defense to preserve your life." Ammon's voice was gentle. "You are no murderer, though even murder can ultimately be forgiven."

Karlinah looked up and wiped her eyes, but she didn't dare speak.

"Your father was forgiven of murder after the veil of darkness lifted and he gained a knowledge of truth. As for me, I knew of my sins as I committed them and willfully rebelled against God until an angel came to turn me and my brethren from our ways." He shared more about his past with Karlinah, and she was amazed at the contrast from then until now.

"Though neither of us is perfect, do your father's and my current actions not show we have been born again and left our former ways behind?"

Her eyes glistened as she nodded.

"One does not have to be struck to the earth to be forgiven. Repentance is shown through our actions. When we make a new mistake, we confess and turn from doing wrong." Ammon paused and searched her eyes. "I have seen your good acts and know of your changed heart. I have heard your confession. Don't you think you should also tell your father what you have told me?"

Karlinah bit her lower lip and slowly nodded. It would not be easy, but it felt right.

"After you confess to God through prayer, your conscience will clear. Confession is healing as well as cleansing."

She looked at him in amazement. "God can heal me of all this . . . guilt I've been carrying around?" She waved out one hand.

"Yes. There is one more thing for you to know. God wants us to forgive others with the same ease as we would have Him forgive us. It heals our hearts to forgive others."

Karlinah sniffed, marveling at the beauty of this doctrine. Wow. Forgiving Masoni would free her from her suffering. It might not come immediately, but she felt lighter already. She would pray for God's help as soon as she was alone.

The hurt caused by Ammosiah and Cumroth also came freshly to mind. Though past caring about the initial hurt Ammosiah delivered, she still felt wounded by Cumroth's actions. Would her heart feel better once she forgave him for breaking it? Ammon seemed to say as much. She grasped Ammon's shoulder and squeezed it. "Thank you so much."

"God loves you, Karlinah. Talk to Him."

A huge grin appeared. "I will."

Chapter Twenty-Six

"STILL THINKING ABOUT HER?" CORIANTHEM asked his silent son as they worked to finish up the designs on the synagogue.

Cumroth's face flushed. "Who?" He started up again with his hammer and chisel.

"You tell me. Something's got you distracted."

Instead of answering, Cumroth posed another question. "Do you think you will ever marry again, Father?"

He shrugged. "I don't think about it. I'm content. I've gotten along well with your company, but the day will come when another will become more important to you. This is as it should be. If I get lonely, I may think about it then."

"Would you ever consider marrying an unbeliever?"

Corianthem looked up from his work. "What are you really asking? This is about the princess, isn't it?" There was no question in his tone.

Cumroth hesitated and then blew out a breath. "Karlinah has not been converted to the Lord. I have tried to get her out of my mind, but I can't." *Her unforgettable face haunts me.*

"So you want to know if it's acceptable to pursue your feelings? To whom—me? God?"

"I don't know." Cumroth lightly kicked at a block of stone. "It's not like she hates believers—she's surrounded by them. I've watched her, and I know she is good and kind. She could easily have become a follower if not for her struggle to accept a Nephite."

Was there more to it than that, a side to her he knew little about? Could a seemingly kind princess who takes her brother on walks and wears handmade beads in her hair manipulate a handful of would-be suitors as Japethihah suggested? It didn't ring true. It also seemed equally unlikely she could find enough value in him to return his feelings. She was only being nice. He told himself to forget his silly notions.

"This isn't something I can answer for you, son. Only *you* can make that decision. Just don't make it in haste." Corianthem looked into his son's eyes. "Let me give you one last piece of advice. Judge Karlinah more by the direction she is moving than where her footsteps are. Is she headed in a direction that fits with your happiness?"

Cumroth flung his hands upward. "It doesn't matter. She wouldn't want me."

"*She* should be the judge of that. Does the sun not rise and set upon you as well as her? Don't be so hard on yourself." Corianthem set a hand on his son's arm. "But you do pose a serious question. Marriage to an unbeliever would impact every day of your life. It could drive a wedge between you."

"I know."

"And it gets tougher when children come along," Corianthem said.

Cumroth sighed. "I just need to forget about her. There are plenty of other girls—ones who would be happy living a simple life."

"True. But would you be happy with one of them when such a girl puts you at ease? She may be more tolerant of Ammon than you know. She has a good heart. Consider her the same as other girls, royal birth or not. Things aren't always what they appear. You've got to find out the truth."

"Here's a truth for you, Father. She hasn't come back to see me. There are too many men for her to care about me. Shouldn't that tell me something?"

"It tells me you're both stubborn. But I don't blame her. Don't you recall your treatment of her?"

Cumroth winced, regretting listening to Japethihah's information. "I've learned enough to know I'm not what she wants." His jaw set. "Besides, our job here is nearly finished, and we'll be leaving. It will be easier to forget her once I'm gone."

***

Karlinah descended the front steps from her porch and breathed in the evening air, washed fresh by rain. She flexed her fingers a few times and worked her shoulders in circles. First glancing up at the stars, she started walking. A shape quietly stepped out from behind the large oak in the public courtyard.

"Something wrong, princess?" the smooth, deep voice greeted. "You are rubbing your hand."

She touched her throat. "Oh, Japethihah! You startled me. I thought I was alone."

"Forgive me." He gave a slight bow. "Now what's troubling you?"

"Nothing, I'm just stiff from grinding maize."

Japethihah assumed his best sympathetic look. "You poor thing—forced to work so hard. Life was better before Ammon preached equality." He clicked his tongue. "But I know how you feel. I spent all morning bent over, trying to fix my neighbor's fence." Japethihah put a hand to his lower back. "I had to lay down with hot rocks on my back afterward."

Karlinah's mouth gaped before she shut it. She lifted an eyebrow skeptically.

"I'm feeling much better now. Let me see your hand," he said, reaching forward.

"I'm fine, really. There's no need—"

But Japethihah grasped the hand and began a gentle pressure with his thumbs spiraling around her palm.

"Ooh. That does feel good." After a minute, however, Karlinah pulled her hand away. "Thank you."

He said, "Your hands are too delicate for such menial tasks. I worry about you, Karlinah. They work you too hard. You are *not* a servant."

"What I do is my own choice, Japethihah."

"Well, then you are an angel—truly deserving of these." Japethihah stooped to pull out a gathering of wild flowers he had set beside the oak tree. The bunch included a variety—some with yellow, spindly petals and a dark center; the large pink blooms of the hibiscus; and tiny, white clusters bending from long stems.

"They're beautiful." She resisted reaching for them. "But I've told you before I don't think of you that way."

Japethihah kept his arm extended until she took the bundle. "Their beauty pales in comparison to your own."

She didn't smell them. "What's this all about?"

"Just showing my appreciation for the finer things in life, unlike *some* men."

Karlinah studied him through narrowed eyes. "What do you mean?"

"You and I are so much alike, both strong-willed. We have both suffered rejection as outcasts. Sadly, the believers cling only to their own kind," he said gently. "But I know what you need to be happy, and I will make it so if you will reconsider our betrothal."

She pressed her lips tightly together, not liking where the conversation was heading.

"You deserve the company of someone who understands . . . being different, not like those others, who look and are quickly gone."

Karlinah glared at him. He paid too much attention to her business.

"I've noticed the competition never sticks around," he said, verifying her thoughts. "They don't know how special you are. Too much religion clouds their judgment. Give me the chance to love you and treat you as you were destined to be treated." Japethihah swallowed, awaiting a reply.

She trained her eyes on his. It was the first time he looked vulnerable, but that didn't soften her response. "I don't think I'm so different from the believers. In fact, I just might join them."

One side of Japethihah's face twitched, and his eyes bulged. He spoke in low, rapid tones. "You'll never be happy with them. No one will accept you as one of them. The young men only choose the most devout women and those who have never been married. They don't care about your royal station as I do. I would treat you as a queen. We can go away from this place and start over where no one would—"

The shaking of Karlinah's head became too distracting for him to continue. Japethihah ground his teeth. "Face it, Karlinah." The silky voice turned gruff. "No one wants you but me. Even your stone artisan has left the city."

She flinched. What did he say?

"Search all you want, but he is gone. He and his father packed their cart this morning. Like the others, he didn't love you, didn't want you. *I* can offer you so much more. I'm your last hope. Think about it, my dear."

Japethihah reached to touch her cheek, but Karlinah slapped his hand away. Suddenly she thrust the flowers into his chest. She was seeing Masoni all over again—polite until angry or drunk, demanding obedience without a care for her feelings, making her feel worthless inside while he lusted after her beauty. "I don't need to think about it," Karlinah said hotly. "I will *never* marry you."

Japethihah's dark eyes burned with anger. "We shall see about that," he whispered, his eyes thinning to slits.

That same look had haunted her before. While she dwelt on the past, Japethihah clutched her by the shoulders, and suddenly his lips were pressing hard against hers. She sputtered, trying to get air and push him away. Japethihah broke the kiss and turned to walk away before Karlinah could do more than growl at him. His actions left her feeling tainted, and she swiped at her mouth.

She turned, lifting her skirt to run up the steps, tears blurring her vision. *Doesn't he know the meaning of never? Ugh!* Why did she let him upset her? He seemed to be an expert at saying and doing things that distressed her. Like saying Cumroth had left. Could it be true?

The question plagued Karlinah all the way to her bedchamber. Something—reason?—told her it probably was. The synagogue exterior looked finished as far as she could tell, and Japethihah had responded with quick surety. What had he said—he saw them packing up their cart? A vision emerged of tools and belongings thudding against the bottom of the wooden cart. It could have been rocks piling up in the pit of her stomach for how weighed down she felt. She sunk down on her bed. Like the sands pouring from a jar, time had run out.

Who knew what land Cumroth traveled to? By the time she could find out, he would have found another woman in another city and forgotten all about her. She would never see him again. Now that she had committed to fight for another chance with him, she was too late.

Feeling empty and cold, Karlinah laid on the bed, her arms hugging herself. All hope of changing Cumroth's attitude toward her fled along with her chance to say good-bye. She wished they could have at least parted as friends. Then maybe it wouldn't hurt so badly. Why did she have to care so much?

The answer was plain.

She should have returned to the synagogue one more time just to see what would have happened, but her stubbornness had gotten in the way. Apparently no other girl had kept him here, so he might have given her that second chance. She groaned and beat a fist against her pillow.

Concern for Cumroth replaced her own desires. Where would he go? Would he be happy there? Would he find someone to marry? Not wanting to think about that, she revisited the question of his happiness. It must be lonely going from city to city with only his father for company. Was Cumroth's belief in God—a Heavenly Father who watched over and loved all His children unconditionally—the steady influence he needed?

"Dear God of Ammon," Karlinah whispered, "please help Cumroth to be safe and happy, wherever he is." It felt good to pray for another person, and a small measure of comfort settled over her. "And help me to feel happy too." Karlinah couldn't quite remember how she had heard her family close their prayers, so she just whispered the only word she could remember. "Amen."

Somehow, Karlinah didn't feel alone anymore. She had a whole household of people who loved her, though this comforting knowledge didn't erase the downward crease of her lips. Her heart mourned the love that slipped through her fingers. Cumroth was gone.

Chapter Twenty-Seven

TOBIAS WRINKLED HIS NOSE AND clamped his mouth shut while Karlinah waved food in front of his face. Karlinah took a bite from the flatbread slathered with soft goat cheese and cucumber slices. "Mmm. Linah likes it," she coaxed. "Just try one bite."

He shook his little head from side to side and made his lips disappear inside his mouth. Just then, Hepka came in and laughed at the familiar struggle.

"I can't say I miss that. Jaros eats everything I fix as if he were an ox."

"Want paba," Tobias said before pressing his lips together again. It was pabapira season, and Tobias found the fruit to be his current favorite.

"We don't have any more pabapiras." Karlinah sighed. "We need to get some."

"Get some." His face brightened.

Karlinah frowned at the thought of changing his loincloths when he ate so many pabapiras. "Mother wants you to eat something else besides pabas." She lifted the bread near his mouth again.

"Have two bites, and then we'll go find some pabas," Hepka promised. She gave Karlinah a smile. "We need more fruit to feed the synagogue workers. We can go together."

The mention of synagogue workers brought on fresh pain, but Karlinah suppressed it in favor of the distracting activity. Hepka's companionship soothed, though it might be hard having Tobias along.

Round, brown eyes blinked up at her. Karlinah held the bread to Tobias's lips, and he took a small bite. "One more," she said, and he obeyed.

"I'll get the bags," Hepka offered.

Tobias tugged at Karlinah's hand all the way out of the house and then squealed as the sunshine lit his face. Hepka caught up with them and took her brother's free hand as they followed the path into an area of the jungle thick with pabapira trees. The chattering birds told them all was well. The sisters enjoyed conversation as they walked with Tobias between them.

Just then a growing din captured their attention. Tobias let go of his sisters' hands and pointed up ahead. "Monkeys!"

Brown fur and dark eyes bounced around in the trees a few rods ahead. The girls stopped, telling Tobias they must wait until the monkeys passed. Tobias got down on all fours and copied the noises he heard, making his sisters laugh. A few of the monkeys took notice of them. One bared its teeth and screeched.

Hepka scooped Tobias into her arms. "Shh. Hold still," she whispered.

The three made themselves small by sitting on the ground, Tobias on Hepka's lap. He continued to watch the monkeys but did so quietly. The girls averted their eyes; the last thing they wanted was the challenge of a stare down. Before long the group of monkeys had their fill of pabapiras and moved on.

The siblings approached for their turn at what remained. A shorter tree with plump, yellow-green fruit beckoned. They scrutinized the color of the smooth, rounded skin, but softness to the touch proved the best indication of ripeness.

"Stay here, Tobias, and fill this bag with leaves while we pick," Hepka told him. She handed the woven plant-fiber bag to her little brother for his entertainment. "We'll fill the other one with pabapiras."

"Pabas!"

Luckily the monkeys had ignored several low branches of ripe fruit. The girls reached high to feel and pick the fruit, enjoying some relaxed conversation as they worked.

Hepka spoke of Jaros's cousin, who wanted to meet Karlinah when he came to visit. "From what Jaros says, I think you'd like him. He's heard all about you, and he's interested."

Karlinah shrugged indifferently but agreed to a meeting. Her hands felt rough and sore by the time they had picked all they could carry.

The girls surveyed the effort with satisfied smiles. Turning to call to Tobias, Karlinah could not see him anywhere. Her heart skipped a beat. "Tobias?" It hadn't been long ago that she'd checked on him, had it? With thick vegetation to hide in, maybe he was playing a game. "Tobias, come out right now!"

Hepka scanned the area but saw no sign of the youngster. She added her voice to her sister's, and they frantically darted around trees, vines, and bushes, calling his name. The only thing they found was the discarded bag, which Karlinah picked up and set by the filled one.

"The game is over, Tobias. You need to come to me now." Thoughts of wild animals filled Karlinah's head.

"Come get a paba," Hepka coaxed.

The girls scurried one way then another, until they had covered a small circle around the area. "Tobias! Tobias!" they called without success.

Karlinah took charge. "You go this way, and I'll go that," she said, pointing, "but stay within sight. We'll meet back at this tree."

When they both returned without success, Karlinah suggested they repeat their effort in the remaining directions. The results were just as devastating. Karlinah could see the terror in Hepka's eyes, hear the panic in her voice. "He's small enough to be prey for some animals! He could climb a rock or tree and fall on his head! He might—"

Stretching out her arm, she put a palm out toward Hepka's face. "Let me think." Karlinah didn't want to hear the list. She knew the dangers.

They couldn't both fall apart; they would never find him then. She closed her eyes and mentally gave herself some encouragement. A small peek at her sister revealed Hepka wringing her hands. Hoping to block the image, Karlinah squeezed her eyes tight and tried to think like a child. What would Tobias do? She could imagine him running and climbing, exploring everywhere. If Tobias wouldn't answer, finding him would be impossible.

Ammon's gentle voice came into her mind: *With God nothing is impossible.* Hope filled her heart. *God knows where Tobias is.* Karlinah's eyes flew open as she realized this certainty.

"Let's pray." Her words were confident.

Relief showed on Hepka's face. "Yes."

Karlinah lowered her knees to the ground, and Hepka followed. She licked her lips, trying to remember the prayers she had heard. Fragments of phrases filled her mind, but they were not hers. She had whispered a prayer for Cumroth a few nights ago but had never voiced one in front of someone else. Desperation spurred her on.

"Dear Lord," she began, "our little brother is lost." Saying the words brought on fresh tears that Karlinah sniffed back. "We know you care what happens to Tobias, for he is young and innocent, even if we—if *I* am not worthy to ask for your help. Yet, Ammon says you created each of us and will hear our prayers."

Encouraging warmth filled the center of Karlinah's body. She felt it slowly radiate outward, filling her. "Please, God, help us to find Tobias. Please protect him from harm that we may find him safe from the dangers of the jungle. Guide us in what to do. We ask for this in the name of Christ the Savior who will come. Amen."

It felt as if she owned the words and they measured up. A Savior: someone who could save Tobias. Someone who could save *her*.

Karlinah lifted her head to see Hepka smile, and the two hugged. An impression entered her mind, and Karlinah spoke it out loud. "He's following the monkeys." She rose to her feet, pointing. "This way."

The girls ran forward past where they had searched and called for Tobias. They hunted for a while around stands of trees but still could not hear their brother or any sounds from the monkeys. No tracks were left in the grass or dirt. Were they going the right way? Doubt crowded into her thoughts. Had she just wanted a logical place to look or was it a prompting? Still, they pressed forward, shouting his name.

She felt weary and wondered how far her brother's little legs could take him. Hadn't they already covered this section? Everything looked the same. Frustrated, she clenched her fists.

"Maybe we should split up to cover more ground," Karlinah suggested.

Hepka shook her head, fear returning to her eyes. "We'll get lost ourselves. Maybe we should go back for help."

Straining to feel guidance, to hear a thought, something, Karlinah closed her eyes. She wasn't certain how divine assistance worked. Nothing happened.

She worked her jaw, gaining control. Her prayer hadn't just been empty words. She had felt something. Wasn't it the same good feeling as when she spoke with Ammon or when she brought food to the workers or when her father spoke of the things of God? Yes, but the feeling never lingered. How could she know what was right?

Trust.

The word echoed clearly in her mind and faded. This time the consequences had to do with a child instead of herself. Any other outcome than finding Tobias safe was unacceptable. She had prayed as a show of faith. It was God's turn now. What more trusting could she do? *Please,* she pled inwardly. No signals came to her mind except a flicker of her own impatience.

"Tobias," she screamed. Nothing.

Karlinah clenched her fists but refrained from shaking one heavenward. "I don't know whether to get help or keep looking." Karlinah heard the hopelessness in her own voice.

Hepka's mouth turned down. "He has to be around here somewhere. Don't lose faith, Karlinah. Didn't you feel led to look this way?"

"Yes, but is he here? No! And clouds are gathering." She crossed her arms. "Is it always this way with God? He lifts you up just to let you down?"

"We have to show our faith, Karlinah."

"Isn't that what I did by praying?" she said, sounding exasperated.

A slight smile crept over Hepka's mouth. "So you did." She inclined her head. "Do you truly believe God will help us?"

"Don't *you*?" Karlinah didn't want questions; she wanted answers. Gazing upward, Karlinah squeezed her lips together and recognized how demanding she could be.

"Yes, but we have to be willing to accept that His answer may not be what we desire." Hepka shivered as if suddenly cold.

Karlinah stiffened. "You mean, we could find Tobias . . . dead? How could God allow such a thing?"

"Life's road is not always mapped out by God. We have choices, you know. We are meant to have trials in this life to see if we will choose to follow Him when it gets hard." Hepka sniffled. "So do you believe God will help us?"

Karlinah nodded, blinking back tears. "I want to believe. Will you pray for us this time?"

Hepka took Karlinah's hands in hers. "Yes, but it will be no better than yours." The two bowed their heads while Hepka spoke a simple plea.

When Karlinah added her amen, she felt more able to accept whatever consequence occurred. They had, after all, neglected to watch Tobias for those moments. *Please, God, if our desires are the same as Yours, let us find him safe.*

Karlinah trusted in the first thought to pop into her head. "We need to go back the way we came. We've missed something." She felt reassured when Hepka agreed. They needed to comb the area more carefully. Tobias could only have trailed so far after the monkeys; they were much faster than he.

Proceeding slowly, fearful of what they might find, the pair searched, calling out their brother's name. It was a slow, careful process, and the light faded as the clouds thickened. Karlinah could feel her stomach churning and her neck muscles getting stiff. She glanced at Hepka and knew she felt just as drained. But giving up was not an option. *With God nothing is impossible*, she reminded herself. With new resolve she walked and scanned, walked and scanned.

After a few minutes more, off to the side, a fleck of color caught Karlinah's eye. An animal? It didn't move. She took steps toward it while her mind recognized the patch of cloth from Tobias's tunic poking out above a fallen log. Her stomach lurched as she ran. Could a log have fallen on top of Tobias?

"Tobias," she cried, but he didn't move.

Hepka came running after her, and they stopped to find the little body curled up behind the log. Kneeling beside him, they could tell his chest had a steady rise and fall. Karlinah wept with relief. She gently shook her brother, rousing him from slumber.

"Where monkeys go?" He rubbed his eyes.

Karlinah held Tobias to her chest. *Thank you, God*, she prayed. *I'm sorry I doubted.*

Chapter Twenty-Eight

KARLINAH WRUNG HER HANDS AS she moved toward her father's chamber. It felt reminiscent of approaching her former father-in-law when he summoned her after discovering Masoni's death. Her heart had been numb then, except for fear over the discovery of her actions. Now she would face another king—one who loved her—to reveal those secret actions she had hidden.

She'd purposefully waited to find him alone, without guards or her mother around. She tapped at his chamber door.

"Who is it?"

"Karlinah."

"Come in."

Lamoni's cheery voice did little to lighten her mood as she moved toward him.

"Sit down." He motioned toward a wooden bench and sat beside her. "Wasn't that a wonderful proclamation we received from my father yesterday?"

"Hmm? Yes." Her mind revisited the news riders had delivered to Ishmael as one of seven cities of believers who united to be known by a new name.

"That last part thrills me. 'I hereby declare that the name by which the believers of Christ shall be known, that they may be distinguished from their brethren from henceforth, is Anti-Nephi-Lehi.' I memorized it," Lamoni said, delighted. "And now there is talk spreading through all seven cities, of laying down weapons of war and never again taking up arms against our brethren." He pumped a fist against his chest.

Karlinah shot him a smile but feared she would spoil his mood. She remained silent, and his eyes turned serious.

"What is on your mind, daughter?"

"I wanted to speak with you about something that happened in Jerusalem—a confession of sorts. I'm afraid it won't be pleasant to hear."

Her father's smile faded, and his brow wrinkled, but his voice remained even. "Go on."

"My husband, Masoni, had a habit of drinking strong wine and would get drunk every few evenings. Sometimes he ignored me or fell asleep. Other times it heightened his desire for me or brought on anger."

Karlinah swallowed at the worried look coming into her father's eyes but told herself to get it all out. "I learned when to make myself scarce. A few times he found me to take me to his bed. Drunk like that, he had no feelings for me, no tenderness. His selfish rush caused me physical pain." She could no longer look at her father and stared down at her hands in her lap.

"I hated my husband and wished he were dead. One night those feelings surfaced again as he desired me. It was too soon after the last time for me to fully heal, so I refused him. I knew he would be angry, would beat me like he had before. I thought I could manage, but I was wrong."

Karlinah heard the intake of her father's breath, felt his hand covering hers. Tears pricked her eyes, and she couldn't concentrate on the well-meaning gesture.

"Masoni flew into a rage, yelling all kinds of things. He said he'd kill me. He pulled his knife from its scabbard and stepped toward me. I backed up with nowhere to go and only walls behind me."

"Oh, Karlinah!"

She paused long enough to lick her dry lips and continued woodenly, staring straight ahead. "He stumbled over his own feet, and the blade went into his side as he fell. It gave me hope that he should be the one to die, not me. I rushed to force the blade in deeper. I wanted him dead, but he fought harder. He grabbed my neck, and we struggled until he lost strength. It scared me what more he might do if he survived, so I looked for something to help me end it. I grabbed a small statue god and smashed it against his head. That was when he went still.

"Relief came first and then fear of Masoni's father finding out it was me who had done this thing. I washed the blood from my hands and returned to my bedchamber unnoticed." She looked into Lamoni's eyes now. "My secret remained safe. I killed my husband, and nobody knew about it but me." What would he think of her now? She searched his eyes for understanding. A pained look settled there, and she swallowed hard.

Gentle arms surrounded her in a hug. "I am so sorry this trial has plagued you. I wish I had never placed you in those circumstances; I did not know. If it eases your mind any, I understand the anguish you felt. I was wracked with the guilt of my sins, having caused the death of scores of men. Praise be to God for his abundant mercy to save us from an awful hell." He took her hands in his. "You remember what I preached on that day the crowd gathered, don't you?"

She shook her head, tears filling her eyes. "I'm afraid I wasn't a good listener that day. I could blame it on how wiggly Tobias was, but I suppose I felt overwhelmed by the strangeness of that which I heard and my mistrust of Ammon."

"We are accountable for actions we know to be wrong, Karlinah, but our Redeemer has allowed us to become clean through repentance."

"I know that now. Ammon explained it to me, and I have sought God's forgiveness. Ammon and I decided I should share my confession with you." She wiped away her tears and curved half of her mouth into a smile. "So you don't hate me or think less of me? Because I would understand if you did."

"Foolish girl." Lamoni chuckled, wiping his own face. "Never think that. I will always love you."

The two embraced again. "What do you think I should do?" she asked. "Masoni's father would demand my head if he knew."

Lamoni nodded. "Your confession to him would achieve nothing since he knows not the meaning of forgiveness. The people of Jerusalem have not accepted the missionaries, and their wickedness increases. It won't bring his son back either." He paused to think. "What matters is that your heart is right. God will forgive you as He has me. Do you believe this?"

"I . . . I want to." Memories floated up of her father's commands that meant the death of a servant or citizen. She had caused only one death, and her father named her actions blameless. In this she agreed, but she had embraced murderous thoughts. What were Lamoni's thoughts when he'd ordered death as punishment for wrongful actions? It didn't matter; he had changed and been forgiven. Perhaps they were not so different. The knot of worry in her stomach loosened, and warmth flooded her heart. She had confessed her deepest secret; it was time to let it go.

"Yes, Father. I am at peace with God. Ammon has agreed to continue teaching me."

Lamoni put a hand over his heart and grinned. "I am certain what this will lead to. You have filled me with peace this day. Think no more on your past."

With lightness in her heart, Karlinah felt her pain already disappearing from memory.

***

The king's cookery no longer bustled with activity now that there were fewer workers to feed. Only a handful of men remained to make log benches or other furnishings for the synagogue. The day's meals were over and the hallway now quiet. As she passed, Karlinah heard a sound and peered through the doorway. She saw a wooden-slab table, three fireplaces, and—Ammon? What was he doing here? He bent over an iron pan warmed by glowing coals on the hearth.

"Need any help?" Karlinah asked, stepping into the room.

Ammon looked up and returned her smile. "*Now* you offer help. My egg is already done." He pulled the pan off the coals and slid the wooden scraper under the egg, tearing the yolk as he lifted. "Oops. It wasn't supposed to do that." He made a face, and Karlinah laughed. Thick yellow drops landed on the dirt floor as Ammon placed the turkey egg on top of a bowl of stewed beans. He tried to cover the spill by scraping dirt over it with his sandal, but the packed ground didn't budge.

Karlinah laughed again. "Don't worry about it. It'll soak in."

"There's enough to share if you'd like some."

She shook her head, smiling. "I'm fasting."

Ammon lifted his eyebrows briefly. "Maybe I shouldn't eat in front of you then."

Her delicate hand fluttered in the air. "Go right ahead." She paused while Ammon scooped a bit of food with his flat maize bread and took a bite. She took a step closer. "But since you're here, can I ask you a question?"

Ammon nodded, his mouth too full to speak.

"What do I need to do to be baptized?"

Ammon coughed and sputtered. "Sorry," he said, pounding his chest. A grin replaced his look of surprise. "Many have been praying for such news. It fills me with joy."

Karlinah beamed. "My repentance is complete. I spoke with my father last night after pouring out my heart to God." She smiled at the memory of her father's arms around her, weeping with her at what she had gone through.

She pushed past those thoughts and said, "I have received an answer to my prayers and feel peace in my soul. A quiet witness had whispered to me all along. I just didn't, or wouldn't, recognize it for what it was."

"Would you mind telling me about it?"

Karlinah put a hand to her chest. "You know how stubborn I am. It took me a while to recognize that the warm feelings were witnesses from God until I sincerely wanted to know." She chuckled as Ammosiah's image floated behind her eyelids. "In fact, one time I mistook the sensation for infatuation."

Ammon's smiling eyes silently urged her to continue.

"I suppose you heard about Tobias getting lost in the jungle?"

Ammon nodded.

"That was a significant time for me. I felt guided by brief, penetrating thoughts leading me to find Tobias. I accepted that I needed God's help no matter the outcome, and then I couldn't mistake the swelling in my heart."

"Then you are ready to be an Anti-Nephi-Lehi? To be called a follower of Christ, bear the burdens of others, and stand as a witness and servant of God? This is what baptism signifies."

"I am." Karlinah's heart leapt within her. "I am!" Tears sprang to her eyes. If there had been any hint of doubt before, it fled like a startled bird. She wanted this more than anything, even more than a chance to see Cumroth again. Following Christ and bearing one another's burdens had the power to see her through the pain of losing love.

Thinking how thrilled her family would be, she asked, "Will you baptize me tomorrow?"

"If it gives you enough time to notify those you wish to attend, then I would be honored. My joy is as full as yours." His eyes shone.

"It will just be my family and Abish, so there shouldn't be a problem." Karlinah bounced on her toes and clasped her hands together. "Thank you."

Exhilarated, she turned for the hallway and bounded toward the porch steps. The cooling air drew her outside. Karlinah spread her arms and twirled on her toes, her ebony braids keeping up after she slowed, slapping against her shoulders. Gazing up at the sky of bright stars, it felt as if God could see her and was pleased.

"Good evening, princess."

Not *that* voice. The feeling of contentment slipped from Karlinah's face as she brought her gaze around and inwardly groaned. She had tried being direct, but he still came around. No more feeling sorry for him; it was time to cut the maize stalk down. Maybe even tromp on it for good measure.

"What are you so happy about tonight?" Japethihah said as he stepped into view.

Karlinah clamped her mouth shut, desiring to share her news with her family first. Irritation gave way to nervousness as the quiet settled upon her. Quickly glancing around, she saw that they were indeed alone. Focusing on the image of him as a maize stalk garnered the confidence she needed. She folded her arms.

"Your little dance must mean something?" he coaxed.

A bold tone slipped out. "If you must know, I'm going to be baptized." She lifted her chin to the towering head above, daring him to try to persuade her otherwise. His temporary loss for words made her smile.

"Well, if you are certain this is what you want, then congratulations." He laced his fingers together and started walking. "You must tell me all about it."

"You're not angry?" She stepped alongside his leisurely pace and checked his look. She found his smile but wondered if it seemed forced.

"You know I care about your happiness, my dear."

"Good, because nothing you could do will stop me."

Japethihah nodded and continued walking. "Will it take place at the river?" He pointed to the river trail just ahead.

"Yes."

"Will I be invited to come?"

Karlinah stopped and gave him a sideways glance. "Are you certain you want to?"

Japethihah took a few more steps. "Of course."

Perhaps it would do him good to witness a baptism; it might be the very thing to soften his heart. "Consider yourself invited—as long as you understand that I can never be more than a friend to you. You must quit seeking me out. On that, my word is my final. I need to be getting back now."

Seeming to ignore her words, Japethihah took a few more steps and glanced behind him. "Will it be down this path at the deepest spot where the water pools?" he asked. Another couple of steps and Japethihah stood where the path narrowed to snake through the foliage.

"Of course, but really, Japethihah, I can hardly see anything. I'm going back." Karlinah turned around. A cry of pain sounded behind her.

"Ouch," he moaned.

Karlinah whirled. "Are you all right?" A scuffling noise followed. She took a few steps toward the bushes but couldn't see him high or low. "Where are you?"

A horse whinnied in the distance ahead. The wind carried no other sound. Just then a hand clamped over Karlinah's mouth and another around her waist as she was lifted from the ground. She kicked back, her heels connecting with the attacker. The body frame was unmistakably Japethihah's. What did he think he was doing?

She wiggled one arm free and beat her fist against him, but she still couldn't cry out. The hand persisted over her mouth, scaring her further. The air flowing through her nose didn't seem enough, and she flailed in a wild panic. Japethihah carried her down the path.

Finding a small grassy spot, Japethihah laid Karlinah down on her back, one hand still over her mouth. His knee pressed onto her abdomen while his free hand went to his pouch. Seeing a good chance to struggle for freedom, Karlinah wiggled and twisted, but the pebbles against her back only dug in deeper. His size and strength dominated.

Japethihah straddled her body, his knees holding down her arms. She went rigid, pleading with her eyes. He quickly thrust a piece of cloth into her mouth then tied another strip around her head to hold it in place. The tasteless fabric made her wish for something fresh and cleansing, like water and air, but it was the least of her desires. She kicked her feet and rocked from side to side but couldn't get loose from his grasp. Panic swelled in her breast.

"Don't be afraid, princess. Surely you know that I love you?"

More strips of cloth came out of Japethihah's pouch, and he tied Karlinah's hands and feet. He ignored her furrowed brow and the tears streaming from the corners of her eyes. Japethihah lifted up his prize in two arms like a sack of grain. She bucked and flopped until Japethihah breathed out a threat.

"You'll be free soon enough. I'm going to show you what you won't recognize on your own—how good we are together. So you can either come along obediently and get used to the idea, or I will violate you right here and then slit your throat. That's not the way I want it, Karlinah, but I *will* have you one way or another."

Her body stilled except for her quivering mouth that let out a stifled whimper. How could this be happening when she finally felt happy? Karlinah closed her eyes and silently prayed. For now, it seemed prudent to comply and put off his threat. Maybe she would know incrementally what to do.

Ample moonlight revealed Japethihah's smirk. He carried her down the path until they came to the place where he had tied up two horses. Supplies draped across one horse, sending a vivid message. His preparedness stabbed at Karlinah's mind, and she reeled at the ramifications.

"We're going on a trip," he told her. "I'll keep your feet tied for now and put you in front of me on the horse. Your life depends on your cooperation." Getting her situated, Japethihah revealed more. "When we're far enough away that your voice cannot be heard, I will untie you so you can be comfortable. Try to fall asleep with the gait of the horse."

His voice oozed generosity, and she felt a wave of nausea.

As her attacker slid behind her rigid body on the horse, Karlinah leaned forward, refusing to give Japethihah any satisfaction through her touch. She told herself over and over that time was on her side. She had to endure this frightening game until her absence became noticed and an army of men came searching for her.

"Everything will be all right, Princess," he cooed. "When you've had a little time to get used to the idea, I'll make you my wife and take good care of you. We'll find a place to build our own village away from the madness we've left behind. I will make you happy. You'll see I've been right all along."

The laden horses meandered northward up the river trail by the light of the moon, farther and farther from her home.

Chapter Twenty-Nine

LEVERS, ROPES, AND PULLEYS AIDED Cumroth and Corianthem in lifting the last slab of stone they had quarried enough to guide it onto the wooden ramps leading downhill to the cart. With the cart holding as much weight as it could take, Cumroth and his father rested in the shade before they would hook up the ox.

Corianthem rubbed his arms. "I'm getting too old for this."

"You say that every time," Cumroth countered.

"I mean it every time." He laughed. Corianthem wrung out his headband. "Do you want to head back to Ishmael? We could chisel these blocks there before heading who knows where."

"Our work there is finished," Cumroth said flatly.

"Yes, but your business isn't."

Cumroth turned to glare at his father. "Why do you want me to go back when I have no chance with the princess?"

"Because you are miserable," Corianthem said with a sad smile. "You've been sullen and silent this whole trip, and I'm just about ready to give you away! You won't even laugh at my jokes."

Cumroth huffed. "That's because they're not funny." But a smile played at his lips.

"I know you. You'll never forgive yourself if you don't find out with a surety. You'll wonder and kick yourself for months, and I'll have to listen to your complaining. Find out now so you'll have no regrets. *Then* you can put her out of your mind."

"Ha! Sounds like you have a lot of confidence in me."

Corianthem put a hand on his son's shoulder. "There was an attraction between you two. Even an old blind man could see that. Then you decided to ignore her. Stupidest thing you've ever done. She's the only woman I've ever seen who could put a spark in you, get you talking."

Cumroth lowered his eyes. "Maybe, but I don't think it meant so much to her." Japethihah's advice passed through his mind, and his eyes lifted to meet his father's. "What about her not being a Christian? I must live by Ammon's preaching, whether she does or not. Could she stand it if I insisted on certain things? She's not used to being ordered around."

Corianthem shrugged. "And you're not the ordering type. Did you know she was married to the prince in Jerusalem? I'm sure she had her share of orders from him before his death."

Cumroth's mouth hung open. "What? How do you know this?"

His mind recalled the slight figure in royal finery who had complimented his carved bench near the king's groves. And her voice—the one surprising him with polite speech—yes, it could have been Karlinah's. Again, this did not match the woman Japethihah described at all.

"I only learned of it two days ago through one of the masons."

Cumroth ground his teeth. If Japethihah were here, he'd punch his lying mouth. "I could kick myself!"

"That would do neither of us any good. But think on this—could she pressure you away from *your* faith? Just how strong are you?"

Cumroth's eyes flashed in irritation. "Whose side are you on?"

"She gets along with her family and other Christians, doesn't she?"

Cumroth grumbled, "I'll bet she even gets along with Ammon." He put his elbows on his knees and rested his chin on his hands, thinking how he'd been fooled by a stranger.

"It will take effort—any marriage does. Only you can decide if she is worth it."

Cumroth remained silent. He believed his faith would remain strong and that Karlinah would live a Christian life with or without baptism. Maybe with time . . . It seemed they could be happy together if she would accept him.

"I'm not trying to push you either way, Cumroth. I just want you to recognize the facts. There is goodness in Karlinah that precedes conversion, but if she never converts, could you live with it? You should get your own answers."

What if her interest in him had been genuine? He would be throwing away the best that could be offered. He reviewed what he knew about her. She'd praised him in Jerusalem when they were strangers of different classes. She'd cared for Tobias with patience and love. She'd served food to the workers with cheerfulness. Nobody besides his father had gotten him to open up and talk like she had. And he felt wonderful around her! He had been a fool to trust the tall stranger so implicitly.

"There's just one more thing I'll say." Corianthem made eye contact with his son. "I think she draws out the best in you. I've never seen you as happy with a woman as those few days before you knew of Karlinah's royalty." He shook a finger at Cumroth. "You need to know you are every bit as good as anyone else—even this princess. We are all children of God."

"So they say." Cumroth smiled then exhaled. "If I could just hear it from Karlinah . . . if she thinks I'm good enough . . . if she'll have me . . ."

Corianthem stood, brushed his knuckles across the top of Cumroth's head, and reached out to help his son off the ground. "So are we heading back to Ishmael?"

A corner of Cumroth's mouth lifted. "What do you take me for, a fool?"

***

The morning song of birds forced Karlinah to open her eyes. She found herself curled into a ball on the ground. A blanket had been thrown over her. She propped herself up, feeling stiff, though she couldn't have lain there more than a couple hours. A line of rope extended from her ankle to a tree trunk, and a length of cloth wrapped around her hands. She winced at the reality of her predicament.

Japethihah hunched over a small fire, cooking something that smelled good. At least he had taken that awful rag from her mouth. She could still taste it and felt the pasty dryness it left. A desire to gulp down water came to the front of her mind, followed by a rumbling from her famished stomach, reminding her she hadn't broken her fast. "Water," she croaked.

"Good. You're awake." Japethihah stood and handed her a waterskin. She guzzled it and looked around. With daylight Karlinah had hoped to know where she was, but she didn't. They were higher in the mountains. The landscape had turned from ferns and large-leafed trees to scrub oak and pines. Only the horses looked familiar.

"Aren't these my father's horses?"

"I consider them an early wedding gift." Japethihah laughed. "They've had a short rest and watering, so we shall be off again right after eating."

From the corner of her eye, she saw Japethihah coming at her with his knife. She gasped. Surely he wouldn't bring her all this way just to kill her?

"Give me your hands," he commanded. Japethihah easily sliced through the cloth. "I'll give you a moment to relieve yourself while I turn my back. Just don't try anything. You won't get far. Remember, I'm the one with the weapon."

Her jaw clamped in anger, but her eyes searched for possibilities. Thick brush surrounded them, and a narrow river ran not too far off. He would hear if she splashed into the water to cross it. Surely her father would send searchers to look for them. If only she could hold Japethihah off from his intended marriage long enough to be found. King Lamoni would never give up, of that she felt certain, giving her hope. An idea flowed into Karlinah's mind.

Japethihah called out, "Shall I turn around yet?"

"No. Wait."

She wanted to leave a clue for those searching. Quickly, Karlinah removed the strip of yellow cloth holding one of her braids together and tied it to a bush. She left the other beaded tie in place. Hopefully Japethihah wouldn't notice the bush if she could steer his eyes elsewhere. She crept toward the river before calling out to him. "I'm just going to wash my hands and face."

Japethihah turned his gaze on the princess.

Karlinah didn't like his greedy smile, but at least his eyes were on *her* and not the trailside bush. To keep his focus on her, she kept talking. "Where are we going? Have you thought this through, Japethihah? You know my father won't rest until we're found, and then he will kill you. Let me go back now, and I'll say I got lost."

Japethihah chuckled softly. "They won't find us. I'll be covering our tracks today. By the time anyone might stumble upon us, I will be the father of Lamoni's coming grandchild. You will plead my case as a dutiful wife, and the king will have no choice but to forgive."

"Never!"

"Like I said, Princess, you were meant to be mine. I *will* have you, so get used to the idea. And after you've been with me, no one will want your unclean body, taken without marriage vows." He clicked his tongue in distaste. "I am your only chance for a husband. You should be thanking me."

Karlinah's stomach recoiled. She wanted to scream. No one else *would* want her. Not when there were so many virtuous women to choose from. Her only hope was for rescue before Japethihah made good on his intentions. From the look in his eye, he wouldn't wait long.

***

By midmorning, it appeared that Karlinah still hadn't gotten out of bed. Abish balanced a tray with a bowl of cooked barley, a pabapira, and a cup of cow's milk on one arm and knocked on Karlinah's door.

"Hey, sleepyhead, you're lucky I saved you some food." Abish waited for a response. Nothing. She knocked louder.

"Are you ill, Karlinah?" Still nothing. "I'm coming in." Abish didn't usually bring a tray to Karlinah's room anymore, but something about not seeing the girl up yet left her worried. She cracked open the door. Surprised to see the smoothly made bed and empty room, an uneasy feeling jerked her stomach.

Abish set down the tray and rushed down the hallways, searching. She saw Jarom ahead and asked, "Have you seen Karlinah this morning?"

"No."

Without waiting, Abish moved on. She glanced in the cookery and asked the servants there, then the guards at the throne room entrance. No one had seen her. Rounding the next corner, Abish caught sight of queen Mierah coming out of her bedchamber.

"Have you seen Karlinah?"

The queen shook her head. "Have you looked outside? Perhaps she is visiting Hepka."

Abish bit her lip. Not trusting her voice, she shook her head. She blinked back the watery image of the queen's face.

"What's wrong?" Mierah said.

Abish swallowed hard. "I don't know. I just have this awful feeling. No one seems to have seen Karlinah at all today, and she's not in her room. Where would she go? Ammon said she's getting baptized this afternoon."

"Yes, isn't it wonderful? An answer to my prayers. I thought it strange for her to leave it to him to tell us though." Mierah frowned. "She might have gone on one of her walks, but you've got me concerned. I'll send some guards out looking."

Abish nodded. "I'll take the path to the river. Maybe she wanted to check on the dam the boys are making and see if the water is deep enough."

Mierah strode off toward the throne room.

Abish stepped outside a moment later to a sunny day, though the wind had picked up. She crossed the courtyard and found the well-worn path through the brush. She hurried forward, calling Karlinah's name. A moment later, Abish came upon fresh horse dung, not more than a day old, right on the path. Her scrutiny settled on hoofprints in the dirt. They lead toward, not away from the river, and some were on top of one another, as if more than one horse had traveled the path. Strange. She hadn't seen any visitors or known of the king's household using the stables recently. Abish pressed on. It wouldn't be long until she reached the stream and the fork in the trail.

The brush opened up to a grassy area where the trail divided. Abish spun around, shouting the princess's name in several directions. She listened for a response that never came. The pooled area of the small river remained undisturbed. Searching the ground, Abish found where the hoofprints continued to the north. If Karlinah had gone on a horseback ride, the stable hands would know of it. She raced back the way she came.

Arriving at the stable, Abish learned that no one had seen Karlinah, but two of the horses were missing. The king had already been alerted, and soldiers were searching the city. She ran back to the house to tell someone of the evidence she had seen on the trail. That should send the soldiers in the right direction. Would Karlinah be found with the horses? If not, where could she be? And why *two* horses? A shiver prickled her neck.

Chapter Thirty

A SINGLE PLUME OF SMOKE rose from the next ridge to the west as Cumroth and Corianthem broke camp after a much-needed good night's sleep. They both caught sight of it at the same time.

"Do you think a Lamanite army could be heading for the land of Ishmael?" Cumroth asked with fear laced through his voice.

Corianthem shook his head. "Not with one plume. Must be a cooking fire from hunters or a scouting party at most."

"Think we should have a look? King Lamoni might need to be warned."

Corianthem put a hand to his chin. "I'd do it if we didn't have this beast to worry about." He yanked a thumb at the ox pulling their cart. "We'd never get away quickly if we needed to unless we left our load. I think we should just report it when we return."

Cumroth agreed. He carefully studied the landscape for landmarks he could use in the report. The pair decided not to call attention to themselves and ate a cold meal of jerky and stale bread, then they packed up their bedrolls and set them in the cart.

Eagerness over seeing Karlinah grew for Cumroth. They expected to arrive in the city by late afternoon. He would need a bath in the river first. As he led the ox over the trail, Cumroth thought about what he might say to her. Apologizing for his rudeness would come first. Then what—declare his feelings? Would she think him crazy?

He repeatedly swung a balled fist onto his other open palm. It didn't matter; he determined to set things straight right away—to let her know she could trust him as the quiet but hardworking, confident man she first met. Delay would only prove torturous and destroy the foundation he had built. Then he could get on with his life, whichever way it headed. If she rejected him, wondering would no longer hang over his head. But it might break his heart.

The ox slowed, bringing Cumroth's thoughts to the present as he trudged along. He whacked at an encroaching branch and some tangled vines with his knife, giving the cart room to pass.

He took a long swig from his water pouch, draining it. They would catch up to the well-traveled river trail soon enough, and he could refill there. Traveling dragged on this part of the trail, and Cumroth welcomed the passing of time with his father's distracting chatter.

At the river, Corianthem unhitched the ox and let it drink. They shared the last of their flatbread and jerky, picked a few berries, and replenished their water. Cumroth sat on the ground and watched a blackbird flit from bush to bush, enjoying its happy chirping. His eye caught something yellow between branches of green. He couldn't make out what it was, so he clambered to his feet.

"Father, come here!"

The startled bird soared away as Corianthem lumbered over.

"This is Karlinah's!" Cumroth rolled the clay bead between his fingers. "She made this to fasten her hair. It hasn't been here long. Look how clean the cloth is. Why would she tie it to a bush? Unless . . ." Fear replaced his worried look. Cumroth cupped his hands, yelling out her name in all directions. No answer returned. Then he remembered the plume of smoke. Could there be a connection? They briefly discussed their options.

"Leave the marker there," Corianthem said. "I think you should hurry and go on ahead."

"But Karlinah might be close enough to find."

"No, son. You can't go alone. There are too many trails on which to get lost and dangers in being alone. Go to the city and get help. That is Karlinah's best chance."

Cumroth frowned and kicked at a rock. They finished letting the ox drink, and Cumroth helped to hook it up before asking, "Are you sure?"

"Yes. You'll need help. I can manage the cart myself for this last part. The trail is good."

"What if the axle breaks?"

Corianthem waved a hand in a shooing motion. "If I'm not there by dusk, you'll know how to find me. Now go!"

Cumroth didn't need to be told twice and took off running in spite of sore back and arm muscles. The journey without the ox would take a few hours. Ignoring his quivering calves, he pressed on, finally passing the spot where Karlinah had found him bathing.

He reached the king's house and raised his knee to the first step then collapsed in a heap. His right calf muscle had tensed and constricted into a ball. Cumroth doubled over, yelping with pain.

A guard came out to check the commotion. "What's going on?"

Cumroth sucked air through his teeth. "Is Princess Karlinah here?" He panted.

"Aren't you the stone artisan?"

The pain intensified in spurts for agonizing minutes. Cumroth alternated moaning with high-pitched shrieks while the guard helplessly stared at him. When would this end? Finally, he could sit up and tend to the spot, rubbing to soften the knot.

"Yes." His muscle relaxed, but his tone grew demanding. "Is she here?" Cumroth licked his parched lips.

"No, she's gone missing. The king just sent troops out searching."

"I know which way she went." That set the guard into motion, and Cumroth soon found himself telling Queen Mierah what he knew.

"Your information is a small addition, but it could be useful," the queen replied. "Though I have confidence in the trackers already following the hoofprints, I want to do everything possible to find Karlinah. Thank you, Cumroth." She clasped her hands together and set them under her chin. Her eyes glistened with tears. "It cost you much to deliver this news. I'm not sure it is wise for you to continue on to the army, as you say you wish to do."

Cumroth crinkled his forehead. "Please. Give me a handful of men and—"

The queen held up a hand. "Sit and rest while I tell you what I know."

Cumroth wondered if she had changed her mind. She *had* to let him go. It might kill him not to know what happened to Karlinah and not to be able to help. But it was not his place to say more. He would act on his own if he had to.

Queen Mierah called for a maid to bring Cumroth some food. Moments later, Cumroth scooped up mouthfuls of a mutton and vegetable stew as he listened. He learned that the tall, slender man who had lied to him about Karlinah was also missing. They suspected he had taken her, traveling on the two missing horses. He grabbed his fist, wanting to punch Japethihah in the face. Karlinah's father and oldest brother led the searchers, who had left midmorning. His longing to join them was overshadowed by the pain in the queen's eyes.

"She's not dead," he told her. "Japethihah doesn't want a dead woman."

"I know. It's what sustains me."

He guessed the queen had his same track of thinking about what Japethihah did want. He desired her most precious possession—her virtue. That was why Japethihah had taken Karlinah. The longer it took to find her, the greater the chance she would be defiled. No matter what happened, Cumroth knew he would still love her. Having her ripped away from him like this had taught him that. But what if she carried a baby fathered by Japethihah? Could his heart accept the child? He hoped so but honestly didn't know. If Karlinah could accept his devotion, the rest might fall into place. Again, he felt the urgency to find her.

"The trackers will surely find your daughter's beaded marker, but the smoke we spotted was off the main trail. They might need me to point out the direction."

Mierah nodded. "That could be important, even with good trackers. You are determined, aren't you?"

Cumroth blinked. "Yes."

"Then I had better find some companions for you." A smile slid onto her face before she left him to finish his meal.

His heart lightened, but his muscles still complained as Cumroth slipped to his knees in prayer. He would need all the help he could get.

***

"This spot will do for tonight," Japethihah declared wearily, though dusk had not fully arrived.

They had traveled on horseback along a narrow offshoot of the river for most of the day. It felt good to be off the horse—the *only* thing that felt good. She wanted to scream, but no one would be able to hear her, so she made a hateful face at Japethihah behind his back instead.

The army must have started their search for her. How long would it take? She watched numbly as Japethihah unloaded the other horse and let both animals drink from the stream.

"You get the women's job—setting up the tent—while I fetch firewood." Japethihah's tired voice tinged with sharpness.

Karlinah's mind caught on one phrase—*the* tent—and her hands trembled. *One* tent. Did it have only one room?

Her first night had been spent traveling and dozing on horseback with an hour or two of sleep on the ground. Exhausted and in need of a good rest, she would attempt to set the tent up, though she had never done this in her life, but she wouldn't go in. He could have the infernal thing to himself. Determined, Karlinah set about her task with angry stiffness.

Japethihah chuckled at Karlinah's exaggerated movements. "I know what you're thinking, my dear, but I hate to disappoint you. We've waited this long, what's a couple more days? You will be sleeping in the tent *alone* tonight. I will sleep outside at the foot of the door to . . . protect you."

Sudden relief flooded in, replacing one of her worries.

"We are both much too tired. I want you fresh for our wedding night festivities." His chuckle deepened. "Tomorrow will be another day of heavy travel, and then we should be safe enough to take a more relaxed pace." His lips curled. "So on the third night, I take you for my wife. Prepare yourself."

A shiver crawled down Karlinah's spine, cold and sharp. Shaking it off and glad to get her body moving, she went about figuring out the tent. As she finished, she noticed his approaching steps.

"It pains me to tie you up, but I'm going hunting." Japethihah grabbed Karlinah by the arm and pulled her toward a tree. "I wouldn't have to do this if I could trust you." He twisted her arms behind the slender trunk, and she spit in his face as he wrapped her wrists with rope. He raised a hand as if to slap her but then stopped himself. She glared back, almost in a challenge, but neither spoke more.

Karlinah watched him sharpen the end of a long stick with his knife and disappear into the bushes. Hunting was the reason they'd stopped before dusk, but it might give the army a better chance to catch up to them. She seethed as the waiting dragged on. Her shoulders ached, her arms scratched against the bark, and the rope rubbed at her skin whenever she moved. Her eyes had drooped by the time her captor returned. He came through the bushes holding a limp rabbit from its ears, a smile of success on his face.

Japethihah cut the rope around her hands, and she made a show of running her hands over the sore spots. He ignored her and went to start the fire. Karlinah turned her back on him.

The rabbit roasting from a stick above the fire smelled good. The last time they'd eaten was that morning. As the sky darkened, Karlinah moved closer to the fire. She peeled off a strip of the roasted meat and stuffed it into her mouth. Earlier there had been little desire for anything more than water, but now her stomach demanded more. Karlinah knew she needed the strength food would provide. Savoring the roasted flavor, she closed her eyes and chewed. A moan hummed from her lips before she opened her eyes.

"Someday you will feel the same way about me as you do that rabbit," Japethihah said. "The pleasure you get from eating will be less than the pleasure I can give."

Wide-eyed, Karlinah made a face of horror and spat the meat onto the ground.

Japethihah laughed. "You wait and see."

Karlinah crossed her arms and looked away.

"In fact," he said, advancing toward her, "the sooner you see that side of me, the better. Would you like me to start changing your mind tonight?"

His voice neared, putting dread into her heart. He reached to tuck a strand of hair behind her ear, and she stiffened. A glint of lust flashed in his eye. Japethihah traced a finger down her jawline. He lifted the hair from her neck and moved in to nibble behind her ear.

She knew she shouldn't make him angry, nor did she want him aroused. She had made Masoni angry a few times, and he had struck her for it. Pushing Japethihah too far could prove equally dangerous. Hot breath prickled her skin.

She ducked away before his lips found her skin. "What, and break your promise?" She kept her voice light. "Besides, you need a bath. You smell of sweat and horses." She pinched her nose.

Again, Japethihah laughed but didn't walk away. He arched a questioning eyebrow. "We could *both* take one in the river. And wash out our clothing since we have a fire going."

Karlinah's breath caught. This was not going the way she hoped. *Please, God, don't let him touch me.* If it came down to it, Karlinah wondered if she could push Japethihah's head under the water or against a boulder. Images of Masoni cropped up. Would God forgive her now that she knew His laws and their consequences? A shudder crept down Karlinah's back. She knew the answer. Only for self-defense could she attempt such a thing, and so far, Japethihah wasn't out to kill her. Maybe he would slip and hit his head. She frowned at the unlikelihood of it. Where was her rescue party?

Japethihah stared at her a long moment before looking away. "Some other time when we're not so tired. A good meal will tame you." He grabbed her by the arm. "Let's find some greens to go with the meat. Do you know which ones are good?"

Karlinah snapped, giving him an incredulous look. "I'm the pampered princess, remember?"

Japethihah's free hand met her cheek with an audible slap.

The sharp sting heated her flesh, and Karlinah gingerly touched the skin. Her lips pressed tightly together. Why couldn't she keep her mouth shut? Her hellish life with Masoni was repeating itself, and Japethihah wasn't even drunk. Hatred rose like bile in her throat.

"See what you made me do?" Japethihah defended. "After all the trouble I went through to spear and cook food for you, you won't lift a hand. Your pampered life will have to wait."

Silently fuming, she rubbed at her raw wrists.

They faced the fire again, and Japethihah turned the stick once more to rotate the meat. "It's nearly done. Go get us some water to drink while there's still enough light for me to watch you. And don't make me come after you."

Throwing him a glare, Karlinah headed toward the stream. She passed the grazing horses, seeing the tight knots in the rope around the tree, then glanced back at Japethihah. His watchful eye penetrated into her soul. She stormed off to fill both pouches.

When she returned, Japethihah took his water pouch and thanked her politely as if nothing was wrong. He tore off strips of hot meat to taste. "Mmm." Then he tore off more and handed them to Karlinah.

The morsels were tender and tasty, and though grateful, Karlinah ate with a stony face. The cold water refreshed her, but she wouldn't show Japethihah any satisfaction.

"A meal fit for a queen," he said, licking his fingers. "The land will provide. We will have a garden and plenty of meat to live on."

Karlinah barely heard his words. One thing stuck in her mind now that darkness descended and the end of the day neared. "You just keep your promise. The tent is mine."

Chapter Thirty-One

QUEEN MIERAH APPROACHED THE STONE cutter with a filled water skin in one hand, a pouch of trail food in the other, and three men trailing behind her. He took the pouches when she held them out to him. "These men serve as runners and will assist you in reaching the army. This is Johab, Omar, and Aaron," she said, pointing.

She studied Cumroth's face and thought his color looked good. The meal and rest had revived him. "Is there anything more you require?"

"Thank you, but no. We need to get going. The army is several hours ahead of us."

Mierah dipped her head and watched the four men turn to leave. They headed toward her precious daughter, who seemed to be slipping farther away from her. She turned her thoughts from what awful things Karlinah might have to endure before they found her to the thousands of prayers said in her behalf. The entire city must know by now, and all that could be done had been set in motion. It was in God's hands now.

***

Though toned, Cumroth's muscles protested his second run. His foot travel didn't typically require running, and he tried to ignore the dull ache in his legs. Encouragement from Aaron, the friendliest of his three companions, and a focus on his purpose kept Cumroth going. When they met Corianthem with his cart, they stopped to give him a brief explanation, enjoyed a few swallows of water, and continued on their way.

Finally a decent break was allowed as dusk filtered through the trees, casting eerie shadows around Cumroth as he sat catching his breath. He learned more about his companions as they sat in conversation. Johab, the oldest and leader, perhaps a dozen years Cumroth's senior, maintained good physical shape. He had a wife and three children. Young Aaron had large eyes and a mouth to match, though his speech remained positive. The quiet, practical one, somewhere between the two in age, was Omar.

"I have to admit," Aaron said, "I thought you might slow us down, Cumroth. You know, not having army training and all, but your mother would be proud." He chuckled.

"My mother is dead," he answered matter-of-factly.

"Oh. Sorry. Well, maybe your legs will match those muscular arms of yours by the time we're through with you."

Aaron's words didn't bother him, but something did. Cumroth's body tingled with the unwelcome sensation of being watched. He glanced around before leaning back against the tree trunk. Knowing that jaguars preferred to avoid humans, he shook off the feeling. Between four noisy voices, animals shouldn't be a problem. It would have to be something big and starving to bother them.

Cumroth raised his water pouch to his lips and tipped his head back. The refreshing liquid cooled his throat. A thick vine dangled near the side of his head, and Cumroth swatted at it absently. Stabbing pain shot into the fleshy part of his forearm. He howled. Something cold twisted around his back, moved past his torso, and curled around his leg. Before he could release the scream begging to escape his throat, he was knocked to the ground. There was no wind left in his lungs to make a sound.

***

Karlinah spotted the same blackbird staring down at them from a familiar tree. "Didn't we just come this way?"

A chuckle gurgled in Japethihah's throat. "Yes. We've made two different circles back to this spot, and we'll make one more."

Karlinah frowned. He was making it more difficult to be tracked. Earlier they had ridden into the stream, now he made false trails. After a third pass, Japethihah continued on through bushes that scratched at them, horses whinnying, until they found a deer trail to follow. When they stopped, she wondered what he had in mind now.

Japethihah looped a length of rope around one of her wrists and fastened the other end to a tree. "Take care of your personal business while I brush away our tracks."

It made Karlinah down-hearted to see him take these precautions. The only good thing about it was the extra time it took. She wasn't about to give up hope. Her presence would be missed, and searchers were on their way. When she got back on the horse, she would secretly leave the other yellow hair tie on the dirt trail behind them. With only a small, clay bead to weigh it down, Karlinah wondered if a breeze might cover it with dust or blow it off the trail, but it was the best she could do.

The trackers needed to find her soon; she had one more night before she would become Japethihah's so-called wife. They rode in silence, and her mind scrambled for a plan. Not knowing if she could trick him, her best chance of getting away was to make sure Japethihah was injured.

Never having needed to think of such things before, Karlinah also paid attention to the location of the sun as they traveled and was nearly certain they were headed northwest. Scanning the surrounding hills, she decided the mix of jungle and forest undergrowth was not so dense as to mask her colorful clothing. Her yellow would peek through the green of ferns and pines. This would be good for the trackers but not for escaping Japethihah. She couldn't see any caves or boulder clefts in which to hide.

Japethihah's mood soon lightened. He babbled on, telling her of the wonderful village they would build and name after him. There would be others he could flatter away to join them. They would reign together as king and queen. The pack horse carried a sack of grain and seeds to plant. Hunting would provide animals for meat. "I've thought of everything," he concluded.

All she wanted was to get away from this evil man who had given her no choice in the matter. He said he would kill her if she didn't comply with his wishes. Would she see her mother again? If so, would it be after her belly was rounded with child? Karlinah wiped her wet cheeks.

"We already have two horses, male and female." His voice came warm just behind her ear. "I will build us a house first, and then we will acquire more animals to reproduce. When I am certain you are with child, I will go to the waters of Sebus and take from the flocks that get scattered. We will multiply and replenish in our own corner of the earth." Japethihah laughed darkly, deep in his throat.

Endure it quietly, Karlinah told herself. *Japethihah's plans will never get that far.*

Chapter Thirty-Two

CUMROTH COULD HEAR HIS COMPANIONS moving and shouting as a heavy weight pinned him facedown to the earth. His good arm pressed against his side, and the other throbbed where fangs had pierced it. The pressure of the reptile's squeezing became evident as he struggled to take quick, shallow breaths. Panic filled his mind as he couldn't gulp enough air. His body writhed in vain to get away. He could barely lift his head off the ground, but he couldn't see anything over thick, scaly skin.

Cumroth didn't want to die. A thousand memories flicked behind his closed eyes in the briefest instant. Had his chance with Karlinah come and gone so quickly?

His next ragged breath wouldn't let his ribs expand, and he prayed they wouldn't be crushed. Movement bustled around his body—he could see men's heads now—but pressure still closed in. He wondered how long until his lungs collapsed. A tingling sensation prickled over his leg as it numbed. His companions must be attempting something, but all he could think about was it being too late. His eyelids fluttered open, and he struggled to kick with his free leg, to flail the bitten arm.

Voices shouted at him to hold still. How could he hold still when his life was ending? Panic told him to fight, to thrash until the snake released him, because he was barely breathing.

"Hold still," a voice commanded with such intensity that Cumroth obeyed.

Cumroth concentrated on breathing, hoping his stillness would make it easier. He required more air, and instantly it came. He felt the pain of blood flowing again through his leg. The heaviness remained but not the gripping pressure. "What . . . ?" he squeaked.

"The snake is dead, but it still has you in its grasp. We have to cut it off, and we don't want to cut you. Now don't move."

Cumroth stilled. The pounding of his heart sounded in his ears. All at once, the pressure around his midsection released. He guzzled air. The weight slipped off his back, and he didn't feel pinned to the ground anymore. He rolled over and saw the fellow runners dragging large pieces of the cut-up boa—each as long as a boy and as thick as a tree trunk—away from his body, blood dripping from each piece.

Cumroth saw a dark smear across his arm where the sharp pain had first occurred. Though the light was dim, he knew it was his own blood. He found the source—two jagged holes penetrated and tore the soft tissue of his arm. At least it oozed rather than spurted, but it was deep. He applied some pressure with his hand. Though the reptile's sharp, hooked teeth had pierced his arm, Cumroth knew a boa's bite was not poisonous. Its purpose was to grab hold of its prey long enough to wind its body into a suffocating squeeze.

"Thank you," Cumroth said, panting, "for saving me."

Aaron shrugged it off with a laugh. "That was one enormous snake."

"Would be good meat if we didn't have a more important errand," Omar said.

Johab came to check Cumroth's arm. "You'll end up with a jagged scar, but you'll live."

The blood was coagulating. Johab searched and found a nearby plant. He took a leaf and tore it in half, rubbing its oozing liquid over the puncture. "This will guard against festering," he explained. "The flowing blood helped clean your wound." Johab ripped a length from his girdle and tied the cloth around Cumroth's forearm. "That will keep it clean."

Feeling shaky, Cumroth sat up. He knew he was in no shape to run the rest of the way. All feeling had returned, but he felt bruised and battered, weak and shaky. The group discussed their options.

They couldn't leave Cumroth, but somebody had to reach the army tonight in case they decided to move before dawn. There were too many paths the army could take, and Cumroth might be the only one who knew the proper direction, should the trackers encounter a difficult time.

"I didn't come all this way just to tangle with a boa. I need to show the commander where I saw that campfire. A description won't be enough." He didn't want to reveal his personal concern for the king's daughter.

They decided to split up. Johab and Omar would run ahead, and Aaron would help Cumroth follow at a slower pace. They would make it to the camp before dawn if the army stayed put through the night. Aaron helped Cumroth to his feet. Seeing him walk on his own power, Johab and Omar took off, wishing them luck.

With slow but steady momentum, the faster two pressed on and reached the camp without further incident. Cumroth ignored his throbbing arm by listening to Aaron's chatter, which reminded him of his father, giving a measure of comfort. At last they reached the army, who had waited for them through the night. Cumroth collapsed for a couple hours of sleep until first light, when someone woke him and took him to Karlinah's brother.

***

It had been a horrible sleep on the thin mat, and Karlinah awoke feeling stiff. She scowled, angry she had been tired enough to sleep the whole night away. With only a shred of hope, she listened to the quiet. If she could just step over Japethihah's body without waking him, she might make it to one of the horses and ride away.

A quick peek out the tent flap was all it took to dash her hopes. Japethihah was up and checking supplies by the horses. Just then he glanced her way. She stomped from the tent.

"Good morning, Princess," Japethihah said. He raised both eyebrows and grinned.

Did she look so amusing? Without thinking, Karlinah smoothed her hair and rumpled clothing before realizing there was no one to impress. Her plaits had come undone, leaving her with tousled waves. Once again she set her mind upon her predicament.

"I trust you slept well?" his silky voice said.

Karlinah put her hands on her hips. "No. Where is this life of treating me like a queen that you promised? No fire to warm myself this morning? And I suppose it will be a cold meal? I wanted hot biscuits like yesterday or even maize mush."

She sought to shame him into making a fire and spend time cooking. The best thing she could do now was to delay further travel. Certainly father's army was out looking for her. "I'll get some firewood." As she stooped to pick up a stick from the ground, her back muscles complained.

"Don't bother," Japethihah said. "We are leaving as soon as possible. Get the tent down, and I will give you something to eat once we are on our way. Your pampered life will have to wait."

Karlinah glared at him and went back to the tent. She found a fist-sized rock to pound against the sides of the stakes to loosen them from the ground. Maybe someone would hear the sound or a louder noise. A new idea formed, and she gathered courage to use it. She thought of a reason to scream and jumped back from the tent.

Japethihah turned toward her with a sharp look.

"Something slithered from under the tent," she lied. "I think it was a snake."

The rock remained in her hand. She wasn't certain of her aim and decided she needed to be close enough to hit him without throwing the rock. She didn't want to kill him, just disable him so she could get to a horse and ride off.

Japethihah marched over and slipped his foot under the floor of the tent where Karlinah had been. Nothing happened.

Karlinah edged closer, gripping the rock tightly with a shaky hand. Her hand had been steady and quick when she smashed the statuette against Masoni's head. She flinched at the memory.

His tall body bent lower to inspect the ground.

This was the moment. She raised her hands high overhead, ready to strike. Karlinah's shadow appeared against the tent wall. They both saw it at the same time. Fear halted her movement for the fraction of time it took to catch a quick breath. She knew she was discovered. There was no choice left but to follow through. Her arms came down hard and fast as Japethihah twisted to the side in a rolling crouch. The tent cushioned his fall as he slunk to the ground, and her swipe remained unbroken.

She'd missed!

Eyes blazing, Japethihah scrambled to his feet and lunged after Karlinah. She ran, screaming in terror. A quick glance ascertained he was less than a body length away. Her breaths came faster. Feeling the weight of the rock still in one hand, Karlinah pitched the stone at the towering figure pursuing her and continued running. It hit him squarely in the chest with a dull thud. She heard a snarl. With arms pumping, Karlinah sped up as she aimed for the trail instead of the horses ahead. Japethihah was too close, and she didn't have the skill to mount quickly.

Karlinah felt a hand yank her tunic. Her feet slid out from under her, and she landed in a puff of dust on her backside, eyes squeezed shut and mouth groaning. Warm fingers encircled her neck. Her eyes flew open to see Japethihah's face a hand span from hers, his panting breaths hot on her face.

"Don't ever try that again." His grip tightened to emphasize his words.

Panic set in as she struggled to breathe. For the second time in her life, she thought she was about to die.

When he released the pressure, Karlinah gasped and coughed. The knot of fear sank to the bottom of her stomach.

"It's up to you, Karlinah." The hands slipped off her throat as he spoke. "You can be my queen, or you can be dead. Either way, I will not lose. You will be mine or no one's. It's as simple as that." He paused, a sneer on his lips. "Go take the tent down so we can get out of here!"

Karlinah rubbed at her throat then inspected her scraped elbow as she stumbled to the tent. Soon the ties were released, and the canvas walls came billowing down. She looked around the camp while Japethihah tied the tent onto the packhorse. A glimmer of hope surfaced that the tent left stake holes and a matted down spot on the grass. Last night's ashes from the fire also left evidence. It would be an obvious indication *if* it could be found, but how long would that take?

***

As Cumroth was presented to the prince, the smile on Lamonihah's face eased his nerves.

"Ah, the stone artisan," Lamonihah said. "I've seen your clever work. Tell me about this snake attack you endured."

Cumroth's face heated at the extra attention. He gave a brief account that focused on his companions' help.

"Remarkable. How are you feeling?"

Visions of a soft bed came to mind, but Cumroth replied, "I can manage."

"Good. I understand you have additional information. Take a look around. Which way do you think they went?"

In the growing yellow haze of morning, Cumroth found and pointed out the direction.

"Excellent, the same direction we were headed."

Cumroth said, "Karlinah left a beaded marker, so there may be other clues ahead."

"Yes. She had two braids that day, so we expect to find one more if we haven't already missed it. I will spread the word before we march. For now, the prints are detectable, but the clouds show signs of coming rain." Lamonihah placed a hand on Cumroth's shoulder. "You have shown great courage in your assignment. Words cannot adequately express my thanks. After you eat, you may go back to the city with a few of my men who will be returning the king. He received a nasty sprained ankle."

Cumroth shook his head. "I can keep up. I wish to see this through."

Lamonihah narrowed his eyes dubiously and then shrugged. "Have it your way."

Cumroth nodded and drew back a few paces, feeling foolish. What had he expected—to be put at the head of the trail? The trackers didn't need him anymore. All he'd gotten for his trouble was a battered body and a life-threatening tale to tell. *Maybe I shouldn't have come*, he thought as he ate a hunk of cured peccary flesh and maize cakes. *Lamonihah doesn't need me. Karlinah won't need me either. But what would they think of me if I turn around?*

Moments later Cumroth fell into place amongst the line of two score soldiers. His legs resumed their dull ache as he marched. Someone from behind bumped into him and muttered a quick apology. He realized he had slowed because his mind drifted, tumbling with self-doubt.

Not today, he determined. *I'm going to find Karlinah.* Cumroth picked up his pace and prayed silently for himself and Karlinah to have strength.

An hour later the company halted as Lamonihah held up a hand.

"There are too many tracks here," Hirum, the head tracker said. Lamonihah frowned, staring at the ground beside him.

Hirum motioned for his team, and a dozen men surged forward to read the trail.

Cumroth watched them spread out, studying the ground and lifting the skirts of nearby bushes. Lamonihah signaled for the remaining men to sit and rest. Cumroth chewed on some dried guava and jerky sent with him by the queen while Lamonihah spoke to all.

"Pay attention to everything but especially anything yellow. Her skirt or tunic may have caught on a branch. There may be another hair fastener tied on a plant somewhere."

"You get cut or something?"

"Huh?" Cumroth lifted his head to see a man pointing to his bandage. "Something like that," he quickly answered, wishing the man would let him listen to Lamonihah.

The first pair of trackers returned, and Cumroth leapt to his feet, edging close enough to hear. Hand movements of the trackers suggested the hoofprints led in circles. They looked perplexed.

"It can't lead back here," Hirum snapped. "They've gone somewhere. Go back and extend your search line."

Another pair came out into the open to report. "We've got a trail jump. Our group is taking the west side, and Sam's group will take the east. The others will continue north."

Hirum nodded. "Let me know if you need more men." The two went back to their job.

Another long moment passed before Cumroth could see a few men returning with puzzled faces. He counted them and paced, impatient for the last four trackers to return. Finally, the western searchers slipped through dense foliage, whooping with elation.

"Almost had us fooled," Cumroth could hear a tracker say. "The hoofprints were dusted away, the undergrowth undamaged. Then we found this." The soldier dangled the dirty yellow cloth by its bead. "Just beyond is a deer trail where the horse tracks begin again."

Karlinah was still alive and leaving clues! They couldn't be too far ahead.

"On your feet, men," Lamonihah ordered. "We have a trail again."

Cheers of hope echoed all around as the army settled into a line. They ignored the protruding branches raking across their skin as the army blazed through the section that met the deer trail. Cumroth pressed forward with new vigor for a while before he felt his steps and eyelids growing heavy under increasing heat. He took a long swig from his water skin.

The sun was high overhead when the group came to signs of Japethihah's previous encampment near a stream. They weren't as close as Cumroth hoped, and his energy plummeted. He joined the soldiers in filling their water pouches, hoping the cool liquid would refresh him.

Lamonihah raised both hands high, and the group quieted. "Men, this is where Karlinah and her kidnapper camped last night. That means we are still half a day behind them. We have done well to follow the trail and get this far, but it is not enough."

He waited for all eyes to meet his. "I want a small party of the fastest, freshest men to thrust ahead. I need Karlinah found before nightfall!

Those who had guard duty last night or have injuries will rest here."
He motioned for the brawny tracker to come forth. "Those in the best
condition, stand with Hirum."

Several men moved near the tracker, and Lamonihah counted them.

Cumroth knew he didn't qualify, and it was somewhat of a relief.
His body was nearly spent. He tried to take comfort in the fact that his
contribution had helped them stay in the right direction, but he felt little
reassurance. Karlinah was still out there with a crazy man.

Chapter Thirty-Three

THE PLAN MADE SENSE IN Karlinah's mind. She went over the numerous ways it might play out. The most important thing was for her to stay on the horse so she could ride off alone. She would have to wait for the right opportunity, for that moment when Japethihah would relax his hold around her waist.

Japethihah had often switched trails or made new ones. He had dusted their tracks with an evergreen bough and buried the horse droppings. With hope for her rescue diminishing, Karlinah knew she must act on her own. Time was running out.

Japethihah never permitted her to sit on the horse by herself except as he mounted. The only way to escape with the horse was to knock Japethihah off. A mere shove wouldn't do it. She needed to catch him unaware, or he would pull her down with him. She shuddered to think of his anger if her plan failed. Japethihah had threatened her life, but Karlinah felt certain he would allow her to give in to his terms over carrying out this threat. Masoni never would have given her that chance. It was kill or be killed on that fateful night.

Japethihah's voice pulled her into the present. She wondered if he liked the sound of his voice. His mood to talk smothered any hope he might become drowsy. The horse's gait and the warm sun peeking through the clouds could have worked in her favor, but no. His voice rambled on about the home he would build for her.

"Your cooking area will have a bricked fireplace with a metal bar across to hang pots."

"And a small brick shelf on the inside wall where I can fire-harden my beads."

"Yes." Japethihah's voice took on a pleased ring.

If he insisted on talking, she would help him loosen up. "We have to grow garlic," Karlinah said. "It perfectly flavors many vegetables from the garden or—"

"—or what I might hunt," Japethihah finished excitedly.

The tension at Karlinah's waist eased slightly. "We already know there are deer, peccary, turkeys, and rabbits out there," she said, spreading one arm out in front of her. "We will find enough food." She hoped he might also use his arms expressively, but he didn't.

"I look forward to our first venison stew," he said.

Karlinah thought she could hear him smack his lips together. Growing impatient with this new game, she decided it a good enough moment for a distraction. She raised her arm and pointed ahead of them just off to the left, the direction her legs hung over the side of the horse. "Look!"

"What?" Japethihah said, leaning out to view around her. As he did so, his arm at her waist sagged.

Karlinah guessed at the position of his head as she anticipated his gaze. She swung her left elbow back hard and high. The aim was intended to break Japethihah's nose, but she cracked it against his right jaw due to his height. The result worked just as well.

A piercing howl rent the air as he reached for his face, and the horse took a few jumpy dancing steps. Now free from his grasp, Karlinah twisted around and pushed at his chest with both hands. She could feel the momentum of her body follow into the push, the weight of her upper body going too far to the side. She flailed an arm backward to counterbalance. At the moment when her fear of falling evaporated, the horse started forward again. Japethihah teetered back then forward with the rocking of the horse, his hand lunging to grab her. His fingers tangled into her hair, and he latched on while pitching backward once more with the horse's movement.

Karlinah screamed; the startled horse crow-hopped.

Karlinah could feel her legs sliding out from under her. She reached wildly for the horse's mane, but she fell too quickly. One last tug pulled at her scalp just before she landed on top of Japethihah.

Fear and repulsion drove her to roll off him without thinking. She scrambled to her feet in time to see the packhorse stepping over Japethihah as it whinnied. Running with all her might, Karlinah could hear Japethihah's moans growing distant.

Moments later she heard her name, heard the rage in it, and wondered if he just might kill her after all. Her heart pounded in her chest. With some distance between them, she could stay on the trail longer. She must push herself as hard as she could for as long as she could.

Several minutes went by as Karlinah's breath came in short, hard gasps. She panted, drying her throat. Her lungs felt like they were burning. She tried to swallow but found little moisture. *Keep going*, she told herself. Closing her mouth, she forced the air through her nose and blew it out her mouth. She concentrated on this for a short while, and it helped reduce her terror.

The trail ascended a hill, and she slowed to a jog. She glanced quickly behind her. No Japethihah. *Good.* The fall surely injured him to some degree, or he would have been in view on this straight stretch. Grateful he had cushioned her landing, she regretted not managing to stay on the horse. Why couldn't the plan have gone as she had imagined?

At the crest of the hill, Karlinah checked her bearings. The sun peeked through patches of gray clouds to her right. Daylight would last a couple more hours, and she knew the hilly terrain would continue for a while before she reached the wider river trail, before she could reach water. She licked her lips and felt her throat thicken but pressed on. At least she could take advantage of the downward slope and let momentum carry her.

Over the next hour, Karlinah interspersed jogging and walking, but she kept moving. Her biggest fear was that Japethihah could reclaim a horse and easily catch her. She kept glancing behind her and listening for horse hooves as if he might appear at any time.

The mountain was blanketed in shadow now that the clouds had thickened. The warm wind pushed at her face, blowing her long hair out of her eyes. The southern breeze became a directional aid but also signaled a coming storm.

Countless worries ran through her mind. Would she get lost in the dark? How soon until she found water? Where was Japethihah? *God our Father, please help me*, she prayed.

A few minutes later, Karlinah heard a chilling call carried by the wind. The syllables of her name were distinctly separated.

"Kar-li-nah. I for-give you. Come back!"

A shiver of terror struck through her body. Japethihah must have seen her or her yellow clothing. She ran hard again, feeling a surge of new energy.

Just when she found her momentum again, one of Karlinah's sandal straps broke, and she tumbled to the ground, rolling into the scraggly branches of a bush. She glanced at her reddening scratches while an urge filled her mind.

Risky as it was to be alone in the jungle, she had to get off the trail.

***

Dusk approached, and Lamonihah was worried. Dark clouds rolled in, threatening to wipe away any tracks with wind and rain. He cursed the delay Japethihah had given them. They should have caught him by now. The hoofprints on the deer trail had abruptly disappeared, and they'd wasted precious time searching for markings that didn't exist. Finally, the trackers found fresh marks on a parallel trail.

He trudged behind his best trackers, reminiscing about his sweet sister. She had stubbornly stuck with him even when he played with other boys, not wanting to be left out of anything. It gave his weary body something to smile about.

"Look, a sandal!" One of the men straightened from the ground and held the shoe aloft.

Lamonihah rushed over. "It's Karlinah's." He noted the broken strap. She was on foot, heading their way. Had she passed them? "What happened?"

Hirum held up his hand, searching the ground. "There was a scuffle here. She had a southward running stride until here," he said, pointing at the ground. "Then she stumbled and rolled where the sandal was found. The prints leave the trail from there."

"A broken sandal shouldn't spook her off the trail," Lamonihah said, frowning. "Something else happened."

Hirum nodded and waited for the trackers he had sent northward. After a few minutes, he could see them coming back. They verified finding a second set of prints.

Lamonihah felt a knot form in his gut. "She's running from Japethihah, and he went after her on foot."

Solemn faces nodded in agreement. The situation screamed danger.

Hirum spoke. "She's south of us now, but so is Japethihah. If she had stayed on this trail, we might have run in to her."

Lamonihah ground his teeth and gave orders. "You three continue northward on the trail. Those horses had to go somewhere. See if you can find them." He pointed to two more men. "Stay on this trail while heading back to the main group. Don't miss any prints that might come back to it. If you reach the men before you've heard from us, enlist their help in searching. Trade off with a rested man if you need to."

They scurried off.

"The rest of us will spread out, searching both sides of the trail, two by two." He cupped his hands to his mouth, facing the direction of the prints. "Karlinah!" he called as the first drops of rain fell from the sky.

***

A loud crack of thunder woke Cumroth from his spot on the weed-filled grass. Drops of rain hit his face as he looked up. Slivers of daylight filtered through the clouds. Other soldiers murmured, rising from their places on the ground. Though renewed by his nap, he didn't welcome the rain. It would make tracking more difficult.

"Any news?" Cumroth asked Aaron. The two had kept in close proximity since their partnering after the boa attack.

Aaron shook his head.

Cumroth couldn't just sit around and think about Karlinah. "I'm going to find something fresh to eat," he told his companion. "Want to come?"

"I'll make you a deal," Aaron said. "You find something better than dried mutton strips, and I'll make us a hollow."

"Sounds like I got the easy part," Cumroth said.

"Not if you can't distinguish wild, edible plants."

Cumroth laughed. "My father taught me a few things during our travels."

"Lucky for both of us."

As Cumroth tromped off, fat drops pelted him from the sky. Then the clouds let loose like the slitting of a sack of grain. He heard Aaron's voice calling after him, "Don't worry. Boas hide when it rains." Cumroth rolled his eyes.

Wading deeper into the wet shrubbery, Cumroth gathered pebbles to leave stacked trail markers as he went. He could hardly see a thing through sheets of rain but predicted it wouldn't last long.

In a clearing of weeds and other greens, he carefully checked the plants, the rain less harsh now. Most of the edible plants had leaves too mature to be anything but bitter, but Cumroth selected the youngest ones he could find, nipped off several leaves with his fingers, and stuffed them in his pouch. Then he was lucky enough to spot a small berry bush. It had been picked over by birds, but he managed to reach into the center of the thorny canes with his good arm for a small handful of choice, hard-to-reach berries. He popped his share into his mouth and savored their sweetness.

Cumroth's sandals slid over muddy grass and old leaves as he entered a thicket of trees with vines. The rain slowed to a drizzle. Seeing a large-leafed tree, he opened and raised his water pouch to catch several small collections of water pooled there. His eyes foraged the ground in the dimming light. Round patches of white grew at the base of a stand of trees. Too bad the mushrooms were a poisonous variety. Disappointed, he knew it was time to head back before total darkness fell. His offering would have to do.

The rock stacks were helpful in finding his way back to the army. Cumroth found Aaron fastening the last of the branches together for their shelter. How much good would it would do? They didn't yet know if they were staying here through the night. The warm rain stopped, leaving them to feel the chill of night. They were soaked, with nothing dry enough to make a fire, but at least the food gave them some pleasure. The two men popped the greens into their mouths. It was nothing special but gave some variety. Cumroth took one berry to freshen his taste buds and gave the rest to his partner. They were just finishing some jerky and water when they heard the whinny of a horse. As this was a marching army, it could only mean one thing.

"Karlinah!" Cumroth cried in hope. He didn't wait for Aaron but made his way toward the din of gathering men. From the moonlight peeking out from clouds, he could see one rider. His heart plummeted as he noticed the form of a man.

"Fellow soldiers," the man's voice rang out. "The good news is Karlinah has fled from her captor on foot."

Cheers erupted. Cumroth felt a surge of gratitude and hope. Maybe the worst was over.

"She veered off the trail on the east side, heading this way. If she stayed to that course, she is not an hour's jog from here. But she could be anywhere, and the man who took her is pursuing her. She hasn't answered our shouts from the trail. Lamonihah calls you back to action."

***

Karlinah crouched behind a boulder, hoping her hard breathing wouldn't give her away. The rain muffled her sounds but also made it hard to tell where Japethihah was. Darkness was both a curse and a blessing. She'd heard his steps crunching leaves nearby an instant ago. Now there was nothing. Holding still and feeling the cold, she saw bumps rise on her arms. Should she dash from her spot? A feeling told her to stay put.

His deep voice resonated seemingly right next to her. She clamped her hand over her mouth to stifle a cry.

"Don't fight it, Karlinah," Japethihah cooed softly. "We belong together. I've known that ever since you returned from Jerusalem. The gods sent you back to me for this reason."

He was walking; she could hear sloshing sounds from puddles that hadn't yet drained into the limestone below the soil. Did this mean he wasn't certain of her position?

"You were starting to know it too, until that worthless Nephite came along."

Karlinah's heart thudded in her ears. The voice seemed closer.

"We had the perfect match—the priest and the princess. I am your desti—ouch!"

Did Japethihah stumble into the boulder or a jutting branch? It didn't matter. *Run now!* She obeyed the voice in her head. Karlinah shot off in the direction she had been heading. The warm wind pushed past her face. South, she hoped. There were evergreens at this elevation, and her one bare foot felt sharp pine needles that poked and stones that pressed into her delicate skin. Twigs grabbed at her, but she kept moving.

"Karlinah!" a voice called through the wind.

She kept going with her hands out in front of her, feeling her way; otherwise, she would have smacked into several tree trunks. Something cut into her foot, and she grimaced, avoiding any sound other than one sharp intake of breath. The rain came hard with a burst of lightning, and she ducked to hide from the flash of light. When she could hear nothing more than her heart pounding and the wind in her ears, she moved on until her foot grew bothersome.

Stopping, she cupped her hands and drank a few swallows of rain that slid down her throat. The offering made her stomach rumble. This she could ignore, but her foot she could not. She tore a long strip of fabric from the bottom of her skirt and wrapped it around her foot.

The brief rest rejuvenated her, but now she needed to run.

Chapter Thirty-Four

CUMROTH LISTENED AS THE CAPTAIN on the horse finalized the orders. "If you have no leads to follow by daylight, meet back here one hour after sunup. Any questions?"

A man took a step forward, saying, "Was the other horse recovered? Can we assume Japethihah is on foot?"

"Yes to both questions. The other horse is in our possession. Be on the lookout for this adversary. Beware of the danger he poses and take him alive if you can. But our priority is the king's daughter. Do nothing to jeopardize her safety. Anything else?" He looked around. "Then partner up and don't get lost."

Anger built within Cumroth as his chest heaved. He wanted to rip Japethihah apart with his bare hands, to snap his neck like a twig. He seethed, counting off in his mind the possible sufferings Karlinah had endured.

"Ready?" Aaron said, interrupting Cumroth's thoughts.

"Yeah, let's go!"

The two started off at a quick jog up the trail. The men traveled in a pack for some distance until they neared the search area. Partners turned off into the undergrowth ahead of them here and there, calling out Karlinah's name. Cumroth plowed straight ahead, pleased with the improving conditions. The waxing moon grew increasingly bright as the clouds parted, and the wind had mostly calmed.

Aaron gazed at his partner with a questioning look. "You want to go farther?"

"Yes." The jog and renewed purpose had infused warmth into his body that counteracted the chill of wet clothing. "Maybe we can find that piece of dross."

Aaron laughed. "I take it you aren't talking about the princess."

"Not even close." Cumroth wished he hadn't said that aloud.

Aaron stopped and stared at him with wide eyes. "You've got feelings for her."

Cumroth stopped and turned. His silence gave answer enough. He pictured the whole army finding out and teasing him in front of her. Definitely not the way he wanted Karlinah to find out.

A silly grin widened on Aaron's face. "I wondered why a stone-cutter would go through all of this. Sure, Queen Mierah wanted your information delivered, but you had plenty of chances to return." He shook his head. "Pure craziness."

"You say a word and I'll . . ." Cumroth laid his hands on Aaron's shoulders but stopped short of shaking him. He didn't know what he would do. Crawling into a cave came to mind.

"Hey, you don't have to worry about me—your secret's safe. After what we've been through together, I consider us friends." Aaron's sincerity changed to a mock-hurt tone. "I hoped you would feel the same."

Cumroth rolled his eyes at the guilt flung at him then smiled. He hadn't been in one place long enough to have someone call him a friend since the death of his mother and sister, when he and his father began traveling.

"Sorry. Thanks for sticking with me."

Aaron banged his fist playfully at Cumroth's shoulder. "Yeah, well, let's get going."

They spent hours creeping around the terrain, listening for sounds and following false trails. Sometimes it was the wind rustling leaves. Sometimes they tracked a small woodland creature. Often they could hear the sound of Karlinah's name in the distance. It seemed no one had found her or her captor. All they seemed to get for their trouble was cold and tired. It was bound to be a long night.

***

Karlinah woke to the sound of her name. Japethihah! He was after her again. She couldn't believe she had dozed off. She only meant to rest for a few minutes. Now he was catching up to her. Would this night never end?

Then she heard her name from a different direction. How could Japethihah get over there so quickly? The sounds in the jungle were playing tricks on her. She shook the fog from her head. Where to go?

The wind had stopped, leaving her without a clue of direction. She didn't remember which way she had come. Maybe she could find a place to hide until daylight. She was so tired, wet, and muddy. Karlinah struggled to her feet like a new lamb trying to stand right after birth.

"Dear God," she whispered, "I have done all I can do. It is up to you now."

***

Cumroth listened to the sound of Karlinah's name being called out from somewhere on the next ridge and kicked a rock. "There's no way Japethihah would stick around here with these men combing the hills," he growled.

"Yeah," Aaron said. "I'd get out of here if I were him. Being caught would mean death as sure as the sun comes up each morning."

"Then what are we doing so close to the others?" Frustration edged in Cumroth's voice.

Aaron puffed out an irritated hoot. "Finding the princess would be nice."

Cumroth planted his feet and faced his companion. "Two score men are searching for the king's daughter. I want to make sure that filthy snake doesn't slip out from under us. We need to head farther north." He stepped toward the nearest tree to feel for moss on the north side. Aaron followed hesitantly.

"I don't know, my friend. It might be too late. We're supposed to meet the army an hour after sunup."

"*You're* supposed to meet the army. That captain doesn't have say over me."

Aaron folded his arms. "So what are you going to do—kill yourself searching? Let me tell you something, Cumroth. I've been pretty amazed at how you've held up after the beating you've taken, but if you go off by yourself and collapse, no one will be there to haul you back to safety. Face it—we're not going after Japethihah. Hopefully we'll find the princess."

Cumroth squeezed his eyes shut and took in a deep breath. "It's now or never, Aaron. We only have a couple hours until daylight, and it's still reasonable we can capture that filth. I'd be willing to bet my cacao beans Japethihah couldn't get far on a night like this. He's probably been walking in circles. But once daylight hits . . ." Cumroth gave an uneasy laugh.

"My priority is the princess. Besides, you shouldn't go alone, and I need to head back pretty soon."

"Then I won't try to talk you into coming with me," Cumroth said, determined. It seemed a waste to come this far and not rid Karlinah of her threat.

Aaron grimaced, torn as to what to do. "I've got a bad feeling about this."

Cumroth tried to ease his friend's burden. "I don't want to get you in trouble, so I'll make you a promise. If I don't find him by midday when the sun is at its zenith, I'll turn around."

Aaron stared right back. "You think you can take him all by yourself in your condition? You're crazy!"

"If Japethihah gets away, Karlinah may never truly feel safe. No one should live with that hanging over them."

"And you're going to be the one to save her." Aaron shook his head. "If I don't see you back in Ishmael by nightfall, I'll know where to look for your body."

There was no mirth in his friend's voice, so Cumroth punched Aaron lightly on the shoulder to improve the mood. "That's a bargain. Now go find a pair of soldiers to join." He smiled at his partner, who stood watching him. "Go on."

Aaron folded his arms against his chest and frowned. "Don't be a fool."

There was no time to waste. With a heavy heart, Cumroth turned and headed north, ignoring the warnings of his friend. He jogged for the next hour, sloshing through mud and stopping only to drink from the pooled rain on broad-leafed vegetation. The sky faintly glowed, aiding his search for muddied indentations or broken vegetation. All he had to do was come across one set of northbound tracks. Yesterday's dry prints may have washed away, but there were muddy imprints somewhere.

The sun fully announced its arrival by the time he found Japethihah's path. Cumroth stared at the fresh sandal prints disbelievingly. He'd done it! The steps were close together in a walking pace. His heart thundered, and his scalp tingled. He was close. Looking ahead for movement or discolorations, he crept forward, quickly and quietly, with his ears finely tuned. He took caution at each bend in the trail and finally saw a patch of white through the bushes ahead.

New energy surged through Cumroth's tired body. He scanned the terrain, thick with vegetation except where the trail was cut. Once noticed, Cumroth wanted it to be too late for Japethihah to do anything more than run. Or fight.

When Cumroth had closed the distance between them within the length of a young tree, the tall figure turned, crying out in surprise. But Japethihah did not run. Instead, he pulled on the dagger at his side and held it out in front of him, hunched in a fighting stance. A wicked smirk lingered on his face. "Well, if it isn't the stone artisan come to save his true love."

A hearty laugh rang in Cumroth's ears, but it didn't unnerve him. The man looked as beat as Cumroth felt. He held his own blade and edged slowly forward.

"Too bad you are too late. The princess is already dead." Japethihah took a couple steps forward. The two were a man's length apart. "I warned her that if I couldn't have her, no one would. She should have believed me."

Cumroth pinched his lips together and held his tongue while searching his enemy's eyes. They taunted. He didn't believe what he was hearing, didn't want to, but if it turned out to be fact, then Japethihah deserved his punishment. Death for death. The artisan took another step.

The silky voice continued, "Once I knew the army had arrived, I cut her up in little pieces. The army will find them sprinkled under jungle growth." This time the laugh was a deep, throaty chuckle. "I would love to see their faces."

"You're lying," Cumroth said and then regretted his words. His tone exposed his fear. His eyes searched but found no blood on Japethihah's clothing. "But no matter, you still deserve to die a coward's death."

"Not if you're dead first," Japethihah replied. He lunged at Cumroth, swiping the blade near his throat.

Cumroth ducked. Japethihah whirled back, and the two faced one another again. Cumroth mimicked Japethihah's steps in opposite, trying to get the feel of his movements while avoiding contact. His foe likely took it for a sign of cowardice and grinned, but when Japethihah lunged again, Cumroth knew which way to shift. When Cumroth dodged two more attacks, Japethihah's grin evaporated. Cumroth grabbed the chance to kick his enemy's arm, knocking the knife to the ground. Japethihah's face transformed from horror to rage.

It should have been Cumroth's turn to laugh, but he couldn't make the mistake of getting comfortable. He had to stay sharp, vigilant with this unpredictable enemy. Japethihah rushed at him like a wild boar. Cumroth switched into defense. All he could do was tighten his grip on the knife and bend his legs for impact. Japethihah's head pushed into his chest, knocking out his wind, and the two fell rolling to the ground.

Fingers like claws reached toward Cumroth's eyes, but his good arm caught the outstretched hand before any damage occurred. Just when he cocked his other arm to strike with the knife, pain shot through it as Japethihah squeezed the bandaged area. Cumroth barely kept his grasp on the knife while he growled in pain. A surge of determination pushed him to roll over on top of Japethihah. He panted hard as he looked into the wild eyes of his foe. Long legs thrashed underneath him as he pinned the pitiful man to the ground.

"What did you do to her?" Cumroth yelled in his face.

Japethihah stilled and cracked a smile. They both realized Cumroth wouldn't know the difference between truth and lies.

Bile rose in Cumroth's throat along with a wave of desire to punish this wicked man. Punish rather than kill? The distinction flickered through his mind. Now that the advantage was his, he had choices. *I am not a killer.* He only partially wanted to obey the notion in his head. Wasn't killing what he had come to do? He had been the zealous pursuer when all that was needful was to rescue Karlinah. But Japethihah had committed a dreadful crime and needed to be stopped. What might he do in the future if Cumroth didn't take care of this now? He had to keep Karlinah safe, so Japethihah must be stopped. Stopped, not killed. He made his choice.

Wedging Japethihah's arm under his knee, Cumroth held his knife just under the wicked man's chin. "This is for Karlinah."

Japethihah's eyes widened as Cumroth lifted and pressed the blade against the pinned man's cheek. He made a careful swipe from the cheekbone to Japethihah's mouth. Red liquid oozed from the line as it spread open. Japethihah held still, wide-eyed, while Cumroth repeated the mark on the other cheek. "You can show your beauty scars to the king. I'm taking you back."

Japethihah made his move as the knife was withdrawn. He thrust his body to the side with enough force to swing his pinned arm out and rock his upper body forward, knocking Cumroth off balance. Japethihah yanked his other arm free and grabbed his opponent's wrists. He squeezed and shook them, trying to force the knife to drop. His fingers found the bandage and pressed into the wound. Cumroth let out a high-pitched wail and released the knife. Japethihah rolled free and got to his feet.

Cumroth lay panting on the ground for a second, exhausted. He glanced at his arm; the bandage around it was soaked bright red. The deep fang cut had opened. He leaned over and scooped up his knife with his good hand, the injured arm cradled against his abdomen. Scrambling up and turning toward his foe, Cumroth gasped as he saw Japethihah's arm raised overhead with a rock as big as his grasp could hold.

Time seemed to slow as the gray blur came closer and closer. He sensed what was coming and reeled back. The stone connected just above his right eyebrow rather than the top of his head. Flashes of light went off in front of his eyes as his knees went slack. He fell to the ground surrounded by black nothingness.

Chapter Thirty-Five

"LAMONIHAH, OVER HERE!"

The frantic voice quickly caught the prince's attention. He ran over to meet the man whose arms waved in the air. As he neared, he saw the body of his sister against a log at the soldier's feet. She didn't move. He knelt down, the hem of his loin skirt dipping in mud. "Karlinah?" His hand gently shook her shoulder. Nothing. He felt for a beat of life in her neck and thought he felt something, but his hands were too cold to be certain. He pushed at her shoulder with more force. "Karlinah!"

Karlinah's eyes fluttered open, and she stared for a moment. "Lamonihah?"

"Oh, Karlinah!" He reached his arms around his sister, half hugging her, half pulling her to sit up. "Are you all right?"

"I'm exhausted, but yes." She gave a weak smile.

"Praise the Lord," he said. A few men gathered around them. "Who has water?" One soldier untied his pouch and passed it to Lamonihah. He fed her a couple sips until she grabbed the pouch.

"I can do it myself."

Lamonihah laughed. "Watch out, men. She's feeling better." He received a swat on the arm for his comment.

One of the soldiers gave a long, high-pitched whistle followed by three short blasts of a ram's horn. Those within hearing range would pass the signal along before coming in. The search was over. Now they could join at the meeting spot and all go home together.

"Thank you." Karlinah handed the pouch back to its owner.

Lamonihah examined his sister. She looked tired, but there were no visible injuries besides a few scratches and her wrapped foot. "Do you think you are up to traveling? We have a horse you can ride."

Karlinah brightened. "In that case, I can't wait to get home."

***

Something tickled Cumroth's face, and his cheek muscle twitched. It sent a shooting pain up into his eye. He wanted to scratch the tickle, but his arms wouldn't respond. Fully awake, he was flooded by the realization that he was sitting at the base of a young ceiba tree, tied to it with jungle vines.

The ceiba tree didn't produce fruit its first seven years, so the spiny green trunk served as its protection until maturity. Cumroth felt thorns digging into his back as he squirmed. He tried to open his eyes, but only one would work; the right was swollen shut. His arms were at his sides, his palms touching the ground, with a vine wrapped three times around his torso and then tied in a knot. A couple of bugs crawled up his arm. His head felt heavy on his neck with each throbbing pulse. He leaned his head back on the trunk, but thorns pricked into his scalp. He ground his teeth. Another insect buzzed in his ear.

So Japethihah had decided on this sick form of torture. Maybe it appealed to him more than killing Cumroth while he was unconscious. Yet it seemed odd that the coward would wait around with an army in the vicinity. He wondered if Japethihah would continue north until he came to one of those groups who dwelt in tents in the wilderness, never to be seen again. Good riddance. Or was he near enough to witness the torture before killing Cumroth?

He slowly turned his head to scan the area. Japethihah was nowhere in sight. He he simply left Cumroth here to starve to death or be eaten by insects or other animals? Was he coming back? Cumroth glanced down. His knife was gone. His water pouch gone. His sandals were gone. A throaty groan for no one to hear escaped his lips. It resounded pained and hollow in his ears.

Think, he told himself, trying to banish the self-pity setting in. He tested the tightness of the vines and found Japethihah had done a thorough job. Strangely, his feet and legs were free. Why had Japethihah left them untied? He tried to get his feet under him and push upward, but he couldn't get them close enough. His heels slid over the moist ground. All it did was strain muscles, waste energy, and rub his skin deeper against the tree. Clever. He tipped his chin down as far as it would go but still couldn't reach the upper vine with his teeth.

He thought of Aaron but knew it would be nightfall before he was missed. He could be dead by then. And what about Karlinah—was she alive? Would she know what he went through on her behalf? Thinking of the alternatives, Cumroth decided he would rather be in this predicament than sitting home waiting for the army to do their job. It was no kind of man who wouldn't give his all, though the risks had proven worse than he imagined. The sitting-home kind of man wouldn't have deserved the princess. The thought brought on a bittersweet smile. *I guess I do deserve her.*

Oh, how he needed to get out of this mess!

Prayer came to mind, and Cumroth appreciated having no shame over his choices as he spoke with his Father in Heaven. The only way he would have killed Japethihah was if it became necessary to preserve his own life. Words tumbled from his lips in a pleading supplication for help. He was at God's mercy. He felt grateful to be alive and voiced this fact. A measure of peace permeated his soul by the time he finished the prayer.

The pain in his head lessened, becoming tolerable. It felt like a gift, bolstering his hope. He was alive, and God could protect him if it was His will. He told himself he would get through this. Ideas as to how eluded him.

"Japethihah," Cumroth yelled a few times, wanting to know if the man was truly gone. An empty echo answered. And then he heard the crack of a branch from behind.

Chapter Thirty-Six

YELLOWS AND PINKS PAINTED A promise of warmth with the rising sun, but a chill lingered in the air. Karlinah pulled her brother's cape tightly around her shoulders and relaxed on the horse. No cumbersome arm held fast against her. Safety replaced fear, and the army had found her before Japethihah could dishonor her reputation. No worrying thoughts plagued her of getting away or having to live through a loveless marriage.

The constant suck of mud that regretted giving up its hold on sandaled feet and horse hoofs made her grateful she got to ride. It also masked the sound of her growling stomach. Both her bed and the bathhouse called to her. Interrupting thoughts of which she should choose first, Lamonihah thrust a leather pouch her way with some dried squash and mutton jerky in it. She made a joke about his saving the best for last but chewed vigorously.

With her stomach pacified by the meager contents, she dozed on the horse for the next hour while the sun dried her clothing. She awoke and traded questions with Lamonihah. Her face flushed upon learning she could have been found sooner if she had recognized that the voices calling her name were not Japethihah's.

"At least you had the wits to escape," Lamonihah said, walking beside her as she rode. "It's amazing you got away at all."

Accepting congratulatory remarks made no sense to Karlinah; it could have easily turned to disaster. She picked at some dried mud on her skirt. "He kept saying he was going to make me his wife." Karlinah cringed, not wanting to say Japethihah's name. She never would have dreamed she would encounter another like Masoni. "Even though I got away, he was coming after me. I wasn't truly safe until the army found me. You arrived in time to save me from *that* fate."

"He didn't . . . violate you, then?" Lamonihah asked quietly.

"The Lord spared me that."

"Still, you've been through enough. You'll have nightmares for months." Lamonihah shook a fist. "I'll pierce his heart with an arrow if I get the chance."

Part of her wanted that too. But she would rather know of his capture than who carried out the punishment or how it was done. Then she could sleep at night without reliving images of his death.

Not wanting to dwell on her fears, she recalled Ammon's advice about forgiveness. "What's important is that I'm safe now. I'd rather forgive and forget about him." *That I may also be forgiven,* she added silently.

Lamonihah stared up at her oddly. "You can't be serious! How can you forget about him unless he is dead?"

Karlinah shook her head. Punishment and bitterness about Masoni's abuse held no healing. Only the gospel message and repentance brought peace. In a way, she pitied Japethihah. "If he is found, his punishment will match what the law requires. His death will not be because of *my* wishes. Such ugly emotions only weigh my heart down."

"It sounds like you've been talking to Ammon."

Karlinah glanced at her brother and matched his smile. They traveled in silence around the next bend.

"Hey, you want to hear the story of what happened to one of the soldiers?" her brother asked. "Well, not a soldier actually. It was the stone artisan, but he came with the soldiers."

Karlinah gaped at him. "Cumroth?"

"Yes, that's his name."

"He's here?" Astonishment blossomed into a hopeful flutter in her chest.

"Yes, he came with the army runners to alert us as to where you might be. He saw the smoke from your campfire and found your first beaded marker."

"Wait. How could he have seen the smoke if he came from the city with the runners?"

"He did a lot of traveling. Poor guy must have run for half the day." Lamonihah shook his head from side to side. "He and his father were coming from the stone quarry when they first saw your campfire smoke."

"So they *had* left the city," Karlinah interrupted. She felt her chin quiver.

"That's right. Cumroth found one of your beaded hair fasteners tied to a bush and recognized it, but that's not the best part of the story." A puzzled look crossed his face. "How did he know it was yours?"

"We became friends," she said woodenly, "but he left and didn't say good-bye." She stared straight ahead, letting her body bobble with the gait of the horse.

"Karlinah." Lamonihah's voice intoned new understanding, and he waited until she looked at him. "The stone artisan?"

She dipped her head once. "But he doesn't care for me."

"Oh, you must be wrong. They were heading back to Ishmael, not somewhere else. You have no idea what he went through for you."

Karlinah held her breath, not daring to hope.

"He ran from where he found the beaded marker all the way to Ishmael to see if you were in trouble. Then he ran back to tell me what he knew of your location. He helped us find the right trail."

A smile tugged at her cheeks.

"That's not all." Lamonihah paused for effect. "On the way, Cumroth was attacked by a boa constrictor and was minutes from dying."

Karlinah's hand flew to her mouth. "How awful!"

"His companions saved him. I offered him an escort home, but he insisted on continuing the rest of the way. Now I know why."

Did he simply want to help after learning of her plight and got more than he bargained for? She sunk her teeth onto a fingernail, not wanting to make too much of it.

"He wanted to be here, Karlinah. He could have given the message and gone back for a much-needed rest, but he stayed to search for *you*. If that doesn't tell you something, I don't know what will."

There was a lump in her throat. "Where is he?" She twisted to look behind her.

"He must be with the searchers behind us. They'll get word of your safety and follow along. You'll see him after we reach the city."

Karlinah nibbled her bottom lip. What would she say to him? Musings gave way to a cold heaviness that filled her insides. Lamonihah only assumed Cumroth was behind them with the other searchers. What if something had happened to him? Cumroth must be in a weakened state. He might need help. Tendrils of these thoughts reached into her mind, fighting for attention with her brother's conversation.

"Did you hear me, Karlinah?"

"Huh? Oh, sorry." She glanced behind again, feeling farther and farther from Cumroth with each step of the horse.

"I was talking about the feast Father will host when we return."

She envisioned the happy scene with a bounty of delicious foods for all to partake. Her father would make a speech and thank the army for their valiant effort. Karlinah imagined she would desire to speak words of gratitude. She searched the faces of the army she imagined standing in rows to one side. Where was Cumroth? His face was not among them nor in the crowd. She swallowed hard.

Lamonihah spoke. "First thing *I'm* going to do is have a warm bath and oil massage."

A strong impression came over her. *Cumroth needs help.* It wafted through her head and vanished. "What did you just say?"

"A bath with rose petal water. Doesn't that sound good?"

She squinted at her brother. "No. What did you say about Cumroth?"

"I said nothing of Cumroth."

Dread pressed against her. This was more than her being nervous to see him. "Something is wrong—I feel it."

His confused face tilted up at her.

She had to do for Cumroth what he was willing to do for her. "I'm going back."

Before her message could register, Karlinah turned the horse. Her brother reached for the rope harness and missed. Startled soldiers stumbled out of the way as she brushed past them.

"Stop her!" Lamonihah ordered.

Karlinah felt a hand grab her ankle. She kicked it free and urged the horse faster.

***

Cumroth heard Japethihah's airy chuckle as he appeared from behind the ceiba tree. He held one palm cupped in front of him, but Cumroth couldn't see what it held. "Hungry?" the former priest asked, picking something small and purple from his hand and slowly moving it to his own mouth. Japethihah closed his eyes and slowly chewed. "Hmm. Looks like you woke up while I was searching for food. Want some?" Then he repeated the exaggerated motion and licked his lips after popping each berry into his mouth.

Cumroth's mouth salivated as he clamped it shut. Through his one good eye, he glanced away in defiance but found his gaze returning. He needed to keep his eyes on his enemy. Japethihah ate the last of the fruit.

"You should have spoken sooner, my friend." His high-pitched cackle rang out.

Cumroth glanced at two full water skins tied at the man's waist then regretted that the look was noticed. The saliva in his mouth felt hot and far too inadequate as Japethihah taunted.

"Yes, I'm thirsty too." Japethihah took the one belonging to Cumroth and placed it to his own lips, making gulping noises before replacing the pouch. "Ahhh."

Cumroth remained tight-lipped as he watched Japethihah's exhibition. He strained against the vines surrounding his chest and upper arms, but they wouldn't budge. The action sent a rush of blood to his head, making it throb. Going limp for an instant, he felt the prickly spines of the trunk and adjusted his sitting. His abdominal muscles provided relief when he sat straighter but could only take the weight off his back for so long before they strained. He eased back against the semiflexible tree spikes in their least prickly direction. "Why am I still here? Why haven't you killed me already?"

A growing smile came to the high priest's face as he hefted Cumroth's dagger. "I was going to, but it gave me no pleasure to do it the easy way. Revenge seemed more worthwhile." His voice grew more intense. "I can never go back to Ishmael to kill Ammon or the king, both of whom took away my favor in the community, my future. Once Karlinah turned to the teachings of Ammon, all hope was gone. Her life had to change or be taken. Now you alone will suffer retribution for the wrongs done to me." He took a step closer to his prisoner and met his eyes. "I shall see fear in those eyes."

Circling the tree, Japethihah continued to speak even though Cumroth couldn't see him. "You'll never have her," he whispered.

The words sent a chill down Cumroth's spine, and he stopped breathing.

The voice continued as Japethihah appeared from the side of the tree and stopped in front of his victim. "You think I don't know why you came after me?"

The held breath slipped from Cumroth's lungs, and he gulped his next. He stared in silence, both angry and petrified.

"Revenge for a lost love is powerful motivation." He chuckled in his throat. "But you can't be with a dead woman." He thumped the flat of the blade onto his palm and resumed his circular path around the tree, stopping at Cumroth's side near his good eye. "She was meant for me from the time I did this to her."

Japethihah knelt down from behind the trunk and pulled on Cumroth's earlobe. He stiffened as he saw the blade lifting to his ear. Did what to her? Karlinah had both of her earlobes. What was he doing? Cumroth flinched as he felt the knife slide against his skin, sending a warm trickle of blood running down his neck.

Words came hot against Cumroth's ear. "Karlinah's lobes were soft, like all of her skin. Soft like her hair as she rode pressed against me on the horse." He sneered. "Her lips are soft too, but you will never know the sweet taste of them." He laughed heartily, enjoying himself far too much.

Resisting Japethihah's taunts grew harder as Cumroth's insides boiled. One arm tugged against the vines as he wanted to throw a punch and couldn't. *He's a liar*, Cumroth told himself. *Karlinah would never kiss him.*

Japethihah circled again with the knife pointed at him. "So with Karlinah dead, what else can I do to a stone artisan besides break his heart? Hmm. I could cut off your thumbs and fingers, leaving you no way to hold your tools. Yes, that might be interesting."

Cumroth tucked his thumbs inside his fists and dug them under his thighs as far as they would go. He glared hard at his captor, and the vicious man laughed.

"Maybe I'll save that for last. I do think it fair to use the same knife that gave me these," Japethihah touched the dried red crevices down his cheeks. He smacked the flat of the blade on his hand. "But I don't think I want another to share matching scars with me. Maybe I'll just thrust it into your heart." Japethihah lunged forward with control, the drying ground less slippery in the warm sun. The sharp tip of the dagger halted less than a hand span from Cumroth's chest. Japethihah held his pose for a moment, his wild eyes searching for a fearful reaction.

Fear was *not* what he got. Cumroth thrust his left leg upward, kicking Japethihah's arm and knocking the knife from his hand. Cumroth grimaced as the spines dug into his flesh. His other foot quickly covered the fallen dagger and scooted it toward him until it lodged under the opposite leg. If Japethihah wanted the weapon, he would have to risk getting kicked again. Instead, the stunned man backed away, but the sound of horse hooves caused him to halt.

"Cumroth?"

They both knew the voice that called. Japethihah's lips pinched.

"Karlinah!" Cumroth yelled. "Stay away!"

Shaking with rage, Japethihah sent him a wicked glare. The former priest grabbed the familiar weapon at his side and took a couple steps forward, raising the blade in his fist. There would be no more torture; Japethihah was ready to finish the job.

He cocked his arm and thrust the dagger at Cumroth, who did his best to duck his head to the side and draw up his knees protectively in front of his chest. Again the spines found raw flesh as the trunk took on his weight. Cumroth heard Karlinah's scream as his eyes shut, his teeth clamped, and his mind prayed for a miss.

Cumroth opened his eyes—a good sign that he lived. A sharp sensation burned at the fleshy base of his neck, hammering out another sign of life. A warm trickle made its way down his chest. He watched the weaponless man, whose mouth hung open, while Cumroth attempted to right his head. Steel met the grazed spot, and he leaned away so the blade wouldn't cut into him more. If he hadn't moved, the knife would have centered in his throat!

Cumroth heard feet swishing through plant life and saw Karlinah come into view. She glanced back and forth between the men, a concerned but determined look on her face. It looked like Karlinah was trying to decide what to do, how to help him.

"No. He's weaponless but still dangerous," Cumroth warned. "Get back on the horse, Karlinah." He was about to say more when Japethihah's wild eyes met his.

Cumroth knew the risk she calculated as she edged closer to the tree, but she didn't know of the knife under his leg. Before he could tell her otherwise, Karlinah lunged for the blade in the trunk at the same time as Japethihah. Cumroth couldn't see who had gotten there first.

Chapter Thirty-Seven

SEEING CUMROTH'S BATTERED BODY TIED to a tree brought on distress that overrode the embarrassment Karlinah felt at her awkward arrival. She'd been right to follow the prompting. A second after taking in the scene, Japethihah drew back his dagger. Blackness through eyes squeezed shut couldn't block out the thwack of steel splitting wood or the scream that ripped from her lungs. Her eyes snapped open with the need to know.

Cumroth's body wasn't limp, and she could breathe again. She heard his groan and stepped toward him. Movement slid into her side view, and without time to think it through, she rushed for the weapon that had just missed taking Cumroth's life. She cringed at the feel of her hand on the handle. *Not another knife.*

Long fingers covered hers as she struggled to free the knife from the tree trunk. She hadn't been quick enough but couldn't dwell on her poor luck now. The weapon popped out with her next grunt, and she struggled with Japethihah for control.

The blade glinted in front of her face as she worked to pry Japethihah's hand off hers. His face shown with confidence, but she didn't care. She clawed at his fingers, but his other hand countered the attack. Their hands broke apart into two sets. It felt to Karlinah as if she wrestled a standing bear with outstretched arms. She knew she could only hold him off so long. Then what would he do? She glanced at Cumroth as she struggled; he seemed to be working at something with his legs.

"You should have obeyed me, Karlinah." Japethihah's voice dripped with venom. "Since you never will, you'll have to pay for it." He shoved her hand holding the knife closer to her throat to emphasize his words. The same desperation that surrounded her months ago closed in again. Kill or be killed. Their eyes met, and he laughed at her terror.

"No! Karlinah, take the horse and get out of here." Cumroth's voice diverted them and they briefly held their pose—listening, quickly considering.

Cumroth's eyes flicked back to their opponent. "I'm too weak to come after you, Japethihah. It'll be easy. Just let her go."

"Cumroth!" Incensed that he would give up so easily, Karlinah pushed her attacker's hands away from her throat. *She* wouldn't take the easy route. Bobbing, jostling, two sets of clasped hands struggled on either edge of her view, almost like a dance.

The face opposite hers spoke. "And leave you with your true love? Not a chance."

What? Karlinah blinked and glanced at Cumroth. Did he love her? Why else would Japethihah say this? Cumroth *had* gone through a lot of trouble for her. Her lips curved upward, and her vigor increased.

"You have the lives of a cat, but I will kick you down as a dog in the end," Japethihah spat. "I'll kill you both."

He forced her hand back toward her neck, and she let her grip barely slacken while ducking her head out of the way. Confused or believing he had the upper hand, Japethihah matched the relaxed tension. She quickly pushed the knife away and simultaneously yanked his other hand to her mouth. Karlinah bit down hard. He let go and shrieked.

She thrust her free hand into his chest and shoved. Knocked off balance yet remaining on his feet, Japethihah stumbled close to Cumroth, pulling Karlinah with him.

As if prepared for the opportunity, Cumroth grunted and pushed both feet against Japethihah's calves, knocking his weight from under him, causing him to land on his back at Cumroth's feet. Karlinah fell forward in tandem, landing on top of Japethihah and quickly pinning him to the ground. They both managed to keep their grasp on the knife clutched at the side of his head. It wouldn't take much for her to press it next to the priest's throat, but old images filled her mind, and terror choked her throat.

Only two days ago, Japethihah had straddled her body before stuffing a vile-tasting cloth in her mouth. Now she had the advantage for this brief instant. Should she put an end to Japethihah while she had the chance? Would these new images only compound her torment? She no longer carried guilt over it, but images of a bloody knife remained locked in her brain. Ammon's teachings flooded her mind. *I don't want to kill anyone.*

"Don't do it, Karlinah," Cumroth said. "Drop the knife, Japethihah. It's over." His feet poised to strike the priest's head.

The man on the ground glowered at the one leaning against the tree making awkward rocking motions. He turned back to Karlinah, and a confident look slid onto his face. They could guess what he believed about it being over.

Karlinah felt Japethihah's body shifting—his legs pulling up—and she quickly grabbed him by the throat while she still had control. His startled eyes stared up at her, and Cumroth thrust a foot sharply to the side of his head. Groaning, the man's eyes rolled back for a moment before returning his focus. He let go of her hand, and it prickled as blood flowed through it. Karlinah pressed the blade just under his chin as she scrambled off to kneel at his side.

"You'd do it, wouldn't you?" Japethihah spat. "You'd murder a man who loved you."

Karlinah didn't blink. "What you did was not for love. You love only yourself."

Japethihah's cheek twitched.

"I *would* kill you if it meant protecting my life or someone I loved," she glanced at Cumroth, "but that wouldn't be murder. So don't try anything." She tightened the press of the blade. "God will deal justly with you. Roll over onto your stomach toward that tree."

Japethihah sent her a hateful look before complying.

Karlinah turned to Cumroth, who looked impressed. "Can you help me hold him down with your legs?" she asked.

He nodded and followed through to put pressure over Japethihah's back. She heard his breath catch, but she could do nothing for his pain until she secured the man lying on the ground. A knife blade became exposed when he resumed sawing at a vine. So he hadn't planned on giving up after all; he just wanted her safe.

Karlinah whistled, and the horse walked over to her. Pressing one knee over Japethihah's calves, she fumbled for the rope tethered to the mare and sliced off a length before setting the knife in her teeth while she executed wrapping the rope around Japethihah's ankles. He cursed but couldn't meet her eyes with his cheek pressed against the ground. She tore a strip from her dirty skirt and stuffed it in his mouth with a nearby twig so he wouldn't bite her fingers. Her lips curled up in a satisfied smirk.

The next part would be tricky. When she reached to pull Japethihah's hands behind him, Cumroth loosened his leg pressure over the body. Japethihah rolled slightly onto one shoulder, slipping the opposite arm from under Cumroth's legs, and snatched for the knife between her teeth. Karlinah had expected something like this and pulled her head away in time. Cumroth gritted his teeth and retightened his hold. His abdominal muscles had to be killing him.

Taking the knife from her mouth, she sliced across Japethihah's knuckles until she saw red. "Behave or I'll do worse."

The priest grunted but held still while she tied his hands together behind his back.

Turning toward Cumroth, she saw a look of admiration that lightened her heart.

Cumroth gave the tied-up body a shove with his feet, rolling Japethihah over onto his back. "Just needed to kick the dog out of the way," he explained with a grin.

Kneeling beside Cumroth, Karlinah sawed carefully at the remaining vines. Amazement flooded her mind that she had found him before Japethihah could succeed. Surely she was led straight here. Grateful tears brimmed as she considered this. At times she had slowed the horse to call Cumroth's name but felt spurred on when no answer came. When she had stopped at the top of the last hill, a tingling sensation covered her skin, his nearness practically evident.

"Are you all right?" Her voice quavered as she took in the cut above his swollen eye, the blood below his ear and neck, the red-streaked bandage, and the raw vine indentations on his arms. She sawed at the last vine, freeing him from the barbed trunk.

"I will be, thanks to you." He gave her a smile, and the relief it sent comforted her. Cumroth soon slumped from the tree and curled onto his side.

She gasped at the rips in his tunic and dots of blood covering his upper back and knelt beside him. "Oh, Cumroth! I didn't know how much you suffered." She choked back the tears in her voice. She wanted to take him in her arms, but he couldn't even sit up.

Japethihah gargled his disgust, but only one person consumed Karlinah's attention. "What do you need? What can I do?" she asked, her voice urgent.

"Water. But tie Japethihah to a tree first."

She watched Cumroth for a moment, questions running through her mind. He reached for her hand and gave it a squeeze. Her brow smoothed, and a smile came to her lips. He cared for her. That fact was no longer in question.

The remaining rope barely reached around another trunk and connected to Japethihah's ankles. Karlinah took the fullest water skin and handed it to Cumroth just as she heard her name on the wind.

Chapter Thirty-Eight

KARLINAH RODE IN FRONT ON the mare with Cumroth's comforting arms around her. Japethihah was no longer a problem. Lamonihah had sent a soldier on the packhorse to fetch her, and now the man she wanted to forget was tied to the stallion, heading toward the army. It was this soldier who had called out her name and would deliver word of their safety. No fear fed her lungs; she could breathe easy now.

Karlinah let her back relax against Cumroth's firm chest, enjoying the rhythm of its rise and fall. She felt something press against her scalp and smiled at the kiss. His arms encompassing her waist tightened in a squeeze, sending a thrilling shiver through her abdomen. As naturally as the dry season led into the wet, she crossed her arms and placed them on top of his, letting her fingertips slide over his skin. They moseyed down the path, silent for a while in both contentment and exhaustion.

Cumroth broke the calm first. "You better tie me to this mare because I just might fall asleep."

Karlinah twisted to see how serious he was. His drooping eyes were far from enjoying the romantic moment she wished for. Poor Cumroth. He had been through too much. She gave in to practicality. "We're coming up to a stream. You need more water and some sleep."

"Yes," Cumroth agreed. They tied the mare to a tree near the bank, allowing her both water and grazing. The riders both drank freely, and Cumroth moved a few sticks and rocks from the best grassy patch. He lay on his stomach, his head resting on his good arm. He fell asleep instantly.

Karlinah could tell he had avoided contact with his tender injuries, and her heart pained for him. The best thing she could do for him now was to let him sleep. Better take this chance to wash in the stream. Both her clothing and body needed a good rinse.

***

Cumroth woke to a buzzing in his ear. He swatted at the pesky fly, and his muscles protested the movement. Realization returned, and he sat up to find Karlinah staring at him from her roost on the grass two rods away.

She grinned. "Feeling better?"

"A little," he lied. She looked beautiful with her hair dripping wet, her clothing clinging to her shapely body. He wanted to go to her, to taste her lips, but his stiff body groaned as he awkwardly rose. His own stench reached his nose. He smelled of dirt and sweat and horses. "I need a bath."

Grinning widely, Karlinah nodded. "The water should feel . . . invigorating."

"That little stream is cold?"

She shook her head. "It's not bad. I was thinking of the cuts on your back. I've found some numbing leaves to apply after you bathe."

Cumroth grinned and ambled over to the stream. It only came to his knees, and he pressed his lips into a line. He would have to bend and splash, maybe even lie down to rinse his hair or reach the dried blood on his neck.

The water stung, but he did a thorough job nonetheless. He squeezed out his tunic, climbed onto a rock in the sun, and unfurled the fabric across his lap over his loincloth. The setting reminded him of an earlier time at the river. "I've dripped all over the place, but there's plenty of room." He patted a spot next to him on the boulder, inviting her near.

Karlinah laughed and sat beside him, breaking one of the gray-green leaves in her hand to reveal the soothing liquid inside and dabbing it on his back. "It might not be proper, but I don't believe you'd hurt a mosquito."

It pleased Cumroth that she had remembered. He leaned toward her, and the tilt of her head invited him closer. Tingles rippled through his body as his eyes closed. His lips met softness, and he pressed more firmly. She let her supple lips mold to his. He willed the moment to last forever. His hands reached for her back, and he pulled her closer. Too soon, she pushed back, but her face looked radiant.

There was no judgment in her eyes—only equality, acceptance, and . . . happiness. Emotion escaped his lips. "I love you, Karlinah." There. It was done. And he hardly had to think about it.

Her eyes said everything he longed to hear, and her lips left no doubt. "I love you too," she whispered.

She was going to let him care for her. He knew it.

Could this peaceful feeling last through eternity? He needed one more kiss—just to be sure.

Chapter Thirty-Nine

ACHES AND PAINS SEEMED TO cover every speck of Cumroth's body. He lay on his bed waiting for the smooth stones his father heated in a pot of water. They would bring wonderful relief to his leg and upper back muscles. The salve on the rest of his back stung but would shortly soothe. He knew he would fall asleep quickly. His father would be the one to remove the pebbles, pull up a covering, and leave him until the following day. Cumroth knew he would have no trouble sleeping past daybreak.

It was late morning when a rumbling in his stomach woke him. He rose and discovered a pot of hot maize mush and a basket of fruit near the hearth of their borrowed hut. He was eating when his father came through the door.

"Ah, the dead has risen. How are you feeling?" Corianthem's cheery voice called.

"Much better. I can see out of my eye as well as ever. How does it look?"

Corianthem came closer for a check. "The swelling is gone, but your bruises are blossoming. You'll look the hero's part at the king's feast tonight. He has invited the whole city to celebrate the safe return of his daughter, and *we* are to be honorary guests at the king's table." His father looked as if he would burst with pride. "I, for one, am in the mood to go."

Cumroth frowned, hating the gossip that would circulate and the attention it would draw to him, but it was inevitable. He sighed. At least Karlinah would be with him, and he could meet more of her family.

"Don't give me that look. You're going. I need a companion." Corianthem tousled the hair on top of his son's head as he had done since Cumroth was a boy.

"Stop, Father. Of course I'll go. I just don't like crowds."

"I know." Corianthem's eyes sparkled. "There's one more thing you need to know."

"What?"

"King Lamoni is celebrating something else at the feast."

Cumroth rotated his hand, indicating his father should get on with the telling.

Corianthem reached for a tunic and handed it to his son. "You better put this on first. I'll let the young lady tell you about it herself." He stepped to the door and motioned to someone outside.

In walked Karlinah, looking more beautiful than ever. Her hair was plaited and coiled on top of her head. Jade earrings dangled at her ears. She wore a simple, long tunic of white cotton. She grinned at him, and he beamed with pleasure as he stood and walked toward her. His mouth went dry, so he was glad she had something to say.

"I planned on doing this a few days ago before . . . you know, but now I can invite you to come." She smiled at his befuddled look. "Ammon will be baptizing me today!"

"Really?" Cumroth blinked. "I'm not dreaming?"

She laughed—the sound delightful to his ears. He took her hands, and the pair spun in a circle, both of them laughing for joy.

***

Karlinah gazed with tears in her eyes at the small group gathered at the river's edge. Everyone she loved was in attendance—her parents; brothers and sister; Cumroth and his father; Abish; her sister-in-law, Evah; her brother-in-law, Jaros; and of course, Ammon, who would perform the ordinance. Her heart swelled within her, and she desired to say a few words to them.

"Thank you for being here and for your examples. Each of you has patiently helped me get to this point. This might have happened sooner if I wasn't so stubborn."

Catching Cumroth's eye, she thought again how he wouldn't have witnessed her baptism had it been sooner. His presence warmed her as the sun. "Well, I don't want to give a speech. Just know I love you all and thank you for being a part of my life."

Ammon took his cue to step forward next to Karlinah. "This is a happy day, one where a chosen daughter of God will join His fold and be called one of His people. This is a necessary step to receive the fullness of salvation."

He faced Karlinah and took her by the hand, leading her into the water. A startled bird flew from a rock in the river, making the only sound besides the rippling water. Giving them both a moment to get used to the cool temperature, Ammon proceeded with the words of the prayer.

Karlinah's grip tightened on Ammon's arm as he leaned her backward and immersed her in the river. He quickly lifted her up, and she sputtered with the cold. A huge grin spread over her face, and she basked in the happy smiles of the people waiting on the shore. Arriving at the bank, Karlinah let Queen Mierah place a soft cloth over her wet shoulders and then draw her into a hug. King Lamoni came next, and then a line formed for the others to have a turn.

When Cumroth placed his arms around Karlinah, he hunched over, his head next to hers. They stood that way for a moment. She could feel his chin quiver on her shoulder. Finally he stepped back, and she could see the tears in his eyes, could feel them forming in her own. Peace and contentment intensified within her being. It was as if she not only felt how much Cumroth cared for her but also how important this event was to him. Her tears overflowed, sending a trail down her smiling cheeks. Cumroth still had no words, so he stepped back out of the way.

Barely hearing the congratulatory words of the last few in line, Karlinah thrilled at the joy within her heart. Cumroth had loved and accepted her as she had been, but now she was washed clean from sin, having taken the first step toward salvation. The past no longer mattered. Memories of Masoni and Japethihah could evaporate. With this fresh start, there was only one man's image she wanted in her mind.

Chapter Forty

Hepka tucked the last of the tiny white flowers into Karlinah's hair while Abish and Evah fluffed out her tiered, purple dress and added gold bands to her arms and neck. The bride's nerves were nothing of the sort she'd experienced with her marriage to Masoni. It was excitement she felt this time, not trepidation. She was glad Cumroth had talked her out of secretly going to Ammon to be privately married. "Your parents deserve this. They will never let you hear the end of it," he had told her. She knew he was right, but she hadn't wanted reminders of the ostentatious wedding of her first marriage.

The couple settled on inviting family, their closest servants, and Cumroth's three army companions to join them at the synagogue. Inspecting the preparations after his arrival, Grandfather had toured the synagogue and made a small fuss over the lack of decoration. Karlinah had kissed him on the cheek and told him how glad she was that he came. He didn't say much afterward.

The synagogue looked beautiful to Karlinah as she entered. Her mother and the servants had placed colorful pillows on the front benches. Garlands of leaves and flowers lined the aisle. The scent of rose petals and plumeria filled the air. A row of beeswax candles burned across the edge of the platform. The building seemed even more spacious with only two rows of benches taken, but they were filled with the people she loved.

Karlinah caught her breath. Standing at one corner of the platform was Cumroth in a fine, calf-length tunic. A golden girdle was tied at his waist, and a shiny medallion hung from his neck. He was scrubbed clean, and his shiny black hair hung straight—the tips of his ears poking out. The sight of him did Karlinah's heart good, and she beamed. He stared back with a boyish grin and eyes that twinkled.

Evah, with rounded belly, played a soft melody on her flute as Karlinah walked up the aisle to meet Cumroth. They stood face-to-face and reached out to place right palms together between them. Ammon approached the couple, and the music stopped.

"We have gathered today to witness the joining of a man and woman as commanded by God from the days of Father Adam and Mother Eve. I council you to multiply and replenish the earth as the scriptures say. I would also have you live as followers of Christ and treat one another with kindness all your days. There will be moments to soften your hearts and apologize to one another. Be quick to forgive and show forth more love than you think you have in you."

Karlinah heard her mother sniff but couldn't make her eyes stray from Cumroth's.

"Cumroth, do you covenant to take Karlinah unto you as your cherished wife, to cleave unto her and none else, and be as one flesh?"

"Yes."

Karlinah felt a tingle ripple down her skin. Still, she did not break the pressure between their upright hands.

"Karlinah, do you covenant to take Cumroth as your beloved husband, to listen to his council, and be as one flesh?"

The word came easily. "Yes."

"Then, by the authority given me of God, I join you in the sight of God and these witnesses here, as husband and wife."

Karlinah and Cumroth lowered their fingers from pointing heavenward into an interlacing lock, palms still touching, representing joining as one flesh. Now they could share their first kiss as husband and wife. Right hands unclasped as they reached to wrap their arms around one another. Karlinah closed her eyes as they pressed their lips together in a moment where everyone else seemed to melt into the distance. It was just the two of them—the beginning of the next generation of Lamoni's legacy here in the seventh city of the people of God.

Group Discussion Questions

1. Masoni was portrayed as more abusive than typical Lamanite men. However, this was a time when men dominated and a bride became a man's property, to do with as he saw fit. Do you think Karlinah, with her strong personality and pampered life, could have learned to submit to her husband rather than rebel? Before that one night of danger, should she have submitted to Masoni's will and made the best of her situation?

2. Have you ever traveled to a foreign land? What cultural differences did you encounter? What adjustments do you think Ammon had to deal with?

3. Hepka's marriage was delayed by circumstances she couldn't control. What setbacks have caused you similar frustration, and what were your feelings toward the thing or person blocking your path? Did you overcome your frustration? If so, how?

4. Karlinah's prejudices against Nephites were strongly ingrained. What things contributed to breaking down those barriers? What can we do to dismantle our own prejudices?

5. Was it more than love that drove Cumroth to see the rescue efforts through to the conclusion? What part did vengeance play? Did Cumroth need to prove something to himself? If so, what? What things motivate you during your struggles?

6. After understanding the meaning of repentance, Karlinah states she would rather forgive and forget about Japethihah. She sees harboring ugly emotions as distasteful. We find out it is more important to Karlinah to show forgiveness that she may also be forgiven. How can this attitude find importance in our own lives?

7. How important do you feel it is to leave a legacy for your children or the next generation to follow? What do you want to pass on to others, and how will you make it happen?

Scriptures Referenced

Chapter One
Alma 3:6; Alma 21:2–3

Chapter Three
Exodus 25:3–4; Alma 47:23

Chapter Seven
2 Nephi 5:3, 4, 7, 11; Alma 17:14, 19–25

Chapter Eight
Mosiah 27:8, 10; Mosiah 28:6–8

Chapter Nine
Alma 17:11, 26–39; 1 Nephi 1:4; Alma 18:7; Mosiah 28:7; Alma 26:12; Alma 3:4–5

Chapter Ten
Alma 3:4–5

Chapter Eleven
Alma 47:23; Mosiah 23:6–8; Alma 18:1–42; Alma 3:11–12

Chapter Twelve
Alma 18:43

Chapter Thirteen
Alma 19:1–2

Chapter Fourteen
Alma 19:2–16

Chapter Fifteen
Alma 19:16–36

Chapter Sixteen
Alma 34:30–31

Chapter Seventeen
Alma 20:1–27; Alma 54:17, 23–24

Chapter Eighteen
Alma 23:4; Alma 12:31; Alma 34:16; Alma 37:9; Alma 9:15–16; 3 Nephi 10:18

Chapter Nineteen
Alma 17:3, 9

Chapter Twenty
Alma 32:42; Alma 19:13; Alma 21:20–23; Alma 23:1–3; Alma 20:29

Chapter Twenty-One
Mosiah 3:15–16; 2 Nephi 9:7; Mosiah 4:2; Alma 9:12; Alma 12:34

Chapter Twenty-Five
Alma 30:44; Alma 46:13–15; Alma 32:28, 38, 39, 42; 3 Nephi 14:20; Alma 19:6; Mosiah 27:8–30; Mosiah 26:29–31; D&C 58:42–43; Alma 39:6; Alma 54:7

Chapter Twenty-Eight
Alma 23:7–13, 16–17; Mosiah 18:8–10

Chapter Thirty-Five
Alma 22:28

Chapter Forty
Proverbs 31:22; Alma 23:6

About
Renae Weight Mackley

RENAE WEIGHT MACKLEY DOESN'T CLAIM to have experienced that lightning-bolt moment of belief in the gospel; she's always been a line-upon-line believer. So the chance to vicariously live the life of a spunky Lamanite princess who has a hard time being convinced of anything is tempting—as long as she eventually reaches that inspiring, happy ending. Though no one has called her a princess since childhood, some know her as wife; mother; grandmother; former substitute teacher; and creator of music, fiber arts, good food, and the written word.